HeR

fatHeR'S

by Lori Kohlman

WILL

With gratitude,
Lori Kohlman

CoVeR DeSiGn
bY
Brad Cyca

HER FATHER'S WILL
by Lori Kohlman

P.O. Box 146 Macklin,
Saskatchewan
S0L 2C0

This novel is a work of fiction. All characters in this book have no existence outside the imagination of the author and have no relation whatsoever to anyone bearing the same name or names. They are not even distantly inspired by any individual known or unknown to the author, and all incidents, locales, and places are either a product of the author's imagination or used fictitiously.

Order this book online at www.trafford.com/06-3313
or email orders@trafford.com

Most Trafford titles are also available at major online book retailers.

Note for Librarians: A cataloguing record for this book is available from Library and Archives Canada at www.collectionscanada.ca/amicus/index-e.html

Printed in Victoria, BC, Canada.

ISBN: 978-1-4251-1655-2

We at Trafford believe that it is the responsibility of us all, as both individuals and corporations, to make choices that are environmentally and socially sound. You, in turn, are supporting this responsible conduct each time you purchase a Trafford book, or make use of our publishing services. To find out how you are helping, please visit www.trafford.com/responsiblepublishing.html

Our mission is to efficiently provide the world's finest, most comprehensive book publishing service, enabling every author to experience success. To find out how to publish your book, your way, and have it available worldwide, visit us online at www.trafford.com/10510

 **Trafford** PUBLISHING™ www.trafford.com

North America & international
toll-free: 1 888 232 4444 (USA & Canada)
phone: 250 383 6864 • fax: 250 383 6804 • email: info@trafford.com

The United Kingdom & Europe
phone: +44 (0)1865 722 113 • local rate: 0845 230 9601
facsimile: +44 (0)1865 722 868 • email: info.uk@trafford.com

10 9 8 7 6 5 4 3

FoR

my Dad

whose quiet and gentle ways continue to resonate in my life.
I know you're watching over us all.
I'll always be proud to be a farmer's daughter.

Acknowledgements

To the One from whom all good things come, you always know what's in my heart. Thanks for giving me a channel to express it.

Keith, with you in my life nothing is impossible. Thanks for believing in me.

Tanyr and Ty, sometimes we all need a little affirmation. Thanks for being mine.

Susan Halliday Conly, thanks so much for your professional eye and your valuable time in giving this story a final polish, for sharing your gift of writing, and for setting such a powerful example for me in so many ways.

Brad Cyca, thanks for your vision in creating a great front and back cover design.

Families, relatives, and friends, thank you for your constant support and encouragement.

Darin Steinkey of Trafford Publishing, thanks for answering my countless questions and for always being available. Your professionalism always put me at ease.

Liz Symes of Trafford Publishing, thanks for that day on the phone. You were a real catalyst in setting me on the publishing path and encouraging me to just make that start.

A Farmer's Creed

Man's greatest possession is his dignity. No calling bestows this more abundantly than farming.

Hard work and honest sweat are the building blocks of a person's character. Despite its hardships and disappointments, farming is the most honorable way a man can spend his days on the earth.

Farming nurtures the close family ties that make life rich in ways money cannot buy.

Farming provides education for life. No other occupation teaches so much about birth, growth, and maturity, in such a variety of ways.

Many of the best things in life are indeed free, the splendor of a sunrise, the rapture of the wide open spaces, the exhilarating sight of your land greening each spring.

True happiness comes from watching your crops ripen in the field, your children growing tall in the sun. Your whole family feels the pride that springs from their shared experience.

By my toil I am giving more to the world than I am taking from it, an honor that does not come to all men.

My life will be measured ultimately by what I have done for my fellow man, and by this standard I fear no judgment.

When a man grows old and sums up his days, he should be able to stand tall and feel pride in the life he's lived.

Author Unknown

Very truly, I tell you,
unless a grain of wheat falls into the earth and dies,
it remains just a single grain;
but if it dies,
it bears much fruit.

John 12:24

ProLoGuE

Hana Islander sat on the edge of her mother's bedside and stared into the eyes of a stranger. Yes, it was Priscilla Islander exuding as much strength in her moment of death as she had in her life, but the words she had spoken couldn't possibly be the truth. Hana had believed otherwise for thirty years.

"Hana! Earth to Hana! Have you heard anything I've said?" Her mother reached up slowly to swipe a soggy strand of hair from her daughter's wet cheek, shortness of breath betraying her sharp words. "I wanted you to know before I...," her words trailed off painfully, unable to speak the inevitable. "Well, I just wanted you to know. But I'm warning you, if you try to find him it will be a mistake. Men out there in that *place*—they're like sugar coated poison. Promise me you'll never go there, Hana."

Hana's eyes focused on her mother's and clouded with tell-tale tears again.

"I didn't teach you to cry, Hana. I taught you to be strong, to be independent, and to make your mark on this world," her mother scolded her with same worn out words that had become like Biblical scripture to her since she was a little girl playing with Barbie Dolls.

She remembered the day she'd asked her mother for Ken Barbie and how she'd received the first gospel according to Priscilla Islander. *A woman does not need a man in order to feel complete. She can be successful all on her own. Strong, independent…*

"Hana! Can you hear me dear? You're scaring me."

"I'm scaring you mother? Do you understand what this means? I have a father out there who doesn't know I exist and you made me believe that he was dead," Hana's voice trailed off, barely capable of uttering the lie that she'd accepted so unconditionally.

"Now hold it right there missy. You should be grateful that I told you at all, although I must admit," her mother paused and took a deep breath, "I'm doing it merely to clear my own conscience." Priscilla reached for her daughter's hand and held it tightly then, diminishing the last shred of doubt Hana had initially felt at her mother's shocking news.

"Listen to me. If you know what's good for you, you'll stay away from him. Promise me you won't go to Lone Prairie. Promise me!" she demanded with a desperation that made Hana flinch.

"I promise Mom," she whispered. "I promise."

It wasn't like she'd lied about things on a regular basis, even though she had told a few white ones in her time. Hadn't everybody? She was a good person, despite her momentary lapse of moral conviction, but her mother, as always, had left her tied in knots. Besides, Priscilla was gone now and while her dying wish was important, Hana couldn't quite seem to allow it to take precedence over the fact that it was completely irrational and irritatingly typical of her mother.

For once she asked herself the question that had always seemed so selfish. What did Hana Islander want? She thought about it intensely as she packed the final remnants away of what had been her mother's belongings, secretly hoping that she might find some revelation about her past.

The apartment had been nearly stripped of all evidence of Priscilla's existence there and a chill cascaded across the empty room like a wave, catching her in its haunting grip. It was then that she spotted one last article shoved carelessly beneath her mother's glass nesting tables. With an exhausted sigh she picked it up. It was camouflaged with dust, blending nearly perfectly with the hardwood flooring. Like a child, she drew in a deep and excited breath, imagining that she had just discovered a pirate's map, or some such silly thing that would lead her to a place left to be discovered, a comfort amidst the chaos.

"How to live big in a small space," Hana read the title aloud. Disappointment clutched her heart for the last time. Her mother had nothing left to give and she would just have to accept that once and for all. Carelessly, she shoved the book into the last open box which was, like its packer, over stuffed with musty memories. With difficulty, she closed the flaps of the box and then braced herself against the impending silence. She hated silence. It told her truths she did not want to hear. It told her in an instant that the fervently independent and strong-willed Hana Islander was completely and utterly afraid of being alone.

Pulling herself up off the floor, Hana stacked the boxes, taking extra care to drop them with thuds that echoed and intermingled with the sound of her heels on the hard wooden floor. It was noise, necessary distraction. Besides, who needed to hear the truth? Truth was as tainted as the invisible air she breathed, as real as the untouchable clouds. She stopped at the large show-case window and looked down to the concrete nearly fifteen stories below her feet, but her heart raced on ahead, falling to the mercy of the unimaginable.

She wanted to know who she was. No, she *needed* to know who she was. It was the truth, bare, exposed and ugly. To be validated, to know that there was something more to her existence—she'd wanted that for as long as she could remember.

"Doesn't everyone want that?" She nearly shouted, the silence shattering and then returning again. There was nobody there to answer, although she could hear her mother's timeless reply— *Promise me you won't go there.*

Walking quickly across the room, Hana grabbed her purse, her coat, and nothing else. With conviction, she slammed the apartment door behind her, locking it and all her vulnerabilities tightly shut forever. *Enough of that,* she scolded herself, irritation quickly losing the battle with an emotion that she abhorred, the one that felt like an unwelcome stranger. The thought came to her that she could just give into it and cry, but the tears wouldn't come and she knew regrettably that like her mother, anger would replace them if she wasn't careful. Yet, as certain as the hollowness that crept into her soul, anger was inevitable. In an instant, her entire life had become a lie and she deserved an explanation by the one person that could give it—if he still lived in Lone Prairie; if he was still alive at all.

Questions piled upon dormant memories, bringing them to new life. She understood now so many things she hadn't before about her mother. It was, perhaps, the greatest paradox, the idea that through death, life becomes temporarily illuminated. And there were always ways to find things out, especially if the will for truth was greater than the will to hide it, and in this case, Hana was certain, she had enough will for the living and the dead all rolled into one.

It was only a month later when she stepped reluctantly onto Abner Crawford's creaky front porch, sheer will having carried her through her mother's funeral, and an extremely inadequate period of mourning. She should have waited, succumbed to the natural grieving process and taken time to heal, but there really hadn't been any point to it. You couldn't put a bandage on an internal injury. Somehow, she'd have to heal from the inside out and finding Abner Crawford seemed like the most logical place to start.

Hana Crawford, she allowed the name to roll silently off her tongue as she watched the lazy German Shepherd lift his head for a second and then drop it again, as though her presence was of no consequence to him. She hoped his owner would be more responsive.

Mustering up her courage, Hana spoke her name softly aloud this time, as though in speaking it she could perhaps convince herself of its truth. Shakespeare had been completely wrong. There was something in a name. A rose by any other name might still be as sweet but there was nothing even similar about an Islander and a Crawford. Islander was sophisticated, strong, even a bit mysterious. Crawford—well, what really was a Crawford? It sounded so plain, so simple, so *something*. It was a name that turned mysterious into fishy, eccentric into common. No, a Hana Islander could never be a Hana Crawford. It just wasn't right. In fact, something about this picture was very wrong. Her mother, the perfectly prim Priscilla could never have lived here in this dilapidated shack. With shingles missing and those that remained rippling under the heat of the prairie sun, the house looked as though it could have been condemned. Furthermore, what would Priscilla's favorite home decor magazine have to say about the patchy siding, blotched with spider egg shades of yellow? Priscilla hated yellow. No, Priscilla Islander couldn't have lived here.

Hana formed a tight fist and motioned to knock on the faded screen door. Numbly her arm dropped to her side before her knuckles could make the connection. It was a simple but firm calling that would announce her presence in the life of a man who didn't even know she existed, and beckon him to answer. Capturing a shaky breath deep inside her lungs, she turned to face the farmyard, looking for courage in the tired and worn-out buildings.

The hip-roof barn, once red she assumed, had now faded to a horrible shade of pink. She could almost see right through it in spots where the afternoon sunlight shot through cracks, finding the fields beyond it. To the south of it stood a large shop, its doors wide open and revealing an array of farm equipment as foreign to her as aliens in a space shuttle. A small garage stood near the house, unattached and out of place. Its paint matched that of the house, only perhaps, with even less care and attention paid to the cracked windows and the side door that stood ajar.

Finally, her tour of the yard nearly complete, Hana took note of one last building off in the caragana shrubs. It was, perhaps, twice the size of an outhouse, unpainted and shaded by the thick branches. In fact, she might not even have noticed it had a white entity not just flown out the front door as though the sky were falling. After it, followed several other excitable and noisy characters—chickens she presumed, although she hadn't really seen any close up if you didn't count the petting zoo she'd visited as a child, and there she had kept her distance.

She watched with trepidation as they pecked their way along the ground, coming ever and ever closer to the front porch. Without another thought, she found the courage to knock on the front door.

"Can I help you?" He stumbled to the door and froze. Only his eyes moved to the rhythm of her white silk scarf flapping in the breeze as though it were a ghost. Annoyed, she loosened the knot and slid it off her slender neck. Ridiculous wind. Who could handle such a dry, hot, wind? True enough, she was living in the city of Saskatoon where wind was not a stranger, but this, this was different.

His bottom jaw dropped slowly to match the movements of his arms and his legs as he pushed the screen door open and shuffled out onto the porch. His hair was grey, his shoulders slumped, his hooded eyes clouded and droopy. He didn't look well and Hana immediately feared she'd come too late, but she'd never been one to bother with niceties under any circumstances. Besides, she had a score to settle. He'd never gone after her mother, had never cared enough to find her, to see if Priscilla was managing on her own. He must have loved her enough to at least been somewhat curious about where she'd gone. He must have considered the possibility that maybe, just maybe nature had taken its course. At the very least he shouldn't have been as naïve as to presume that the possibility didn't exist.

Taking a step forward, Hana was met with another gust of wind, this one snatching up the tendrils hanging loosely from the upsweep that kept the rest of her long reddish hair stringently in tact. Annoyed again, she fingered the tendrils, pulling them back and out of her face.

"Mr. Crawford, my name is Hana Islander, and I'm your daughter." She waited for a verbal reply but could see his reaction in his eyes instead, and the tiny bit of a smile that began to curve his thin white lips.

Her spirit felt disheveled, like her appearance and at first she doubted her analysis of the man. Could it be that simple? He actually believed her. It was the only response that she'd accept, like the first step to him passing a test that she'd intricately formulated in her heart, but she had expected that he'd be less than inviting, cautious at the very least, anything but a silly heart.

Abner Crawford stared at his daughter, his eyes growing bright and round. He'd dreamed all his life about what it might have been like to have a child, wondered if Cilla would have stayed if they had, and now here she was. She was beautiful, strong and determined, and real, despite his and Cilla's mistakes, despite all the time that had passed, despite the fact that he had very little time left. There wasn't any cause to doubt the woman who stood before him looking exactly like Priscilla had thirty years ago.

"Ab? What's going on out here? Do you know this woman?" A young man swung open the screen door and stood behind Abner as though protecting him from a dangerous criminal.

"It's my daughter, Jayce. I have a daughter!" Abner's smile was beaming now, but Hana's focus quickly shifted from scrutinizing Abner to tearing a mental strip off the smug man who now came to stand between them.

"Ab, you shouldn't be so trusting. You don't know this woman from Adam. I reckon you haven't seen her before in your life." The man's eyes never left hers as his large shoulders blocked Abner from her view.

"Well, no," Ab replied sheepishly, "but look at her, Jayce.

There's no doubt. It has to be true!"
"Go inside, Abner. I'll take care of this."
"But…"
"Go."

ChApTeR 1

The dusty prairie threatened to swallow her as she sped her car down the narrow dirt path. A person could die out here, or at the very least disappear forever. There were opportunities for it everywhere, old abandoned farm houses, hidden valleys, roads that seemed to lead nowhere.

In the past few weeks, she'd spent hours researching Saskatchewan's farming history on the internet, taking particular interest in the Dirty Thirties. Now, an empty run down and abandoned farm site stood on what seemed like nearly every section. There had been many more farm sites, many more houses, barns, granaries, buildings that had been burned down or carted off, the land ploughed under and seeded by the new generation. An old municipal map that she'd photocopied from the local archives had marked off many sites that no longer remained, proof that some people had truly disappeared, barely leaving their sad story behind for anyone who cared to hear it.

She'd always been fascinated with The Great Depression and remembered a detailed school project she'd done when she was in the fifth grade. It was no longer the Dirty Thirties, but Hana couldn't deny certain similarities. Lone Prairie, Saskatchewan, located in the heart of the nicknamed Dust Bowl, was undeniably exhibiting signs of a reincarnated Depression.

For a moment, conviction caught in her throat along with the uncomfortable feeling that she was making a big mistake. Haughtily, she shook off the uncertainties, took a sip of bottled water, and sought out a new radio station, one which had not become a jumble of irritating muffles and scratches. Within seconds, a local country station came through with fuzzy AM clarity, shedding new light on her old love of country music. Joanne, her best friend since high school, had teased her about it many times. It seemed just a passing fancy. Mentally, she kicked herself for having missed the signs. Too late now, she decided. Thirty years had passed irretrievably in muffles and static, where she had unknowingly developed a very false sense of herself.

Straightening her back and tightening her grip on the steering wheel, Hana sought out her unfailing resolve. She found it in the memory of Jayce Harlow's snide expression when he'd accused her of being a fraud only a few short weeks ago, and the reminder that she was about to change all that. If she could remain disciplined enough to stick to the plan, she had the ability to sculpt an entirely new and improved memory.

It wasn't characteristic of her to be cruel and manipulative. Compared to her mother, she'd always been the rational one, the forgiving one, but Jayce Harlow deserved every little bit of his own distasteful accusation, if not for good reason, then merely by default. By the time she was through with him, *he* would have a very bad taste in his mouth, *his* blood pressure would be soaring and *he* would be left absolutely speechless, if that was possible. If not, she had nothing to lose. It was a long term plan after all. It might take months to see any results but she would eventually.

Hana's thoughts spiraled out of control, thinking about the moment when Jayce Harlow had taken a wound and rubbed it with proverbial salt. She'd driven back to Saskatoon in a huff, wondering what right he had to send Abner to the house like a child, just so that he could attack her right there on the front porch. Luckily, he'd accepted her business card, although he laughed scornfully at the professional title she'd worked so hard to achieve, muttering something boldly opinionated about bankers and farmers, square pegs, and round holes.

Nevertheless, all memory blurs and exaggerated replays aside, Jayce Harlow had been cruel and presumptuous, and if she hadn't been so far out of her element, she might have stuck around to push her way past his completely unwarranted defense of Abner Crawford. For whatever reason though, he'd seen her as a threat, and she was bound and determined to get completely to the bottom of it.

It was only a week later when she'd been informed about Abner's death. His lawyer had sent her a detailed copy of the will and she'd read it in disbelief, finding it difficult to fathom that she'd lost both parents within weeks. Even more disillusioning was the notion that Abner would expect her to prove herself in the most barbaric way possible, this being a total contradiction to his original reaction to her, and probably inspired by none other than this Jayce Harlow. It was all his fault, she was sure of it. He'd robbed her of her one and only chance to get to know her father. For that, she could never ever forgive him.

Turning her attention back to the road, Hana steered her new convertible around a sharp curve. The radio station scratched out her favorite tune by Terri Clark, and she cranked up the chorus that suited her mood perfectly. "I just want to be mad for a while," she sang with Terri, allowing the song to justify her completely irrational mood. Besides, it wasn't as if she was the only bitter person in Lone Prairie. Lone Prairie, Saskatchewan, was full of bitter people, bitter farmers to be more precise.

"Well, who wouldn't be bitter living here?" she mumbled, allowing her eyes to take in the overwhelming expanse of the open prairie. What a joke. Miles and miles of nothing and flat enough so that you could see as far as the *nothing* stretched. There were other highlights, too. The next road was always more primitive than the first and the sun was always directly behind you or in front of you. There was never a way to escape the blazing sun or the dust for that matter. It had a way of settling into every little crevice, in the corners of her eyes, in the pores of her skin, in between her teeth. She was glad she'd had the good sense to keep her top up, even though her shiny car had never looked so gritty and dull.

Glancing swiftly at the tiny scrap of paper on her dashboard, Hana signaled left and turned onto a sandy path. It could hardly be called a road. The sand pulled her back and forth as though she was the coveted prize of a tug of war, and she clung tightly to the steering wheel wondering why anyone would deliberately choose to drive on such a narrow and hazardous trail. In winter it would be closed in with drifts of snow, forcing the nearby residents to stick to the main road, and that would add another ten minutes to their travel time in reaching the closest town.

"How barbaric," she muttered again under her breath just to make herself feel better, but nothing would make her feel as good as the look on Jayce Harlow's face when she was through with him. Just a few more miles and she would be there. Then he would see who had become the brunt of the joke. No one made a fool out of Hana Islander. If there was one characteristic she was willing to admit came straight from her father, it was sheer stubbornness. It was, perhaps, her best trait.

She was grateful that her mother had shared with her a few details about Abner before she'd left the world spinning on its axle, even if the recurring theme had proven to be that he was the most stubborn man that ever existed. Priscilla had been selective and biased in the information she'd chosen to share, but it had been better than not knowing anything at all. Besides, her mother had been absolutely right about one thing. The men in Lone Prairie were a strange breed, and one in particular fit the bill of *sugar coated poison* perfectly.

For weeks after her run-in with Jayce Harlow, Hana marveled at the fact that the fine vision of him always seemed to take precedence over his stinging words. She understood completely what her mother had meant, but she wasn't her mother. She was stronger. She was cunning. She wouldn't get burned and she would make her mark. Oh yes.

A large overhead sign caught her attention and Hana's disparaging thoughts disappeared in a cloud of dust as she slowed her vehicle, annoyed by the squeal of her brakes as she turned into the approach. Silently, she cursed the sand for wreaking mechanical havoc on her most prized possession, but her car wasn't the only thing that had recently been affected by the conditions of Lone Prairie.

The sun ricocheted off the hanging sign, drawing her attention to the bold symbol embossed in its center, a half moon carved deeply into the wood, cradling the letter H. It was obviously the Harlow brand, a symbol of power, pride, and lineage, yet it hung from a set of rusted chains that creaked to the rhythm of the wind. The sun had faded it in spots and peeled the paint right off in others. Somehow it looked vulnerable, and upon further inspection of the place it was obvious that there were signs of hard times everywhere.

Hana could imagine that the farm buildings in Jayce's yard had, at one time, stood proud and dignified. Now they severely lacked a coat of paint, this being a long-term effect of the bleaching sun. The grass, overgrown and parched in the ditches and burnt in the places where it was maintained, would have been more forgiving with just a little rain. A lack of it had transformed the countryside, practically devastating it during the most crucial growing stages. If the intensity of the July sun kept up without rain to compensate, crops would be stunted, feed for cattle would be scarce, farmers would be unable to make their payments. The sneer returned to her lips. It really wasn't her problem.

Feeling like a snake slithering in the sand, she crawled beneath the rickety sign, struck once again by the memory of her mother's version of Lone Prairie. The people of Lone Prairie had an unfailing faith aside from the tangible truths that surrounded them. They believed that if they prayed, God would hear them and save them from the wraths of nature. They were, as Priscilla recalled, very religious, self-righteously so. It was why she'd raised her daughter to believe in—well, what had her mother taught her to believe in? Herself? Yes, she had done that, but Hana couldn't quite contain the possibility of allowing uncertain faith into her life. The faith that she wasn't really alone, that there was someone walking beside her through life who was willing to share the burdens once in a while; someone who wouldn't run away when things got tough, the same *someone* who pinched her conscience for preying on Jayce Harlow. He had already been punished by the recurring paths of nature and an imminent drought. But it, too, was not her problem.

With renewed focus, Hana killed the engine and the moment of weakness that had suddenly made her feel sorry for herself and Jayce Harlow. Everyone had choices, and Jayce had obviously chosen to be a farmer. She, on the other hand, had not chosen to be raised by a single parent. She had not chosen to be raised void of religion or faith, but did it really matter? She'd come this far without religion, without a father, and she'd turned out all right hadn't she?

The answer didn't come, and feeling annoyed she slammed the car door just as the heels of her black patent shoes sunk deeply into the dry and sandy ground. The heat immediately penetrated her black pinstriped suit and she tugged at her skirt, aligning the zipper with the dimple in the small of her back. Then, remembering that she'd left her briefcase in the back seat of the car, she opened the door and bent to retrieve it, perturbed by the uncertain sound that came from somewhere in the distance. If she hadn't been clearing her throat she might have heard a flirtatious whistle, undoubtedly male and chauvinistically just like Jayce Harlow.

Quickly straightening, she tugged at her skirt nervously, wishing that she could lengthen it. She should have worn a pantsuit instead. On her very first day working at the bank, she'd learned that her choice of attire had a tremendous effect upon the way in which she was perceived. Today, she didn't want anything to jeopardize the strict importance of her mission.

However, an air-conditioned office was far removed from the

prairie and the way the sun seemed to penetrate black. She opened the button of her blazer. After all, if she started sweating, Jayce would take it as a compliment. He'd think that he had some kind of an effect on her. Besides, she was a professional. She'd been in the business for years and had earned her stripes, her open blazers and just a smidgen too short skirts. If Jayce Harlow was distracted by her choice of attire, that would be his second mistake. His first one had already earned him a heap of trouble. If he knew what was good for him, he'd come out from wherever he was hiding and give her the respect she deserved.

Using her hand as a visor, Hana swept the yard slowly, searching for signs of life. An old green John Deere tractor stood near a set of fuel tanks. Attached to it was a mismatched Massey Harris cultivator.

Of course, it wasn't uncommon for most farmers to have a mixture of different brands of machinery, even if they had a favorite. Sometimes it came down to dollars and cents and a meager budget, and for Jayce Harlow, that was certainly the case.

Hana flinched involuntarily, reacting to that strange feeling again that told her she was wrong to be so judgmental, but she had spent many grueling hours in the past few weeks studying the business of farming and all its aspects. She'd done her homework and no one was going to trip her up on the jargon. Besides, how much more could there be to farming? Ten carefully chosen and printed pages, with picturesque visual aids from the internet pretty much summed it up.

Seeing no signs of him, she decided to try the house. It was lunchtime, after all. She glanced at her watch to be sure. Farmers had to eat, too. Hana approached the bold character home cautiously. It was the only building maintained in the yard. Painted a butter-cream yellow and trimmed with a soft sage green, it looked almost inviting. Its shutters, too small to fit the window and merely decorative, added to its quaintness and the white lacy curtains frilling the windows convinced her that someone else must be responsible for decorating.

She knocked on the door, waited, knocked again, but heard

nothing. Again, she turned to search the yard. She hadn't noticed any vicious dogs, but the *cock-a-doodle-do* of a rooster shot out menacingly, piercing the quietness with its distorted echo. She could handle dogs and cats but the line was firmly drawn at feathered creatures, chickens in particular. For the people of Lone Prairie, they seemed to serve the same purpose of a well-trained watch dog and she wondered if there was a certain conspiracy among farmers to train their poultry to attack unwanted guests. Since her visit to her father's farm and the silly incident that had ensued, she hadn't even been able to eat chicken and probably never would again.

"Hello! Is anyone here?" Her voice betrayed her uneasiness.

A cow bellowed out from somewhere behind the barn and startled her.

"Humph, regular Old Macdonald," she muttered as she grew more uncomfortable by the minute. Then finally she heard something—a distinctive scraping sound. It was the sound of labor, the sound of a human, the sound of Jayce Harlow hiding somewhere like the coward he was.

She followed her senses and made her way stealthily to the tractor. "Mr. Harlow? I know you're here somewhere. I can hear you," she taunted, hands placed firmly on her hips.

He slid out from underneath the cultivator then and stood to face her, oblivious to her anger or her mission, and Hana raged even further at the fact that he didn't even seem particularly shocked to see her. Like on their first encounter, the sight of him assaulted her senses, only this time her eyes raced to take him all in, especially the parts she had not been privy to on their first meeting.

With his t-shirt tucked into the back pocket of his tattered blue jeans like a rag, he looked boyish and provocative. His bare chest gleamed in the sunlight where beads of sweat clung to his skin, and Hana was quickly drawn to the uneven tan, a farmer's tan. Her eyes followed it involuntarily three quarters of the way up his arm, attracted to the symmetry of white meeting bronze just half way across his defined and well maintained biceps. The pail blue veins added yet another dimension to the stark contrast and she shut her eyes tightly to regain focus.

"Are you lost? The highway is two miles straight north of here. If you take the back road though and turn left at the fork in the road, you'll reach it even sooner." He removed the shirt from his back pocket, wiped the sweat from his brow and stared at her intensely, a slight sheen of irritation creasing his forehead.

"I'm not lost. I came here to see you," her temper flared. Of course the first words to come out of his mouth would be presumptuous ones. She shouldn't have expected anything more from an uncultured, egotistical farmer.

"Well? Now you've seen me," he said with a wink that made her blood thicken and pump forcefully through her veins. She could definitely feel a migraine coming on.

He walked around to the side of the tractor then and she followed, only to see him ascend the staircase purposefully, metal ringing out against the pounding of his work boots.

"Wait a minute! I'm here on official business. I need to talk to you," she stood at the bottom of the steps, suddenly feeling very small.

"Lady, I just spent my lunch hour replacing cultivator shovels. I'm hungry, hot, and behind schedule, so if you want to talk to me, I suggest you step on up into my office."

He had to be joking. This game was supposed to be played on her terms, not his. He wouldn't have the audacity to just walk away and leave her standing there.

The roar of the diesel engine startled her and she stepped backward attempting to distance herself from the machine that had just sprung to life. It wasn't at all like the internet had described it. It was intimidating and ferocious. The smell of diesel filled her lungs and caused her to cough uncontrollably, but Jayce Harlow left her with very little time to think.

As she watched the heavy glass door swing shut, Hana quickly weighed out her options, common sense presenting its argument first. She could jump clear of the cultivator which would surely gobble her up if the large tractor tires made even less than one complete revolution, or she could leap up onto the steps suspended nearly three feet off the ground. That would at least show him that she wasn't afraid.

But she was afraid. The tractor tires towered over her by two feet, their deep treads indicative of their ability to roll over huge boulders without the operator feeling even the slightest resistance, and the cultivator was a mass of iron spades that had the potential to dig deep furrows into the gummy clay of the prairies. Her palms began to sweat, her head throbbed with the weight of the decision and then, as though Jayce Harlow had read her thoughts and declared *time's up,* she watched with horror as the outer parts of the cultivator folded up into the air like wings. The hum of the tractor increased in intensity. The wheels started to roll slowly forward, gravel crunching beneath their treads. Even the cat that had been hovering nearby had the good foresight to move out of the way.

Abandoning common sense she jumped, ripping her skirt directly up the back seam. She watched helplessly as her briefcase went spiraling through the air, falling to the ground in a cloud of dust, the cultivator missing it by mere inches.

Debating whether she would be safer on the rickety steps or inside a tractor cab with a mental case, she opted for the cab. With anger leading the way, she stomped up the steps, but the heel of her right shoe caught firmly in the steel tread of the top step, an unforeseen danger. She pulled at it desperately, securing herself to the rail with her right hand, the stronger of the two, but when Jayce Harlow shifted and jarred the tractor into high gear, both hands instinctively gripped to the rail for dear life, the shoe suddenly becoming a minor technicality.

"Open this door!" She demanded, her eyes pleading with a fear she'd never known, but looking the other way as though he were completely unaware of the woman scrambling for her life outside his door, Jayce Harlow proceeded to fiddle with the radio knobs.

Unable to release the door latch, Hana stood on the landing for what seemed like hours, while the hot breeze wreaked havoc with her hair. Her lips were dry, her skin was filmed with a layer of dust, and she was completely at the mercy of a stranger. In a weak moment, she debated begging, pleading Jayce Harlow to stop, but then like the sweet and soothing tune of a lullaby, she heard the distinct sound of the diesel engine gearing down. He was finally stopping and when he did she was going to give him a severe tongue lashing, or maybe a good slug with her other shoe. Yes, that was a better idea, and she slipped it off her foot, irrationally envisioning what she might do with it.

Jayce opened the door slowly, his expression turning to jaded surprise. "Sorry about that. I didn't see you there," he lied. "If I'd have known you were coming I'd have cleaned up the place," sarcasm seethed through clenched teeth.

Well, at least she'd managed to annoy him, she thought as she stumbled inside, still seriously debating slugging him with her shoe, but proper decorum won. She'd get to him eventually and it would be much more effective than a brief moment of physical rage. She'd get to his heart, right where it hurt the most, just like he'd done to her the day he accused her of being a fraud.

The tight confines of the tractor offered very little space but she managed to squeeze her way in beside him, ducking her head and leaning as far away from him as she possibly could. She was disgusted by his attempt to smuggle his amusement and as he shifted the tractor back into gear, the machine gave a sudden lurch, throwing her sideways. Her body collided with his and she recoiled backward, repositioning herself in order to regain her footing.

"I really don't find this very amusing, Mr. Harlow!"

"Nor do I. If that knee of yours slips any further to the right, you're going to hit my gear shift and throw my transmission out," he said matter-of-factly, while his eyes roved over her legs and up to the hem of her short skirt.

Shifting to the left, she found herself to be even closer to him than she was before. She could smell the languid mixture of sweat, dirt, and some sort of shaving cream, and it attacked her senses, making her perspire despite the air conditioned cab.

"I'm not accustomed to having a business meeting inside of a tractor cab," she spoke firmly.

"And I'm not accustomed to having a business meeting, period. Anything anyone needs concerning my business affairs is usually dealt with over the phone. I don't have time to be..."

"Yes well," she interrupted sternly. "It's come to my attention that you haven't been taking your phone calls from the Lone Prairie Financial Savings and Loans Department. That's why I'm here."

Jayce stopped the tractor abruptly, gearing it down to a dull idle. Then he turned to face her squarely, his gaze rewarding her with a hint of vulnerability.

"I want to introduce myself as the Loan Prairie Bank's new Loans Manager," she pulled back and tried to straighten, although it looked more like a painful stoop. "Your most recent loan pertaining to land 15-37-28 w3 is in arrears. You have failed to pay not one, but two quarterly payments. I am here to collect the money owing or to renegotiate your loan. There are several options available to you. You may want to re-mortgage your house or perhaps sell off part of your cattle herd or maybe get a job that will generate some off farm income."

"Now hold it just a gal darn minute. If you think I'm going to mortgage or sell anything, you are sadly mistaken!"

"You owe the money, Mr. Harlow, and you have made no contact with the bank in an effort to deal with this matter. I'm afraid that if you do not settle this within the next six weeks you will lose the land to the bank."

"So, it's true then," a confident smile curved his lips revealing a tiny trace of a dimple in his left cheek. She might not have even noticed it if the dust hadn't settled into it, leaving an almost perfect dot of gray that seemed to beckon her to wipe it away.

"What's true?" She snapped back at him, diverting her attention to his eyes, his deep blue eyes in which she could faintly see a glimpse of her own pathetic reflection.

"You're mixing a little business with pleasure."

"Pardon me? I hardly call this pleasure."

"Well, let me see what I can do about that," he winked and leaned into her, his breath making her cheek tingle.

Several sharp and accusing words came to her mind but jumbled together intangibly, making it impossible for her to grasp a concise thought. She continued to stare at him blankly instead.

"It's probably hard to talk when your mouth's full of sand and grit huh?"

His shoddy attempt at concern unraveled her even further and she watched with trepidation as he reached down to the floor by his feet and retrieved a blue jug. After unscrewing the white cap, he took a long drink. His Adam's apple bobbed up and down greedily, and when he was through he wiped his mouth with the back of his hand and handed her the jug.

"It's still cold," he tempted her.

"No thank you. I would sooner die of dehydration than drink from that."

"Not hard to do around here but suit yourself," he shrugged as though her rejection was of no consequence to him, and then tucked the jug back down by his feet. "So, you've taken the job opening at the bank. The word's been around town."

"Yes," she replied, irritated by the fact that people in a small town couldn't keep a secret.

"Get used to it," he read her thoughts. "Everybody knows everyone else's business around here." He paused thoughtfully and then narrowed his eyes, a signal that the conversation was about to dive straight into the dust. "So then, I presume you'll be honoring the requests of your father's will?"

There it was. "Yes," she replied confidently, taking the opportunity to set the record indisputably straight. "I certainly wouldn't have come to Lone Prairie to work in a bank. I have a perfectly good job in the city and I intend to keep it. Taking a temporary transfer while I'm fulfilling the terms of this ridiculous will and testament allows me to ensure that my job is waiting for me when I return."

"Humph, that's ironic."

"What is?" Hana kept up her guard, fully prepared for an insult.

"That a city bank and ours should be so closely linked."

"Yes, well, the Lone Prairie Bank is now one of the many small town banks that has recently been amalgamated with ours."

"Tell me about it," Jayce grunted his obvious disapproval, "and it's just one more sign that things really have gone backwards."

"Backwards? I'd call it progress," Hana snubbed, somehow certain that she'd just been personally insulted.

"Well, it's not progress when every time anyone calls the local bank, they get an answering service from the city and then have to be put through the agony of listening to elevator music for ten minutes until they're finally forwarded to somebody from our own facility."

"I didn't make the rules, Mr. Harlow, and change is always inevitable."

"Well, not all change is good."

Now that was something she could certainly agree with, but she wouldn't dare give him the satisfaction.

"So, you're the one they've sent to do their dirty work, a city girl who wouldn't know the first thing about farming. Or shall I say, you willingly volunteered, thinking that it would be the perfect opportunity for you to get the edge on people here. You probably haven't even looked at my complete file. The fact that I've never missed a payment until now or the fact that there isn't a farmer around here who isn't feeling the effects of this devastating drought, I'm sure doesn't matter to you does it?"

His smile had completely faded. She was almost more comfortable when he had practically been laughing at her.

"Well, if that's the way you see it, then, yes. I am mixing business with pleasure and if you think you can use the drought as an excuse to forfeit the terms of your bank agreement, *you* are sadly mistaken. I may have been transferred here by my own request, but don't think for an instant that the Lone Prairie Bank doesn't need me. At times like this it isn't unusual for an outsider to have to come in and clean house so to speak. It's good business sense. I have no attachment to the people here, so I can deal with them more objectively."

"Objectively huh? You know, that's not such a bad idea. And here I was feeling sorry for you and wondering how I could allow myself to just sit back and watch you fall flat on your pretty little behind. Objectively speaking, how you survive the next few months on Abner's farm really isn't any of my concern. All that matters is that *you* don't forfeit the terms of *your* agreement."

"Excuse me?"

"As your father's closest friend and confidante, it's going to be a pleasure to see to it that you adhere to all stipulations of his will. In fact, it's my business to see that you do, objectively speaking, of course. Or did you miss that particular section of the will?"

She hadn't overlooked it at all. In fact, it was the part that had been the deciding factor in her decision to come to Lone Prairie for the nine-month term. She would prove Jayce Harlow was wrong. She wasn't the fraud; he was.

The contemptuous sneer returned to his lips and again she could think of nothing intelligent to say, but she scrambled her brain quickly, jarring it back into the professional mind it should have been in from the start. It was wrong to mix her personal affairs with business and she knew it. She'd heard nothing but disastrous stories about people who did so, but the man was incorrigible. He'd made her feel undeserving, a feeling somehow more repulsive than any she had ever felt.

"The bank awaits your response. I'll leave a detailed document on your kitchen table outlining the terms and stipulations," her voice was unsteady now.

Squeezing her way past him, she flung open the door and darted down the steps, resisting the urge to make another attempt at rescuing her shoe. He'd get a good laugh over it at her expense, but what she didn't see wouldn't hurt her. For now, it was better to leave with as much dignity as she possibly could.

She hopped onto the ground still clutching one shoe, and made an exaggerated loop around the cultivator, fearing that the left wing may fall right on top of her if Jayce Harlow should decide to accidentally hit the hydraulic lever. And he was watching her, too. She could feel his eyes laughing as she walked away in her bare feet, grateful for the sandy road that she had cursed earlier. It actually felt soft beneath her feet, a little hot maybe, or rather, quite hot but she'd be fine, just fine.

"Ouch," she stopped short, her foot throbbing in pain. There were tiny stones hidden beneath the surface. She'd have to be more careful. "A lot more careful," she muttered under her breath, although it wasn't the stones she was thinking about. She'd have to be a lot more careful where Jayce Harlow was concerned. Clearly, she'd have to be content with waiting for the long term revenge. *Sugar coated poison* indeed. Actually, there was nothing sweet about the man. He was pure acidic compound and didn't even try to hide it. No wonder he was single.

By the time Hana reached the yard, a tawny orange cat had been amusing itself by nibbling at the corners of her briefcase, convinced that there would be something pleasant inside. Grabbing her briefcase hastily, she snapped it open and recovered the document, pinching it between the screen doors. No, there was nothing pleasant about it. Jayce Harlow had six weeks to deal with his financial lapse or there would be serious repercussions.

The seat of her car burned her legs and she cranked up the air conditioner, relieved to be back within the realms of her own familiar and safe world. Jayce's tractor roared in the field just across the fence line, dangerously close, and she imagined the expression on his face. He was probably gloating for having turned her carefully constructed plan into a made-for-cable nightmare.

With relief she watched him disappear in her rear view mirror, knowing that her vengeful moment of satisfaction was only temporary. It wouldn't last.

Like the seeds Jayce Harlow had sown in spring, their problems would grow, but not into anything fruitful. No, theirs would be the roots of distrust and hostility snuffing out anything that might have been good between them, like a bad weed. Once again, her conscience sent out a warning signal. It reminded her of the feeling of guilt that had washed over her when she'd left the price tag on a very expensive dress and felt it scratching her shortly after refusing to give her annual contribution to a local charity. Had it been a sign or merely coincidence?

Cautiously, she slowed her vehicle and focused on the narrow gravel road as a farm truck sped towards her. Passing by in a billow of dust and a loud crack, Hana pulled over and stopped her vehicle. When the dust cleared, a mark on her windshield came into clear view, resembling a tiny spider web.

It was a small mark, but like the day's events it would spread out in every direction until the entire windshield was nothing but a big crack. Silently she cursed the prairie and her rotten bad luck. Was someone trying to tell her something? No, it was just her overactive conscience compensating for Jayce Harlow's complete lack of one, she decided.

Cautiously, she maneuvered her car back out onto the road, peering around the mark that seemed to be strategically located smack dab between her eyes.

ChApTeR 2

Hana sat on the front porch and gazed at the prairie sky. It was pink, like yards and yards of silky fabric unfolding across the sky. She watched as the late afternoon sun dyed it a pretty coral, not a cloud in sight to stain the fabulous train that seemed to be attached to an invisible entity.

Her stomach growled, breaking the silence. Reluctantly, she pulled herself up from the porch and turned toward the stark contrast that was Abner Crawford's home, deciding without dispute that it shamefully marred the beautiful scenery surrounding it.

It was a shack really. There was no other way to describe it. She had spent the first few days surface cleaning, but it desperately needed a fresh coat of paint, new curtains, new flooring, the list was endless. Well, it really wasn't her concern. She'd only be here for nine months, well eight months and twenty-six days to be exact. At that point she would sell the place to the highest bidder and they could deal with it. But a touch of sadness settled into its well-worn place in her heart. Abner's farm site would become another statistic, like the many other farm houses that stood dilapidated and empty or had disappeared altogether.

Finding a jar of peanut butter from the bag of groceries she'd picked up earlier that day, Hana prepared a hearty sandwich dripping with honey. She'd become an expert at quick fixes and one-sided conversation, but at the moment, that saddened her too.

Nibbling on the sandwich, Hana leaned over the cracked porcelain sink, gazing earnestly out the smudgy window. From here she could see Abner's wheat crop just across the road, a thick and even patch of new green.

There were several farmers in the area who had already expressed an interest in her father's land, the same old crusty farmers who were probably hedging bets over whether she would fail or succeed. They were probably just jealous, she'd convinced herself.

Abner Crawford had been proud of the prime sections of land he owned, half of which was farmable soil and the other half good pasture land. It was the pasture that attracted them though. The drought had dissipated water supplies and grass for cattle was burning up quickly. Her father's land contained a bountiful dugout of water, *an endless water supply*, she'd heard farmer's say. At any rate, it was obvious that Ab's land had received more rain than other areas.

Rainfall was always unpredictable but they were experiencing times when general rains seemed to be a thing of the ecological past. If there was any rain at all, it usually came in the form of cloud bursts or sporadic showers that were often times carried away too quickly by strong winds. Her father's land looked artificial in its state of thick and even green, a tribute perhaps to his incredible farming techniques or his dumb-luck. Whichever the case, even she could appreciate the value of that, but it, too, was irrelevant at the moment.

The only impending concern that demanded her immediate attention was the barnyard and its array of cosmic-like characters. Truly, they seemed to be from another planet. They were strange and uninviting, and when she wasn't looking, seemed almost to be carrying on conversations with each other about her. Yet as always, her ego rose to the challenge.

Besides, how hard could it be? She'd subscribed to the local paper and the Western Producer, she'd been watching the Agricultural News Station faithfully and she'd been listening to as much of the local coffee shop gossip that she could possibly stomach. In just a few days she'd become quite educated on a lot of subjects. Still, the thought of being in full control of God's creatures unnerved her, like the time her mother had volunteered her to baby sit the Timpson twins and the responsibility had been too much. She was young then, only thirteen, but she'd never forget the moment Mr. and Mrs. Timpson had returned home only to find her completely out of control. The memory of it traumatized her even now.

This time, the responsibility seemed even greater. She was definitely dealing with a full house. There were ten cow-calf pairs in the pasture. They were self-sufficient. They had enough grass and water. Of course it wouldn't hurt to check on them from time to time, take a head count, walk the fence line. It wouldn't do to have them find a break in the fence and get out into the neighbor's field, or worse, onto the road.

Even more pressing though was the loud and obtrusive pig in the corral behind the barn, the twenty pesky chickens and the ornery rooster free reigning the yard, the large and intimidating horse in the small grassy area fenced off beside the barn, the clingy cat, the old German Shepherd dog, and finally her idiotic excuse for a neighbor.

Lost in thought for the duration of her meager sandwich, Hana placed her empty plate in the sink, poured herself a tall glass of milk and flopped herself down wearily onto the old snagged and matted brown sofa, her thoughts wandering now to her most recent experience with Jayce Harlow. Chores could wait until her supper settled. Besides, taking mental stock of each day of her life had always been her trademark for better or worse. She'd always been an analyzer, tearing everything to shreds until eventually she couldn't piece it back together again, but who wouldn't have been rattled by the day she'd just had?

Jayce Harlow was a very deranged individual. Like a typical Saskatchewan farmer, he'd devoted his life to the land, but rumor had it that it disabled him from committing himself to anything else. His fiancée had run off, he'd chased off several girlfriends, and in the end swore off women completely.

Certainly, those were not the actions of a sane individual. If she wasn't quick witted and physically agile, he might have actually driven right over her today. Just what was he after anyway? He had befriended her father, an eighty-year old man. Why would a thirty-four year old man want to hang around with someone, who in the end, was barely even able to hold a conversation?

Well, there could only be one answer. *He* was a gold digger. He wanted Abner's land. He knew that Abner was suffering from Alzheimer's disease, that his immune system had become run down and that if any little virus set in he'd be unable to fight it. He knew that Abner didn't have much time before passing from this world, and he knew Abner's business right down to the final balance in his bank account, she assumed. If that didn't spell suspicion, then what did?

Suddenly distracted by the open Bible on the end table, Hana reached for it and allowed her eyes to scour the page. Funny, she hadn't noticed it in the first few days she'd been there.

"Even though I walk in the valley of darkness, I fear no evil, for you are with me," she read Psalm 23:4 aloud, her hand grazing softly over the yellowed page. She wondered if that very passage had been Abner's strength in the days before his death, like chicken soup to feed his soul. There came a time in everyone's life when they needed a little spiritual nourishment. In fact, it was an entire series now. Everyone was jumping onto the band wagon and feeding their souls in one way or another. She wondered if they'd written a *Chicken Soup for the Farmer's Soul*. Jayce Harlow could certainly use it. And what about herself? What would her book be entitled—Chicken Soup For The Cold Career Woman's

Soul? Why was it that she couldn't find anything that really quenched her spirit, or settled it at the very least, the way a soda cracker muted an upset stomach.

Well, she could blame Priscilla if all else failed. Priscilla hadn't had faith in anyone but herself, and she'd lived a relatively long life. Not surprisingly, that thought didn't cheer her. The truth was, she'd always felt that something was missing from her life, something besides an earthly father. Yet, it was comforting to know that somewhere in her genetic make-up was the ability to have faith. No, that wasn't scientifically correct. Faith was learned. Priscilla had not been responsible enough to teach her anything about God because she did not believe, and Abner obviously believed, but had not taken responsibility for anything including her genetic existence. Like the old rickety shack of Abner Crawford, her soul was in bad need of repair.

A sharp rap on the screen door startled her, reminding her of yet another thing that needed fixing. The door was extremely worn and wouldn't hold out a mouse, or a *rat* for that matter. She approached the door cautiously, pulling herself together and bracing herself for round three.

"Jayce Harlow, what a surprise?" She gave him a false smile. Reluctantly, she pushed open the screen door.

"I thought you might want your shoe back, Cinderella." He handed it to her in two pieces, the heel looking like a mangled twig. "You might want to get some proper foot wear for living out here. A good pair of cowboy boots would probably do the trick."

His smile was genuine, but she was cautious. He wasn't here to return her shoe.

"I see you haven't done the chores yet," he stuffed his hands in his front pockets and peered curiously around the yard.

There it was—the nosey sneak.

"Animals do best when you try to feed them on a schedule of some sort," he pressed with a sly grin that she wanted to wipe away with the palm of her flattened hand.

"That's what you really came here for, isn't it, Mr. Harlow?

You came here to check up on me." She stepped out onto the porch, forcing him to back up and out of her way.

"No, actually there's not much that goes on around here that I don't already know about. And call me Jayce."

"Oh really? And what exactly do you know, *Jayce*?" she inhaled deeply, the warm breeze nearly snuffing out all her oxygen.

"Well, I've just been to town. My tractor broke down shortly after you left, so I had to get some repairs. Mr. Jeffreys at the hardware store told me that you bought a pile of bedding plants and some gardening tools, so I assume you're planning on planting a garden. Mrs. Henderson at the feed store told me you bought some cat food, dog food and horse pellets, and Mrs. Peters at the grocery store told me you bought some milk, bacon and a dozen eggs, to name a few things."

Her mouth gaped open in astonishment. The town really couldn't keep any secrets. She'd have to be more discreet from now on, maybe shop in the neighboring town or—maybe not!

"How dare you? Hana quickly recovered from victimized mode. "It's absolutely none of your business what I do!"

"Oh, but it is. And just so you know, I wouldn't fuss too much about a garden. Grasshoppers will be moving into this area very soon, so anything you plant should be in hanging pots instead of in the garden, and even then they'll get to them eventually. The dog and the cat, Shamrock and Sugar, in case you were wondering, prefer table scraps. Ab used to give them his leftovers, only the best, of course. The horse, King, is getting all the nutrients he needs in the grass he's grazing on, so you won't be needing those pellets and if you're craving pork, the pig out back is market weight."

"Market weight? You mean you weigh that blasted thing?"

"No, I can tell. It's a farmer's gift you might say," Jayce stifled a chuckle, clearly amused by her lack of knowledge. "Abner's been feeding him for quite a while. He's prime for slaughter. That will put enough meat in your deep freeze for as long as you're here and then some. Ab just had a steer taken to the meat packers a few months ago, too, so you'll have enough beef, but if you have checked out the deep freeze, you'd already know that."

"You can't be serious. I'm not going to take a pig to the meat packers for slaughter. I'd rather not eat pork...ever again."

"What about beef? I'm sure you've had your share of sirloin steak in the fine restaurants you've dined at. Is it any different that it's coming from your own freezer rather than the grocery store?"

"Yes," she replied defiantly, knowing how silly she must have sounded.

"And the eggs...you don't need to buy eggs. If you haven't checked by now, you'll find you've already got more than enough. Abner's hens lay about a dozen per day on average. If they cut back in production, then you're not feeding them properly."

"And I suppose I should be talking to them on a regular basis or maybe they have a favorite song they like to hear before bed?"

Jayce paused momentarily, raised his eyebrows and crossed his arms in a serious gesture that showed he clearly meant business. "Actually, that's not as silly as it might sound. There are a lot of farmers around here who believe that talking to their chickens actually increases their happiness and thereby their production levels. But then if you don't say the right things you might actually reverse the effects. In your case, perhaps it would be better if you just kept your mouth shut."

"Very funny," she eyed him viciously, biting her lip so hard she could almost taste the blood.

"Well, whether you believe it or not there is some truth to it and they do actually need to be tucked in, meaning that you make sure they're all in the hen house at dusk with the door locked securely. We have a lot of foxes who love dining on chicken cuisine, if you know what I mean."

"All right, fine," she relented, hoping that they could finally get off the crazy subject of chickens. "I won't buy any meat or eggs, but milk? Now that, even you must agree, I can't produce out of thin air."

"No," his serious expression turned to a guileless grin. "That's why I picked up Betsy from the Veterinary Clinic in Lone Prairie today."

"Betsy?" Hana looked backward over her shoulder at his old beat up truck which pulled a small stock trailer painted grey at one time, she presumed. Orange primer covered patches of rust and made its ability to hold the cantankerous animal questionable. To confirm her fears, the trailer rattled violently to the rhythm of the restless animal inside.

"She's a bit high-spirited but she'll calm down for you if you treat her nice."

"She can't be mine! Ab never said anything about a milk cow," she challenged, wondering if Jayce had simply devised this scheme, deliberately setting her up for failure.

"Well, we weren't sure how things would pan out with the old girl. She's becoming a bit blind in her old age...ran into the barbed wire fence one night, but the vet was able to stitch her up and she's just as ornery as ever. See for yourself."

Jayce led her to the stock trailer parked in the middle of the yard. When the cow heard them approach she bellowed, stomped her hoofs and rattled the old trailer so hard that Hana feared she'd come bursting out.

Hana took a step backward, and clutched her heart. He couldn't be serious. "No! I'm not keeping her here and you can't make me."

"I'm afraid I can," Jayce frowned, shaking his head in disbelief. "If you want to own this place then you must adhere to the stipulations. The will states that you must live off the farm and maintain its revenue. I'll unload Betsy in back of the barn. She needs to be milked morning and night and be sure to do it at regular times. It'll cause less discomfort for her and will result in better production for you. If at any point you get a surplus of milk or eggs, Mrs. Weinstead, your neighbor to the west, is always willing to pay a fair price."

He paused and waited for her reply. When it didn't come, he capitalized, throwing his carefully made point right over the summit and into the realms of no return. "It's not personal. I'm just doing my job, honey."

Her temper boiled, but she followed numbly, watching in disbelief as Jayce unloaded the cow. He left quickly then, leaving her alone with her new cosmic-like character who seemed to be staring nervously at her new owner's hand.

Hana looked downward to find that she was still clutching the dreadful shoe, and feeling somewhat guilty for giving Betsy the wrong impression, she let out a holler, and threw it as far as she could. It landed somewhere in the tall grass, leaving her with no relief from her anger, but instead, another reminder of something else that needed to be done. The grass needed mowing.

Whirling around, she stomped to the house. Where was that despicable will anyway? Finding it pinned to the corked bill board she ripped it off, thumbtacks flying and free-falling to unforeseen places that could only be found by her bare feet when she least expected it, but for now she didn't care. Grabbing her black rimmed reading glasses from the top of the refrigerator, she leaned against the kitchen sink, reading it all again for perhaps the twentieth time.

My Dear Hana;
  You may not be at all amused by my suggestion, but you must understand this from my point of view. I've only just met you. I have no real proof that you are mine, but I desperately want to take your word for it. Now, in my absence I know you can't prove it to me, but Jayce Harlow is as close to a child of my own as I've ever had. He will be watching you. Prove it to him, Hana. If you can live at my farm for nine months, living off its resources, maintaining everything that I've started, then the farm is yours at the end of that time. If you breach this contract through no fault of your own, you will be given a second chance. For example, in the event that an animal should die through natural causes, having no direct relation to your treatment of them or lack thereof, then you will be given

*another chance. The same rule applies to the land. You are
not responsible for weather conditions, but you are
responsible to keep the weeds in control, to cultivate and
fertilize when necessary, and to make full use of the land
within your nine month term. If you should run into any
trouble, Jayce Harlow will help you out in a bind. Although
he seems to dislike you, he is a good man and would never
deliberately misinform you. You can be certain of that.*

*Hana, if I'd have known about you, I would have wanted to
be a part of your life. I regret the way things turned out with
your mother and I. Please don't resent her or me or Jayce.
He's had a whole bunch of troubles of his own and that's why
I hope you'll understand that if you should fail, I want Jayce
to have it all. Anyway, I hope you feel the beauty of the land
in your soul. My life was humble but blessed. My place is old
and not very glamorous but it was mine. I was proud of it
and maybe some day you will be too.*

Your Father?

Abner Crawford

*Oh and P.S.
Betsy likes to be sweet-talked.*

So there was a Betsy after all. Jayce Harlow hadn't been lying.
Tears stung her eyes. Why had it become so important for her to
prove that she was Abner Crawford's daughter? And why had he
died before they could have gone about this like sane individuals.
There were such things as paternity tests. If he was so adamant
about proof, then why couldn't he have requested one?

Hana stabbed the letter back onto the billboard. It was all her
mother's fault. Priscilla Islander had left her husband knowing
full well she was pregnant. She just hadn't bothered to tell him,

and Abner was just as much at fault. Heck, while she was on a roll, maybe it was God's fault too. If there really was a God, why would He leave her in the middle of such chaos? What had she ever done to Him?

At the very least she deserved some answers, and immediately the memory of her missed opportunity flooded her brain. If Abner hadn't gone off on a tangent of some sort and called her *Cilla*, if Jayce Harlow hadn't come onto the scene and accused her of being an opportunist and trying to take advantage of an old man, if she hadn't been so mortified by his accusations and taken off running.

Well, who wouldn't have? She'd been emotionally wrought under the circumstances and had stomped off to her car, unaware of the fact that a feisty rooster was hot on the heels of her designer shoes. She must have looked a sight when she'd finally caught a glimpse of the brown matted monster and taken off running. But the rooster meant business, she was sure of it, and even though the sound of Jayce Harlow's laughter continued to infuriate her, she probably still would have run from the ugly bird with the evil, black eyes.

Nevertheless, Abner had believed that Jayce was honorable, and maybe he was. Maybe he was just doing his job by looking out for Abner, but two could play that game. Her job was just as important. She was the Loan Prairie Bank's new Loans Manager and she had a reputation to uphold. They'd hired her because she was capable of dealing with a bunch of difficult farmers who were defaulting on their loans because of hard times. It wasn't personal. She was just doing her job. Everyone had to be accountable for the choices they made in life, and Priscilla, Abner, Jayce Harlow and all the other farmers in Lone Prairie were no exception.

ChApTeR 3

"Okay Betsy, nice Betsy. Hold still and we'll have this over and done with in no time." Hana couldn't tell if she was attempting to calm herself or the obstinate cow. She'd failed to milk her the first evening and today they were both paying for the missed milking. The cow was severely uncomfortable and Hana had to get to work soon or she'd be late.

For the most part, she'd actually enjoyed the morning. Most of the animals were becoming familiar with her. Not even the chickens scattered in the opposite direction when she filled up their water feeders and gathered the eggs, except for the rooster. He stood always just a few feet behind her, rolling his beady little eyes and cocking his head to the side as though ready to pounce if she should do anything that didn't quite suit him. At one point he'd even taken a run toward her, only to stop short when she turned to face him, as though caught in a crime. She assumed he was nothing more that a fluff of hot air. Perhaps, she could remind him that feather-down pillows were her favorite.

"Okay old girl. Let's give it another try," Hana knelt down in the tall green grass, and Betsy, more intelligent than Hana thought possible, sidestepped to the right and held her head high as though heading up her own dairy strike.

"You're going about it all wrong. You'll never be able to milk her like that."

Hana lurched and fell heavily backward, her butt absorbing the shock of the hardened ground. The milk pail, however, took the opposite effect and flew through the air, missing Jayce's head by mere inches. Betsy, equally as startled, took off running again to the opposite corner of the corral, her suspicions about unpredictable human kind confirmed.

"Jayce! You nearly scared me half to death!"

"And you nearly killed me. I'd say that makes us just about even."

"I wasn't expecting company. Maybe you could announce your visits before just showing up in my yard," she fumed, attempting to catch her breath.

"Likewise," Jayce raised his eyebrows quizzically.

Touché, she thought, but would never have spoken it aloud. Besides, she was happy to see him, despite the fact that he was acting as if he owned the ray of sunshine he stood in. He looked fresh and even handsome in a pair of chocolate brown Wranglers, a brown pair of work boots, and a crisp white t-shirt. Perhaps he wasn't quite the slob she'd originally accused him of being. In fact, today it was she who looked a little rough around the edges.

Wearing an old ratty grey sweatshirt, she quickly tabulated how long she'd owned it. High school? No, couldn't be that long, and sweats? Busted. She'd only ever owned one pair and they'd definitely been a requirement of high school gym class. Oh well, couldn't be helped now. Nor could she fix the way she'd carelessly twisted her hair into a knot and clipped it onto the top of her head—the perfect crown to a plain-Jane face that held not even a stitch of make-up.

"I was worried about Betsy...thought I'd check in and see if you managed to milk her."

"Does it look like I've managed anything with her?" she responded spitefully.

"Not even last night?" His own sarcasm quickly changed to genuine concern.

"No, and believe me I tried. She just won't let me anywhere near her."

"Here, let me show you. You're going about it all wrong. You go grab a pail and I'll get Betsy. Ab has a barrel of oats in the barn. If you fill some into an ice cream pail, she'll follow you like a puppy."

Hana watched him lead the cow into the barn effortlessly and would have felt betrayed if she wasn't so blatantly angry. How was she supposed to know anyway?

"This is her stall. She's used to this stall. Fill up this bunk with some hay from the stack beside the barn and she won't even notice that you're trying to milk her."

Hana went to the stack, grabbed a pitch fork and stabbed a pile of hay. It was dusty and made her sneeze and when she reached the stall, Jayce was laughing. Casually, he handed her a blue and white polka-dotted hanky from his back pocket.

"Do people still use these things?" She stared at it as though it was a foreign object, and in a way it was. She'd only read about them in books, or how did that old song go? Something about *straw hats and old dirty hankies*? But just then another sneeze came, and instinctively she raised the hanky to her wet and watering eyes. Uncertain about what to do with it next, she looked up to see Jayce laughing pitifully.

"What's so funny?"

Her irritation nearly reverberated off the cold stark two by fours, slivered and full of musty cobwebs. She'd never been one to laugh easily, and much to her relief, Jayce pursed his lips and cleared his throat, assuming his serious demeanor once again. "You can keep it," he said and then slowly proceeded to carry on with the lesson, surprising her with his ability to be helpful rather than condescending.

"There's a small stool over there in the corner. Grab that and then we'll get started."

Hana retrieved it dutifully, taking a quick moment to slip the hanky into the front pocket of her jogging pants.

Jayce sat down on the stool and took the pail, slipping it quietly beneath Betsy's udder. "She prefers to be approached on her left side. If you try to milk her from the right, she'll crowd you into the panel. Now, just squeeze gently like this, in rhythm, two at a time," he explained, although suddenly he appeared to be less comfortable.

Well, it was rather embarrassing, intimately embarrassing somehow. She felt her face flush and was grateful for the dark and dingy barn, even though the smell was quickly becoming overwhelming.

"Come sit down and give it a try," he tugged at her elbow, and she crouched down beside him, letting his hand guide hers. His hand was rough and calloused but soothing somehow, and she felt sorry when he let her go and the responsibility to relieve Betsy now belonged solely to her.

"A good way to judge if you're not sure is the amount of milk in the pail. Betsy usually manages to fill it three quarters full."

The milk squirted generously and a few droplets managed to squirt her in the eye. Vexed, she wiped her face with the back of her sleeve and carried on, careful not to allow Jayce to see her irritation. What she really wanted to say was, *here take it, the cow, the land, this old run down shack. Take it all*, but stubborn pride gagged her and she refused to give in.

When they were through, he watched her intently while she released Betsy back out into the corral. A fresh pile of cow dung in the barn posed yet another problem and she stared at it uneasily, waiting for Jayce to break the silence.

"What?" She demanded, immediately becoming defensive.

"Did you know that the average milk cow produces forty cups of milk a day?" Jayce grabbed a shovel from the assorted gadgets Abner had hung carefully on the west wall.

"No, I didn't know that," she replied dryly, wondering why he thought she should find that interesting.

"You don't actually have to drink the milk," he paused, confident that that particular tidbit of information would interest her greatly. "People around here will buy it from you for their animals or you can freeze it and sell it to Mr. Demker, the veterinarian. He uses it for newborn calves that have been orphaned and a lot of other things besides."

"So why did you insinuate I had to drink it?" she prodded, choosing to allow her anger to take precedence over her relief in the fact that Jayce had not left her to deal with the cow pie.

"I just wanted to test you."

"How neighborly of you," she shot back feeling that somehow the score had just tipped in his favor. "Did Abner drink the milk?" she blurted with a strange curiosity that didn't seem to fit the moment.

"Yes, but it does take a little adjusting to get used to non-pasteurized milk. I'm not particularly fond of it myself, but give it a try. Maybe you'll like it."

"Why did Abner insist on milking a cow anyway?" Hana's irritation increased as she struggled to untangle a piece of straw from her hair.

Jayce paused thoughtfully. "Well, Ab was a bit old-fashioned I guess. When people started doubling the size of their farms to keep up with the changes, Ab stuck to his old ways. They called it mixed farming back then. Ab always said, *never put all your eggs in one basket.* He always felt that it was better to run a few cows, pigs, chickens, plant assorted grains. That way if the price bottomed out in one area, you'd always have a back up."

"Sounds wise."

"It is, but the industry has changed so much. It's become more of a business than a lifestyle. I kind of miss the old ways. They were practical to a fault. We're supposed to have so much more in this day and age but sometimes it seems like we have less."

Jayce hung the shovel back in its rightful place and then turned to face her. The conversation had taken a bit of a personal turn and truthfully, she hadn't a clue how to respond. Silence enveloped her, daring to send her most inner thoughts 'priority post' to a man who was a virtual stranger. She reeled them in, returned to sender. Whatever her relationship was with Jayce Harlow, it was certainly not supposed to get personal even though she couldn't deny that it had become just that.

Desperate for a change in conversation, she turned her attention to the cow dung which had now attracted a swarm of black flies in its new spot outside the barn door. She covered her mouth, her stomach whirling unexpectedly.

"I suppose you've thought of a practical use for fresh cow pies, too."

Jayce smiled. "Well, not fresh ones, but the fermented ones make good fertilizer for crops and gardens and the dry ones used to burn well in coal stoves in the 30s when times were tough and they couldn't afford coal."

"You really do have an answer for everything, don't you?" Hana placed her hands firmly on her hips, wondering why she'd still felt the need to chastise him even after he'd helped her out of a tremendous bind.

"You asked," he shrugged nonchalantly. "Anyway, I've got a lot to do today, so I'll be on my way." He turned to leave with a tip of his John Deere hat and a smile that still spelled amusement.

"Wait," she called out before she could stop herself. Who didn't have a busy day? If it wasn't for Jayce, she probably would have been late for work. She owed him something.

"Thank you," she paused, waited, frowned. When he couldn't seem to reply with a traditional 'you're welcome' out of common decency if nothing else, the hairs stiffened on the back of her neck. "It doesn't change anything though," she quickly recovered from rescued mode. "You and I still have some business to settle."

"Well, I should say it does change things. Poor Betsy should at least feel a little better."

Jayce turned to leave, resisting the urge to shake his head in frustration. And just why hadn't he said 'you're welcome'? Because she wasn't welcome that was why. Besides, he was too busy paying attention to the fact that her red hair had fallen from the twist she'd secured to the top of her head. Now it framed her face in rebellious kinks and he thought, for a moment, that he could relate to their obstinate reaction to constant restraint. The woman made him feel a little kinked too, in the neck, and if he wasn't careful she'd think she'd got the better of him. Confidence, real or otherwise, subtly mixed with a touch of arrogance, seemed to work best with the woman he decided, and then quickly ignored the urge to look at her, standing proud and defiant, in his rear view mirror.

He'd convinced himself that he was doing it for Betsy. All anyone needed to do was take one look at the woman in her pinstriped skirt and high heels to know that she wasn't capable of managing a farm. He didn't want to have to haul the poor cow to the vet again. He'd already taken too much time to help Hana Islander as it was.

Yet, he had a pile of fencing to do today just across the road. The fence around Ab's pasture had been deteriorating in the past few years and this morning he'd found one of Ab's calves wandering on the road.

It still seemed a bit strange to think that his old and trusty friend was gone forever, and whenever he was around anything that Ab had taken so much pride and joy in, it saddened him. He recalled the many times he and Ab had walked the fence line together. *Grass isn't greener on the other side, but try telling them that*, Ab used to say, and Jayce chuckled at the memory of the man who didn't miss a beat when it came to farming affairs.

The old Ab would have repaired the fence years ago if he had been in good health, and Jayce would have repaired it for him if Ab hadn't been so stubborn, insisting that he was still capable of doing it himself. Now, he'd have to fix it anyway, despite the fact that the strange turn of events had rendered the fence repair to now be the responsibility of one said and stubborn Hana Islander. Had the idea not seemed so preposterous he might have actually relented to the notion that she really was Abner Crawford's daughter.

"Ab Crawford's daughter, a banker of all things," he mumbled aloud. Could it really be possible? Well, so far he wasn't completely convinced, but today there had been no time to deliberate. Until Hana Islander was thoroughly broken into the realities of living on the prairie, the fence needed to be fixed before a stray calf got itself or someone else killed. Oh, he'd get her into the fixing and repairing shortly. Managing a farm required constant maintenance, but if he had to start somewhere, it had to be with Betsy, and that was about all he could handle for one day.

Besides, it wasn't as though he was working with someone who had grown up around farming, or at the very least had any bit of an appreciation for it. Hana Islander was a cold, harsh business woman who had an edge about her as sharp as a switch blade and every bit as portable. It just seemed to pop up whenever he least expected it, keeping him at bay and making him regret ever having come close.

Well, if it wasn't for old Ab, he wouldn't have either, he tried to convince himself, but her image had stuck in his brain the previous night with more clarity and persistence than the day he'd first met her on Abner's front porch. The heated exchange between them had caused him to toss and turn until he'd finally decided to just get up and start his day. That had been somewhere around four o' clock in the morning, and now he was feeling the miserable consequences of no sleep.

She was beautiful, in kind of a stiff and rigid way. It was that alone that had been his saving grace. He wasn't attracted to that particular brand of women anymore. Prim and proper wasn't necessarily in tune with kind and decent. He'd had to learn that the hard way. But yesterday when she'd come looking for him, when he'd left her standing on the landing of his tractor, when her hair had been disheveled by the wind and framed her face in tiny wisps that flowed into the softened hollows of her cheeks, it was then that he saw her for who she could be beneath all that starch. Yes, a little dirt definitely looked good on the woman and if it could penetrate her cold hard surface and find its way to her soul, then he would know for sure if she was really Abner Crawford's daughter.

There ain't nothing more entertaining than watching a woman pretend to be something she ain't, and then in the end finding out that maybe, that's who she was all along, Abner's prediction took him back in time. Then, he'd thought that Ab was having one of his spells, but now he could see that Ab wasn't perhaps as trusting as he'd thought. Abner Crawford was nobody's fool. He had definitely seen something in Hana Islander that didn't ring true. Now whether that proved to be that she was lying about her identity as Jayce had shamelessly accused her of, or whether it was that Hana Islander had an identity that she was unaware of as Abner suspected, didn't really explain why he had to be the one to tabulate the final results.

"Why me, Ab?" Jayce glanced upward at the clear sky, bereft of any clouds, promises or answers, but it didn't matter. He already knew the answer. He'd made a promise to Abner, and Jayce Harlow was a man of his word. Besides, Ab had made him a deal. He'd promised to pull some strings with the Almighty and send them some rain if Jayce complied with his dying wish. Jayce had laughed at Abner at the time, but the gist of Abner's suggestion wasn't that far from the truth. Without some help from the Lord, Lone Prairie would be dealing with another year of drought. Many farmers would be forced to sell and those who were stubborn enough to stay would have a lot of compromising to do at the local bank. Either way he looked at it, he needed do to an awful lot of praying and maybe a few good deeds for Hana Islander while he was at it.

Jayce shook his head with annoyance as his mother's words came back to haunt him, just as they always did when he'd let his guard down and was feeling completely vulnerable. *You don't pray to the Lord only when you need something and you don't help others if you expect something in return.* She'd said it more times than he could count. But then how was it that he found himself in such a triangle where the lines of difference between good will and *willed* good seemed to be blurred? If he wasn't careful he'd find himself in some sort of self-fulfilled prophecy right along with Hana Islander, and that would prove to be the worst mistake of all. History would not repeat itself if he had anything to say about it, and that meant keeping the lines between he and Hana Islander indisputably clear.

Hana arrived at work just in time. She'd only been working at the Lone Prairie Bank a few days, and showing up late would have jeopardized what little credibility she had with her co-workers. They hadn't treated her unkindly, but they hadn't exactly gone out of their way to welcome her either. Of course, she'd been quick to remind herself that their lack of acceptance was irrelevant.

While the bank would never admit to it, they really did need her. In a small town when tensions were running high at the local bank, it wasn't unusual for them to hire an out of towner to sweep in and clear the air. In this case most of the farmers defaulting on their loans were their neighbors, friends, or relatives even. It wasn't in anyone's best interests to be making personal visits to their farms to discuss financial lapses, only to find themselves sharing a church pew the following Sunday. It was a dirty job but somebody had to do it. Besides, the regular Loans Manager had taken a nine-month leave of absence, the timing of which couldn't have been more perfect.

Hana grabbed a strong cup of coffee, Jayce Harlow's file, and headed straight into her office. She had to admit that her visit to Jayce's farm had been made somewhat prematurely. She hadn't gone over all of the information, but in finding enough to incriminate him with, had stormed out to his farm almost immediately. Now, the information in front of her left her questioning her hastiness. It didn't change the fact that he had defaulted on payments, but it certainly left her with many questions when she'd initially thought she'd had things all figured out.

Jayce Harlow's father had not given him the land as she'd assumed. At the time of Sam Harlow's death, the land remained unpaid and Jayce had resumed payments without a glitch. He'd taken full control of his father's farm, making better progress with the payments in his few short years at the helm than his father had made in all the years he'd been farming.

Hana continued to flip through the files. There were several land deeds that were paid in full. Jayce Harlow owned quite a large farming operation. It was amazing that he'd managed to pay off over half of his loans. On the few remaining, he hadn't defaulted on even one payment. His record was impeccable until last year.

It was then that he'd bought a meager eighty acres to add to his present loans. His financial statements and budget projections showed that he should have been able to make the payments easily, but the drought had set him back like it did every other farmer in the area. So, why the interest in this particular piece of land when he knew it would be a financial risk?

Hana pulled the file on the infamous eighty-acres and looked at the municipal map. With yellow highlighter, she scribbled in Jayce Harlow's legacy. Like a maze, his land spread out all around him, his homestead a strategic island in the heart of it all, but the eighty-acres was nearly five miles to the west. Well, there went her first guess.

Removing her glasses, she massaged the bridge of her nose. She could have understood if he'd put himself out on a limb for a piece of land that served as a strategic bridge between his existing property, but this seemed rather strange. Her mind worked overtime, coming up with only one conclusion. It had to be prime property.

Searching the file for some specs on the eighty-acres, she came up empty-handed.

Who could she trust in this office building, she wondered? Her secretary, Rosey Pinkerty? No, she was too much of a busy-body. But she'd know something, Hana created a subconscious argument, weighing out all the odds. Rosey probably knew a little something about everything. But she was sharp. She'd probably catch on if she tried to pry her for information, and maybe even tell Jayce that she'd been snooping around. There had to be someone else that she could skim information from, someone who could give her an insight into the people and the history of the town without suspecting her motives.

Unable to think of any viable sources, Hana decided to take matters into her own hands. Clutching the land title, she made her way to the filing cabinets.

"Can I help you with something?" Rosey snuck up quietly behind her, her arms behind her back as though she'd just caught the mouse eating the cheese.

"No, thank you, Rosey. I'm fine. I'm just trying to find Mr. Bolter's file is all," Hana quickly thought up an excuse and smothered her annoyance with a brilliant smile.

"Why don't you let me do that? I'll bring it in to you right away," Rosey also seemed to be forcing a smile as she ushered Hana back to her office.

"Great, just great," Hana muttered under her breath. Finding answers would be a challenge, especially with *nosey* Rosey poking around. She was probably the kind of woman who didn't get sick a day in her life, either. She was too organized for that. Well, there were other ways to get answers.

"I'm going for an early lunch break, Rosey, and I'm not sure if I'll be back. I'm going to check in on Mr. Bolter this afternoon to make sure he's sticking to the agreements of his farm plan. After that, I'll head home."

"Shall I phone Mr. Bolter to let him know you're coming?" Rosey slammed the filing cabinet shut before the job had been complete, suspicious that finding Mr. Bolter's file had been nothing but a bogus mission. "The farmers around here don't appreciate surprise visits."

That was for sure. "I'd appreciate it if you didn't call, Rosey. It's our right to check in. It's all in the agreements which they have signed."

"Yes I know, but…"

"See you tomorrow, Rosey," Hana interrupted firmly.

Rosey returned to her desk in a huff, her short, blonde, curly hair bouncing curtly. A few others looked on with curiosity but were wise enough to pretend they hadn't noticed. That's what she liked to see. Blending in and making friends wasn't part of her job description and the sooner they all realized that the better. She had an impression to make on these farmers for the good of the bank and it was in the best interests of everyone to stay out of her way.

ChApTeR 4

On her way out of the office, Hana grabbed three more files while Rosey was in the washroom, having decided that if she was going to make any headway at all with over-due accounts she'd have to work around Rosey. She'd also decided that if she organized her time, it would be possible to squeeze in a visit at the Bailey's, the Benton's, and the Bentley's before reaching the Bolten's. Then at least she'd have the B's covered.

Hana stopped at the local diner, deciding to grab a coffee and a sandwich before heading into the country. Several older farmers sat together around the table by the window, dressed in typical work clothes as though they'd just walked in off the field. Grey and black striped bibbed overalls seemed to be the fashion for the older men, and as she'd been noticing, their caps were the only thing that set them apart from their comrades.

Some bore the ironed on embroidered symbol of John Deere, while others prided the Case International brand, or New Holland. Hana smuggled a distasteful sneer. Until she walked into the shop, they probably had nothing better to do than to argue over which brand of machinery was superior.

They graced her with a hush and watched her intently as she ordered a cappuccino and an egg salad on rye.

"I'm sorry, honey. Our cappuccino maker broke down a week ago and Hank says there's no point in fixing it, since nobody around here drinks the stuff," the waitress smiled sheepishly, knowing that while she'd been attempting to be truthful, she'd somehow managed to incriminate her boss as a small town thinker and to insult the personal tastes of her customer.

Hana heard the cluster of men snicker and immediately her back stiffened. "Well never mind then, Cindy," she squinted to read the name tag pinned to the young girl's uniform. It was a trick she'd learned in her years of business, to use people's names in conversation, and she was good at remembering names, too. She was good at a lot of things, she reminded herself, her confidence returning defiantly. "I'll just take a regular black then, to go."

"Certainly," the girl replied and then hustled to fill Hana's order with a smile of relief.

Within minutes, Cindy had the sandwiches wrapped and the coffee poured. Hana paid her the exact amount, digging deeply into her change purse and her confidence bank as the chants of the men behind her grew louder and more distinct.

"Yep, she's just like her mother, flashy and refined."

"I give her a month," another piped in and they laughed simultaneously.

"She probably don't know much about the price of land either. When she leaves she'll be in such a hurry to go, she'll take the first offer."

It was all *she* could handle.

"Excuse me gentlemen, but if you're going to gossip about me then you might want to consider doing it when I leave. Some of us aren't deaf," she lashed out and then headed for the door. "Oh, and by the way," she swung around purposefully with a flare that she knew would make her appear *flashy and refined*, a maneuver she'd learned from her mother. "I will last the nine months, and then at that time we'll see who doesn't know anything about the price of land. Good day, gentleman," she offered them a sweet smile before heading out the door.

Hana slammed the door of her car and sped out of town in a stream of dust, angry with herself for having lost her cool. She should have just held her head high and left, not given them a second of her time. What did she think anyway, that the people here would accept her with open arms?

If she was smart she'd get to know them, the old timers especially, and let them fill in the empty spaces about her past. They had a lot of farming knowledge, too, more than she'd ever have. She had no right to be getting high up on her britches.

Hana rounded the curve and spotted the first farm on her list of stops. Getting to know people in Lone Prairie would not be an easy feat, especially since her job was not the kind that would place her in their good graces. For the first time since she'd been working in the cut-throat business of the banking world, she doubted herself. It was a feeling she despised.

Deciding to ignore it entirely she made her way to the front door of the Bailey residence. She'd been in the banking business far too long to lose her focus. Besides, in retrospect, the bank had done these people enough favors already. Their mortgage payment was now three months overdue.

Hana knocked firmly on a door that looked as though she could blow it over, if she was the big bad wolf, which she wasn't. She was fair and not at all the kind of person who preyed on the weak. Besides, these people had issues far greater than a mismanaged bank account. The place was a mess. Even without money you could still take pride in things and keep them neat and tidy. It was a value she'd learned since arriving on Abner's farm. In hindsight, it really hadn't taken her very long to appreciate Abner's farm for its simple beauty, like he'd merely borrowed a plot of God's earth to use with tender care, unlike this place that looked as though everyone, including God, was indebted to them and responsible for their hardships.

After several unanswered raps on the rickety door, Hana turned to leave, stopping in her tracks in response to the tiny prickles that webbed their way throughout every nerve ending in her body. Since her recent episode with the rooster, her senses had become very keen to the protective instincts of certain barnyard animals.

Without another second to think, a black Labrador crawled out from beneath a caragana shrub. Positioning itself in the middle of her path, it barred her way with threatening growls and a presence that seem to embody the identical personality of its owner.

"Butch," a frumpy woman appeared behind the screened door. "Lay down!"

Hana looked up at the woman with a relief that was quickly swept away by the stern and disapproving glare that met her. Clearly, Mrs. Bailey was every bit as unhappy with her visit as her temperamental dog was.

"What do you want?" she grumbled, peering at her through the holes in the screen door.

"I'm Hana Islander from the Loan Prairie Bank. Do you have a few minutes to discuss…"

"Do you have an appointment?"

"No, I…"

"We don't take kindly to unexpected visitors."

"But I…"

The woman slammed the door shut.

Appalled by the lack of reception from the woman who expected a phone call, Hana swung around to leave. Mrs. Bailey did not look like the kind of woman who cared a hoot about proper decorum in any fashion, and Hana left to the tune of the barking Labrador who found it in his decorum to escort her to her car.

At her second stop, she was relieved to have been invited inside, but disappointed to find that the Bentons were not even capable of paying their power and heating bill. How could she possibly expect them to make a land payment that was due on one hundred and sixty acres that had been ploughed under the last two years due to grasshopper damage?

At her third stop a little girl met her at the door, swiping her skirt with her little hands as Hana entered the tiny porch. Here she was treated kindly by Mrs. Bentley who invited her to a cup of tea, intent on enjoying female companionship despite the purpose of the visit. Occasionally, she stared longingly at the string of pearls Hana wore to accentuate her lavender sundress.

"You must miss the city," Mrs. Bentley said, assuming rather than asking.

Hana smiled and tilted her head with a sigh, allowing the woman to believe that she did, but it wasn't the truth. She didn't miss the city at all, but it was obvious that Mrs. Bentley herself held a secret longing for the things she believed came from the city, like a string of pearls, a silky lavender dress, and a job that came fully loaded with confidence, attitude, and a generous income.

The little girl watched intently as she sipped her own tea from a little china tea set, glancing back and forth from mother to stranger as though comparing the two possible versions of her own future. Hana turned to smile at her on occasion and saw, like the child, a possible version of herself twenty some years ago had her mother not ripped her away from Lone Prairie.

Before leaving, Hana handed the little girl, Molly, a package of red licorice that she had stowed away in the console compartment of her car. She smiled as Molly's eyes lit up and watched her stare wide-eyed at the package before bringing it to her nose to smell the sweet smell of strawberry.

Out of her rear view mirror she caught a glimpse of Molly skipping down the sidewalk and up the front steps with the package clutched tightly in her hand. Mrs. Bentley scooped her up into her arms and carried her inside the house, but not before taking a stolen glance at the expensive red car that seemed to complete the perfect package stamped *Hana Islander*.

Hana turned her attention back to the road, unable to bear the thoughts that pressed her heart. Her car alone could have fed this family well for a few years. It could have clothed Molly, affording a few toys and treats besides. Hana swallowed hard, wondering why her afternoon was quickly turning into one type of disaster after another. Molly was loved and Mrs. Bentley cared deeply for her husband. That was obvious in the way her eyes lit up when she talked about him. Was it so important then that Molly not receive an abundance of toys and trinkets that she would eventually discard?

By the time Hana reached the Bolter's, she was completely exhausted. Having taken a grueling mental stock of her day so far, she'd come to the realization that out of the three visits she'd made, there were no guarantees. None of them could promise a payment anytime soon and it made her genuinely sad, not for the bank but for the people—yes real people, not just clients with seven-digit numbers beside their names. She'd invaded their homes, their privacy, and their pride. Suddenly, she felt ill.

Walking blindly to the next door, Hana wondered what had ever made her think she could handle the position of Loans Manager in Lone Prairie. It was different in the city—or was it? Images of the homeless shelter in Saskatoon flashed through her mind. She had worked there one Thanksgiving through a school outreach program. There were many unfortunate people in the city, too, she had just closed her eyes to them, and there were banks that dealt with people's more immediate financial problems. It had been her choice to work in an institution that catered to the upper class.

"It's true what they say. You look just like your mother."

Hana now stood on the front porch at Harry and Elizabeth Bolter's, her teeth clenched in anticipation of a typically cold welcome. She waited, but it didn't come. Instead, Elizabeth Bolter smiled at her warmly, an apron printed in apples and bananas, tied around her hips, and a voice that sounded like a mother-to-all, an angel on earth.

"Well, don't just stand there. Come on in, dear. Harry and I have been expecting you. I'm Elizabeth Winter-Bolter. I keep my maiden name because it has a nice ring to it, don't you think? Kind of softens the boldness of Bolter," she smiled.

Hana could think of nothing to say. She'd expected defensiveness, doors slamming even, but this was beyond belief. Rosey must have prepared them for her visit. She'd have to deal with her when she got back to the office, thank her or reprimand her though, she wasn't quite sure.

"I'm here to check on how you're doing with your farm budget. I hope I haven't come at a bad time." Hana attempted to recover some semblance of formality, although the thought monopolizing her attention was that Elizabeth had obviously known her mother.

"I've got things all laid out for you on the table there, Miss Islander. I stayed up late last night. Had a gut feeling you'd be passing through." Mr. Bolter pulled a chair out for her and waited politely for her to sit.

"Harry! I knew you looked exhausted today. How late were you up? I didn't even hear you," his wife scolded tenderly.

"Well, it was darn near three o'clock in the morning I reckon. Just couldn't seem to make heads or tails out of these forms. I hope they make some sense to you, Miss Islander."

"Can I get you a coffee or tea perhaps?" Elizabeth took off her apron and looked embarrassed by it. "I didn't take the time to dress up properly I'm afraid. I've been rather busy helping Harry with the farming."

"Oh that's fine. I'm not used to dirt underneath my finger nails, but running a farm seems to keep me in close contact with dirt. I'll have some tea if it's not too much trouble."

Harry and Elizabeth laughed simultaneously. It was what she'd hoped to hear. She wanted more than ever to put them at ease.

"And how are things going for you, Miss Islander? If you ever need any help, Harry and I are just a few miles away."

"Please, call me Hana, and I've been doing fine. Not sure why I'm doing it at all, but I'm fine."

"I can imagine how difficult it must be for you to adjust to country living," Elizabeth's eyes were soft and sympathetic.

"It just doesn't seem to be in my nature," Hana attempted to keep the conversation light.

"Well, your mother didn't have it in her nature either," Elizabeth paused. "I'm sorry dear. It really wasn't my place to say that. Tea's ready."

Elizabeth turned from the table then and hurried off to the steaming kettle, while Harry sat quietly, studying her. She'd been about to ask Elizabeth about her mother, but Harry's suspicions quickly put her in her place. She was here to scrutinize their finances, to put some pressure on them to pay their bills, and all while they were serving her tea. Her stomach churned.

"Well, let's take a look at these forms shall we?" she suggested, wishing only to get it over with so that she could leave before her heart bled all over the kitchen table.

"You'll notice here, I made a list of the products I've used to spray my crops. I've switched to some of the lower grade products to try to stay on budget but I'm not real happy with the results. Wild oats are tough to kill. I should have stuck with a product I trusted and tried to cut costs somewhere else."

Hana looked over the figures that Harry had mulled over until the early hours of the morning. He was right on target with his projections. The bank would be pleased with his ability to stay on track, and he would be able to make his loan payment to the bank in fall. All was well in the world of commerce, but something just didn't sit right in her heart.

Elizabeth served the tea, along with a plate of homemade chocolate chip cookies. "You're looking a little pale, dear. Are you all right?"

Elizabeth's kindness stung her eyes with tears of self-pity that fell sloppily into her tea. Unlike secret thoughts, tears could not be retrieved. Unless Elizabeth had served onions with tea, she'd have to get creative.

"Oh my, can I get you a tissue?" Elizabeth quickly grabbed one from the flowered Kleenex box on top of the refrigerator.

"I have allergies," Hana sniffed, feeling completely ridiculous but proud of her quick wit. Like a few too many glasses of champagne, the lie would dull the ache temporarily, but later, when the silence spoke, it would come back with a vengeance.

"Maybe it's the marigolds. Elizabeth, move that vase out of the windowsill," Harry ordered and Hana watched helplessly as the two fumbled around their kitchen, trying desperately to accommodate her.

She faked a sneeze and then another until she was so caught up in the lie that she'd almost fooled herself. This one would leave a hangover of gigantic proportions.

"There we are. I set them in the other room. I'm so terribly sorry about that," Elizabeth smiled uncomfortably.

"Oh please don't feel badly on my account. You just never know what's going to assault my sinuses," Hana avoided eye contact, knowing full well that it was her conscience that had just been assaulted.

"I'll get you a fresh cup of tea," Elizabeth reached for her cup.

"No, thank you," Hana placed her hand over top of Elizabeth's, the warmth of their hands meeting nearly bringing her to tears again. She thought of Lucy Maud Montgomery's, *Anne of Green Gables*. It had been her favorite series. Now, she could understand what Anne Shirley had meant by a kindred spirit. Elizabeth was a kindred spirit. In her presence she could feel the possibility of truth and friendship, if only she could open herself up long enough to let it in.

"Why don't we just leave this for another day? I can see that you have things in order here. You haven't exceeded your budget in any way. I'll check back in with you at the beginning of harvest."

"But there's the matter of the repairs that need to be done on my swathing machine. I pulled it out of the shop last week and gave it a thorough check. It won't make it through the harvest without some repairs. We haven't worked that into the budget." Harry scrambled to find the sheet of paper that outlined potential expenses. He handed it to her reluctantly, as though he were revealing a page in his private journal. "Here's the list of things I already know will challenge that budget and I'm not sure how I can manage things around here without them."

Hana glanced at the sheet, wondering how she had become privy to information that this man wouldn't have shared with his closest neighbor. Again the tears threatened to fall, and this time she wouldn't be able to blame it on the marigolds.

"Why don't I take these forms with me to the office and have a look at them there? I'll get back to you on your proposed expenses and we'll take things from there."

"Well, all right," Harry hesitated. "But I'd appreciate it if you could get back to me as soon as possible. The mechanic in town is awfully booked up. He'll need some notice and time to order in some parts, and I certainly don't want to be running into harvest without having all my equipment in tip-top shape."

It hurt her that Harry didn't trust her to act in his best interests. He'd obviously dealt with all kinds of callous business people. People like her. Normally she would have kept her dignity, reminding herself that it was the farmers that had gotten themselves into such predicaments. They'd over extended themselves, were poor budgeters, were even in the wrong business perhaps, but she couldn't do it today. Today, they were victims of unfortunate circumstances.

Hana excused herself politely and walked quickly to her car, the heels of her shoes clicking against Harry and Elizabeth's cracked cement sidewalk. Her car looked out of place, frivolous and flashy against the dilapidated buildings, buildings that had once been painted white and trimmed neatly with red. Her car could easily have covered the cost of a total yard make-over and perhaps even the cost for repairs on Harry's swather, and the old Ford truck on blocks near the garage.

Hana wondered if the truck was their family vehicle, if Elizabeth would need a ride to town to get groceries for the week, if—she stopped herself firmly. It just wasn't her concern. She could never help all the people in Lone Prairie and it wasn't her responsibility to do so, but then why did she feel so guilty?

Taking the short cut home, Hana wound her way past the

Harlow homestead. For the first time since her arrival she took a moment to sweep the countryside without the usual criticism. She'd heard people say that a wheat field could look like a turbulent ocean, rippling like waves in rhythm with the wind. She watched as the heads of wheat swayed back and forth revealing various hues of green, with the subtle hint of something even more magnificent. In weeks the countryside would be transformed to shimmering gold, if only the rain would come and the grasshoppers would leave.

Nevertheless, at this very moment Lone Prairie, Saskatchewan looked beautiful and Hana wondered why her mother had not been able to see it as she could today, cloaked in the colors of promise.

Truthfully, it had been easier not to notice it, to delay forming her own opinion, since her mother's had been drilled into her since she was a child. She'd never understood why her mother had been so adamant about independence. Now, it was obvious that everything Priscilla did, she did in spite of the life she ran away from.

But Priscilla wasn't the only one who had fled from Lone Prairie. There had been others who escaped the bleak existence of farming and its false promises, but then there were the chosen few. Somehow *they* found the strength to carry on despite fickle rains, early frosts and grasshoppers. They were invigorated by each season, called to it by each generation before them, bound to it by each generation after. They could feel the beauty in their souls and they touched it everyday, always mindful of their mandate, their call to stewardship.

They could see the abounding potential of something as simple as an ample hay crop, and Hana couldn't help but notice that already the ditches were becoming thick with purple and blue alfalfa, golden brown brome grass, and sweet clover. Not even the keenest scientists could replicate the scent. It couldn't be captured in a bottle, but Hana logged it in her memory along with the nostalgic feeling that she would miss it when she left.

For farmers, it meant hours of cutting and baling. Then, it

would be harvest and time to bring the cattle home from the pastures. The hay would be used to feed them throughout the long winter months until spring and green grass returned again.

Hana drove on, her father's land meeting her around the next bend. Ab had seeded wheat in the spring. It had been his last journey across his soil, planting the seeds that he would not be able to reap, but the fruits of his labor stood tall and thick now, swaying dutifully to the shifting breeze and blessed by a perfect balance of rain and sun. It was no wonder other farmers looked at her enviously. What had she done to deserve such a bountiful possession? Nothing. Not even living here for nine months could justify her right to own a piece of the soil here in Lone Prairie.

The ocean of promise lured her in. She parked her car on the side of the road and waded into its depths, the stalks stretching up to her knees and tickling her with their thick green blades. She allowed her hands to graze softly across the heads and then plucked one, observing it intricately.

"It's looking good, isn't it?"

She jumped and clutched her chest, turning abruptly to face her intruder.

He sat high on top of his horse, looking down at her with a grin that took her breath away.

"I didn't mean to scare you."

"I thought all farmers traveled by noisy diesel engines," she choked, fighting her usual sardonic tone and losing the battle.

"Well, riding horses around here has become a bit of a dying art but I still try to find the time to do it when I can. It kind of puts the country back into the country. Farmers sometimes get so caught up in making a living that we forget why we're doing it."

Hana reached down and absentmindedly plucked a thick green blade from a stalk, distracting herself from the man who looked so self-assured. He'd changed since early that morning. Now, his blue jeans molded tightly to his thighs and a tan t-shirt contrasted gently with his skin. He wore a white straw cowboy hat instead of his usual farmer's cap, and exuded the same strength and confidence that seemed to surround him no matter what his choice of attire.

"If you place that blade between your thumbs and blow just right, you'll create a whistle that can be heard for miles." He hopped down off his horse. "Here, take the reins and I'll show you."

Reluctantly she took them, but the horse, sensing her nervousness, tugged and twisted his head attempting to get a taste of the lush green wheat.

"Twister! Stop it!" Jayce scolded. "Don't give the lady a hard time."

Immediately, the horse obeyed and Hana felt her knees weaken. Fortunately, the horse didn't give her any more trouble, and while she was grateful for that one small thing, she couldn't help but wish that perhaps Jayce would stop giving her a hard time too. She shouldn't have cared, nor should she even have considered that he might get to like her if he just got to know her, but somewhere between Mrs. Bailey's and Abner's wheat field, she'd lost sight of the facade that had led her to believe she could exist for nine months without a soul to guide her.

Hana watched as he placed a blade strategically between his thumbs and then brought it to his lips, blowing until the sound echoed throughout the hot humid air. It was a simple gesture of fun, but the sight of his lips pressed softly against the blade of grass made hers dry and parched.

"Give it a try," he said, oblivious to the effect he was having on her.

"No thanks. If I did that it would probably come out sounding like a croak," she shook her head to refuse.

"It's easy. It's all in how you shape your lips and…"

She was staring at his lips and he caught her, his explanation breaking off into silence and a wide grin.

"What?" she accused defensively.

"Oh nothing, nothing at all," he continued to smile, finding his way under her skin once again. "So, what do you think?"

"Of what?" she snapped back too quickly. *What did she think of his lips?* Well, she thought they were sensuous, perfect really, and probably very...

"Of the crop," his eyes narrowed suspiciously.

"Oh,the crop. Well, it's looking very luscious, I mean healthy," she quickly straightened, regaining her composure.

"Harry sprayed it a while ago to kill the wild oats. I'd say he did a good job."

"Harry?"

"Yeah, Harry Bolter."

"I know who he is. I was just there to see him today, but he didn't mention anything about spraying my crop."

"You went to see Harry today?"

"Yes, I was there on business. I didn't realize that he, well, that I was indebted to him in any way."

"Harry's been spraying Ab's crops for years. When Abner started showing the obvious signs of Alzheimer's, Harry took it upon himself to do all his spraying...sprayed this crop before he sprayed his own. That's why his wild oats got a little out of control this year."

"He said it was because of the chemical he chose," Hana didn't even try to conceal her insecurities. Somehow, finding out what was going on with Harry seemed much more important.

"Yeah, that sounds like something Harry would say. There's more to folks around here than what meets the eye. He'd rather tell a little white lie than have you think that you're indebted to him in any way."

Feeling vulnerable, she allowed his eyes to pull her into a mysterious place, a place she longed to explore. She might have even liked him if they had met under different circumstances, but that was ridiculous. Jayce Harlow hated her, and she loathed him. He was probably telling her all of this just to make her feel bad and it was working.

"Well, I'll have to settle up with him the next time I see him. What's the going rate for custom spraying?"

"Oh! Don't offer Harry any money. You'll insult him if you do that. If you want to repay Harry, I'm sure there are other ways you can think of."

He jammed his hands into his pockets then as if to stop himself from saying anymore, but he'd said all he needed to. She knew exactly what he was suggesting, that she be flexible about his loan payment. People around here really did know absolutely everything about each other and she wondered how long it would take before the entire town knew that she had practically cried a river at Harry and Elizabeth's kitchen table. As for Harry's loan, while she would have liked to excuse him from it and all its stipulations, it really wasn't within her power. She didn't own the bank after all.

"Well, I should be heading on back. You might want to think about getting these ditches cut though. They belong to Ab and you'll be needing hay to feed to your cows when you bring them home from the pasture in fall."

Hana watched with envy as he mounted his horse expertly, her eyes squinting against the brilliance of the sun—or the sun god—Jayce Harlow, the controller of her universe, the determiner of her fate in Lone Prairie.

"Does Abner own a baler or does he contract the work out to someone?"

"Yeah, to me."

Of course. Who else? "So you'll do it then?" she asked with uncertainty, unsure about his agenda.

"For a price," his grin turned from friendly to sly.

"Name your price," she replied nonchalantly ready to do business.

"We farmers try to avoid cash deals. Usually there's some sort of an exchange of services rendered."

"Well, I'm almost certain there's nothing I could offer you in return. In case you haven't noticed, I'm not exactly *Farmer Brown*, so just name your price and we'll call it a deal," Hana's voice grew increasingly agitated.

"Oh, I wouldn't be so sure about that. I think you have a lot to offer," he raised his eyebrows and winked without even a hint of a smile. Then he turned his horse around and rode off, having had the last word once again.

She stood for a while unable to move, and marveled at the fact that his potential to be nice only seemed to be a part of his strategy to take her off guard.

Well, she'd had enough of him for one day. She would head home in the opposite direction, although the thought of testing out her car horn as she was passing by his temperamental horse would prove to be an interesting experiment. It had obviously been named Twister for a good reason. Sensibly, she opted for the opposite direction and complete avoidance.

The roads were unfamiliar beyond the point of Abner's wheat field but she did have a good sense of direction. Besides, all the primitive back roads had to connect somehow. If she just followed the setting sun, she'd find her way back home, she reasoned, but an hour later she slowed her vehicle and pulled safely into an approach, strongly suspecting that she'd just been driving in circles.

She was tired, hungry and too embarrassed to stop and ask for directions. That little tidbit of information, if placed in the wrong hands, would be sure to reach local ears before she even made it home, and she couldn't stand the thought of the farmers in the local coffee shop having just one more thing to laugh about at her expense.

Remembering her municipal map, Hana rattled it open hastily, smoothing the incorrect folds with the palm of her hand. If she could just make sense out of it, maybe she'd be able to make her way home.

Stretching it out across the steering wheel, she searched for landmarks, hoping to find something familiar. She hadn't noticed it initially. It called to her, beckoning in a way that made the hairs on the back of her neck prickle. She'd nearly driven right over it. In sheer disbelief, she squinted, double checked the map and nearly laughed out loud. It was a small monument taking the place of an old country school, not uncommon and even somewhat insignificant if it hadn't been for the numbers. She'd lived her life by numbers. They, unlike people, never lied. She was sitting on the infamous eighty acres that had been causing Jayce Harlow a heap of trouble. She couldn't resist something that had just fallen her way. Besides, it was her right to know, wasn't it? What kind of land would make someone put themselves out on a financial limb? This had to be good.

Hana cut the engine and got out. She doubted that anyone had passed this way in quite some time. Shielding her eyes from the sun, she visually scoured the expanse of the land that led farther than the eye could see. She grazed the marble memorial with the tips of her fingers, feeling something she couldn't describe, a strange combination of doubt and affirmation.

Returning to her car, she reached through the open window to grab the map. A yellow fluorescent streak confirmed that she was, indeed, in the right place.

Early pioneers who had come from distant lands couldn't have felt any more overwhelmed. Why would Jayce Harlow buy eighty acres of unbroken soil? Hana took a step back and felt the heel of her shoe sink into a gopher hole. Cautiously she made her way back to her car, afraid to step any further into the mass of overgrown weeds and unyielding prairie grass.

It was nothing short of a waste of potential and she could hardly believe that Jayce, a man who seemed to be in complete control of everything, would financially put himself on the line for this. Well, even if she wanted to cut him some slack, her good business sense wouldn't allow it. This was preposterous. It would take him years to work this soil so that it would be ready for seeding, and in that time when the land wasn't able to generate income, it would be costing him money that he'd have to find somewhere else.

What was with the farmers around here anyway? The words of her mother came back to her, bringing with them new meaning. *Pride goes before the fall—sugar coated poison—a strange breed of men.*

Harry's generosity was noble, but she could afford to pay him with the money Abner had in his farming account, and Harry could certainly use the money. Somehow she could find a way to straighten that one out, but Jayce was quite another issue. How could she make him see that his investment was a high risk to the bank?

Hungry and frustrated, Hana got back into her car and headed for home. Strangely, she had no trouble from that point on. The creek led her home like a kind and gentle friend, and the sun seemed to strain itself to stay above the horizon until the moment Ab's farm came into view. She watched it sink quickly then, taking her sword and shield and all of her armor with it. It would bring it all back again tomorrow, when it hailed a new day, but for now she was home, released from the combats of the world and the heat of battle.

The animals, sensing her presence, let out a few barnyard calls that cheered her. They were waiting for her. They needed her. At least someone did. The people in Lone Prairie certainly didn't. Her terrible day played back to her in torturous slow motion.

How many visits like that could she survive? There were stacks of farming loans that needed to be reviewed. What had ever made her think she could handle such a position? There would have been others more qualified, people who had a stomach for that sort of thing. And Jayce—well she couldn't handle him either if she was being completely honest.

Again she did a quick count of the time she had left in Lone Prairie, like a child waiting for Christmas, but she wasn't a child. She could make her own decisions. No one was telling her she had to stay, so really, what was keeping her here? A slip of paper pinned to Abner's bulletin board? Yes, it was definitely the root, but it had grown into so much more. Now, it had had become a rather large weight around her neck clearly labeled P-R-I-D-E, and if pride really did go before the fall, then she was in great danger, although which was the greater fall, she couldn't quite decide.

Returning to a life that now seemed to belong to a different person would be nothing more than a planned bungee jump. Sure, her heart would momentarily fall to her feet, but she would spring back again, the memory of Lone Prairie nothing more than a brief adrenaline rush. But what if she stayed the full nine months? Now that was a deliberate jump out of a burning building into the safety of a fireman's net for her pride's sake—fairly safe, but she'd feel it in the morning. Then there was the third option. It was nearly unthinkable. She could stay forever, but it would be the riskiest fall of all, more like a push off a craggy cliff, no nets, no cords, only a pile of faith that somehow she might be saved from inevitable destruction.

Her life flashed before her eyes and was sadly lacking the right to redemption. Sorting through the ashes, she found anger instead of a Phoenix of hope. Who had started the fire in the first place? Ab and Priscilla? And if so then Jayce Harlow was fanning it with a vengeance. She resented them—all three of them. She'd never allowed herself to become vulnerable to anything and now it seemed as though the very person who was nearly pushing her over the edge was standing below her, net in hand, ready to save her only to say *I told you so*.

Well, they'd all be waiting a little while longer. There'd be no jumping today, despite the fact that the events of the day had succeeded in wearing down her defenses. If Priscilla, Ab, and Jayce Harlow had set her up for a fall, then they had just better turn up the heat.

ChApTeR 5

The crops were burning. Even Ab's crops were starting to show the detrimental effects of the moisture shortage. Hana parked at the edge of the road and peered in at the stalks that hung limply, wilted and battered by the heat of the day. It was devastating to watch something with so much potential lose a bit of its brilliance and worth everyday. She had never thought about it in that way before, the fickleness of farming.

She wondered how farmers could push themselves from day to day with no guarantees that all their hard work would pay off. Could they ever claim that their revenues were in direct proportion to all the long hours of work? She was sure that in the history of farming the two never balanced out, and that was certainly true of Jayce Harlow.

He worked endlessly, tirelessly, like a machine. Hana wondered what motivated him, with no wife, no children, nothing in his life to balance the day to day demands. It was a thought that haunted her, bringing with it a reminder that it was not far removed from her own existence.

The sight of Jayce's tractor tilted dangerously in the ditch caused her heart to seize up momentarily. He was hauling in another load of hay and Hana relaxed again when she saw the tractor level out onto the road and head back to the Harlow homestead. It had become a part of her daily routine to look for signs of him and she did it automatically, almost as though knowing what Jayce Harlow was up to was as important as looking both ways before crossing the street.

Her own hay had been delivered by Jayce a few days earlier, stacks and stacks of square bales, and it baffled her that he would take care of her needs first. At first she imagined that perhaps he was just a gentleman, but on second thought she decided that there must be some ulterior motive.

Consequently, she avoided him and he hadn't made any efforts to approach her either. The lack of contact made her nervous. Sooner or later the fact that she was now indebted to him would creep up on her like a rebellious shadow. Jayce Harlow couldn't be nice. It was only a matter of time before he'd blow a fuse, she was sure of it.

Her mind conjured up all sorts of images of how he'd demand repayment. In just a few days his payment was due to be paid to the bank, or at the very least some agreement was to be made in lieu of payment. More than likely he expected her to waive the deadline. Well, he'd be extremely disappointed if he expected any such favors. She had people to answer to as well.

Hana turned into her yard and cut the engine, another long day's work at the bank behind her. Normally, she'd felt some relief in returning home to the place that often felt tranquil and inviting, but today the grass needed to be cut, the flowers were in desperate need of watering and as always, the chores needed to be done. The work never ended and she wondered how women on the prairie tolerated the constant pressure. *Priority* had taken on a new meaning. It was the only way to deal with the long list of things to do, and today the first priority was the grass. Luckily, Ab had the good sense to purchase a riding lawn mower. It would have been almost impossible to maintain the grass on a farm site without one.

Hana quickly changed into an old pair of blue jeans and a tank top and sprayed herself thoroughly with mosquito spray. Now that was one major thing she did miss about the city. Environmentalists studied the breeding grounds of mosquitoes, determining when to spray most effectively for their removal. Out on the prairie it was up to the individual farmer to take such preventative measures and it was a costly deal. Most farmers chose to buy a case of good mosquito repellant instead.

She found the mower in the shop and immediately began to search through drawers and boxes for an instruction manual. After several minutes of searching Abner's disorganized work bench with fruitless results, she stopped. How hard could it be anyway?

She hopped on and turned the key. The engine whined and she kicked it into high gear, steering it into the tall grass. Lowering the blade, she proceeded cautiously until she'd managed to cut three strips into the patch of overgrown grass. On her fourth turn she heard a terrible grinding sound and turned in time to see shreds of black scatter in all directions. At that moment the blade ceased, sending off the flashing red indicator which warned her to stop the machine.

"Great! Just great!" she muttered, as she investigated the shredded pieces that had caused all the trouble. She picked up the fragments that had once been her black patent shoe and immediately remembered having thrown it into the grass the day Jayce had delivered Betsy.

Like a cataclysmic sign, it had come back to haunt her with an unlearned lesson. What was she supposed to learn from the rapidly increasing moments where she'd felt utterly helpless? Immediately, the answer of a true believer came to mind. *They* would probably say that without God, man is helpless. Everyone needs a little help once in a while. Hana cursed the thought even though it echoed a sort of common sense truth for believers and non-believers alike.

With resignation, she hopped back onto the mower and drove it back to the shop. Mentally, she chalked a phone call to a mechanic onto her list of things to do. It was just one more expense to add to the list that had been multiplying like ant hills since she arrived on Abner's farm.

Spotting an old push mower in the corner of the shop, she let out a heavy sigh. The terms of the will specifically stated that she was to maintain the farm. Allowing the grass to get out of hand would be a breach of contract.

The old mower sputtered and rattled as she heaved it through the tall grass, and then with a physical exhaustion she'd never known she stumbled through the chores, annoyed that she was getting quite an excess of milk and eggs. She would have to give Mrs. Weinstead and Mr. Dempker a call in the morning to see if they'd be interested. It all seemed like such a hassle.

With only the flowers and her meager vegetable garden left to be tended to, Hana took a detour to the garden, deciding that a haphazard water was better than no water at all.

She'd only planted a few petunias, some packages of wild flowers, carrots, peas and few potatoes. It was such an exhilarating feeling to have the potential to grow and nurture something so beautiful. On a small scale, she could almost understand the love that a farmer could have for his land.

Since rain seemed to be a no show, she'd taken Elizabeth's advice offered up during a surprise visit only a few days ago. She'd come bearing a chocolate cake and a vase of orange tiger lilies by way of apology for the rude and disrespectful marigolds.

It didn't take a genius to figure out that Elizabeth had seen through her melt-down completely. She'd never been a good liar, but in the large scheme of things, it really didn't matter. Elizabeth didn't seem like the kind of woman who would let the incident leave her kitchen table. Her visit was sincere and greatly appreciated and at the moment, Elizabeth seemed to be the only person in Lone Prairie without an ulterior motive.

Elizabeth had spoken firmly on the matter of plants, and her advice had been that all plants grew best with water tenderly warmed by the sun. It was the next best thing to God's water and Hana had watched with great interest as Elizabeth set up a rain barrel strategically near the eaves trough and the garden hose. *Sometimes we have to make our own rain my dear,* she'd said and Hana couldn't help but smile at Elizabeth's positive and nurturing disposition as she filled the barrel to the brim with water from the garden hose. *The sun will warm it and it will be right as rain.* It was just one more expression that took on new meaning here in the place that had taken her to a different layer in time.

It struck her as odd that Priscilla should feel disdain at the roll of a farmer's wife, as though they were subservient creatures without goals and dreams of their own. She couldn't have been further from the truth. Elizabeth, the wife of Harry Bolter, was Harry's equal business partner, a good mother, a good cook, a horticulturalist, the one who could always see the silver lining in a storm cloud, the sirloin in the stew meat, could weed out the gossips from the intellects, was unfailingly sympathetic and compassionate. Elizabeth Winter-Bolter was truly a very wise and educated woman.

Feeling a bit cheerier than she had before, Hana filled the watering can and carried it to her waiting flowers. After pouring the water generously into her petunia bed, she paused to pinch some of the dead flowers, remembering that Elizabeth had said to do so, but Elizabeth hadn't mentioned what to do with browning leaves. In fact, upon closer inspection it was obvious that several of the leaves had been nibbled at. Even some of the purple petals showed signs of marring.

Dropping her watering can, Hana surveyed the garden carefully. Nothing obvious. She stepped into the long grass that still needed to be cut. The culprits flew in swarms, scattering frantically in all directions.

"Grasshoppers," she spoke the obvious. *And hundreds of them.* Jayce Harlow had been right. She'd heard that the southern regions of the area had been plagued by them in previous years and that they continued to move north. Her crops, or rather Ab's crops would be next.

Saddened, she watered the flowers slowly, taking in their beauty one last time. Soon they would be gone. Moping to the house with an overwhelming sense of defeat, Hana took a mental note to check on her cattle in the next few days. There was no telling what the lack of moisture was doing to the pasture. Maybe it was already overrun with grasshoppers and the cattle were running out of grass to eat. If that was the case, she'd have to move them home and feed them with the hay supply that was supposed to get them through the winter. Complicated, it was all getting way too complicated.

That night, Hana made herself a cheese omelet, still unable to overcome her finicky dislike of meat from the freezer. The pig out back was gaining weight at a steady rate and while it had become a permanent fixture in her daily routine, she knew that the pig had a greater purpose. She'd have to take it to the meat packers as soon as she could bear the thought.

The cat nudged her, crawling onto her lap but refused to sit still long enough for her to cuddle it. "That's right, I haven't fed you yet have I, Sugar?" She gently stroked the black cat's fur, grateful for the companionship no matter what the species.

In anticipation of something as exciting as some left-over tuna fish, or a partially eaten piece of bologna, Sugar followed Hana to the kitchen and then out onto the front porch, where her meal was graciously divided into two dishes. The old German Shepherd was nowhere in sight, but Hana suspected he'd come when he smelled food. Subconsciously, she ticked off the last chore of the day and went inside, her body aching from the stress of responsibility.

The heat of the day hovered heavily in the old house even as darkness tumbled into the quiet farm yard. Hana turned on the electric fan in the living room, hoping to circulate the air. Air conditioning, it was another thing she missed about her apartment in the city, but the heat wouldn't last. Before long she'd need to worry about where to find enough fire wood for the large stone fireplace that was, perhaps, the most attractive feature in Ab's house. Yet, although attractive, it too indicated a higher purpose, that it was needed in order to heat the poorly insulated structure and somehow she knew she'd have her work cut out for her when snow fell on the prairies.

Unable to think about even one more thing, Hana ran herself a hot bath, pouring in a healthy dose of bubble bath to soften the hard water. It was yet another thing that she hadn't ever stopped to think about until now. Water in the city was clear and fairly soft. It didn't leave the toilet bowls looking dull and brown and you certainly did not stick to the bottom of the bathtub while taking a bath. It had taken several trips to the local drugstore to finally find a product that worked in Abner's water. Now there was a novel idea. Maybe she could just forget about banking and farming and develop a home-based business specializing in products that worked in hard water. Hana giggled out loud, her mood softening with the fluffy and delicate fragrance of the water.

Just for one tiny moment she didn't want to care about the old porcelain tub that was stained orange by the elements in the hard water. Tonight, she'd forget that she was Abner and Priscilla Crawford's daughter, that she hated her job at the bank, and that she liked her neighbor more than she was willing to admit.

Needing desperately to soak her troubles away, Hana watched carelessly as the iridescent bubbles floated softly on top of the water. The small chunk of moon peered through the thin and faded champagne curtains, and for the first time since her arrival she felt totally relaxed.

With her hair clipped up, she eased her head down onto the back of the tub and closed her eyes, thinking about nothing beyond the lilac scented fragrance of the bubbles. Her eyelids grew heavy and she remembered first her mother's sullen warning to never fall asleep in the bathtub, but sensing no imminent danger, she did just that.

It was only a few short minutes later when the piercing screech of chickens awakened her. Forgetting where she was, she jumped to her feet, while her heart fell to her knees. Dizzy and disorientated, she struggled to maintain her balance, as water sloshed onto the floor. Then, in a thrashing haze of helplessness she slipped, her cheek bone smashing the side of the porcelain tub. Pain immediately surged through her body. She should have listened to her mother.

Hana fought back the urge to cry and waited until the wave of pain and nausea settled. When the room came back into focus, she wrapped herself tightly in a bath towel and ran to the kitchen window, peering anxiously out into the soft glow of the farm yard.

The door! She'd forgotten to close the door to the coop where the chickens were perched peacefully in their nests. Something had crept in, a wild animal of sorts, and she had absolutely no knowledge of how to protect herself or the vulnerable chickens.

Eying up her father's rifle hanging in the mounted case on the wall, she attempted to think clearly. It would be the best protection. At the very least she could shoot into the air and scare the thing away, but she hadn't a clue how to work it. She'd never even touched a gun. She'd probably wind up killing herself or an innocent farm animal.

That left only one option. She found it in her nightstand. It was a remnant of her city life, of city mentality. If anyone in Lone Prairie knew that she kept it around for protection they'd laugh themselves silly, but tonight it would certainly come in handy.

She ran out into the humid summer night, stood on her porch and faced the chicken coop. Extending her arm, she pressed the button and clasped her ear tightly, turning the other ear away to protect it from the shrill sound of the signal horn.

The chickens continued to squawk and Hana pressed the button again, determined to scare the predator away. This time it worked. The glow of the yard light revealed the quick flash of rusty brown fur dart out of the chicken coop and slink off into the night. The old saying, *as sly as a fox in a henhouse*, came to mind and irritated her, another cliché that she now could relate to completely. The cowardly fox had crept into the quiet safety of her farmyard and preyed on innocent chickens. Sly, sneaky, conniving and a few other choice words came to mind.

She ran back into the house to slip on a pair of shoes. Her Stilettos stood closest to the door and she slid into them quickly, deciding not to take the time to dress. It was a warm night and the towel would suffice. For the time being it was more important to assess the damage and close the chicken coop door as she should have done earlier that night.

For her own protection she grabbed the baseball bat she kept discreetly hidden behind the door. She was a single woman, after all. It was wise to be cautious. She'd always been cautious. It was why she was utterly disappointed in herself for having forgotten such an important detail. It was completely irresponsible and out of character, and while she tried to blame it on her disillusionment with the grasshoppers and the heat, she knew she'd just been careless. Now there was nothing left to do but face the consequences.

By the time she reached the chicken coop, the chickens had calmed down considerably. Feeling like an irresponsible parent, she crept inside, almost tripping over the two dead birds that lay at her feet. The bloody sight made her clasp her hands over her mouth to stifle a scream that would merely have sent the chickens into another frenzy, but the evidence of her negligence was more than she could handle and she quickly stumbled back outside, desperately needing a breath of fresh air.

The sight that met her eyes as she stepped out into the stifling and humid air, however, was every bit as imposing and she screamed despite the chickens.

"What on earth do you think you're doing skulking around here at night? You nearly scared me half to death!"

"I nearly scared you?" Jayce shook his head in disbelief. "You scared half my herd right out of the fence. What the heck was that awful noise anyway? And what are you doing outside dressed like that?"

Her choice of attire was really none of his business and he stopped short knowing that he'd overstepped his boundaries, but how could he ignore the fact that Hana Islander was standing there in nothing but a blue terry bath towel, looking more attractive than anything he'd seen in a very long time.

"I don't make a habit out of walking around like this," she fumed. "There was a fox in my hen house and I used a signal horn to scare him off."

"Oh, is that all," Jayce's serious expression turned to amusement. "And do you intend to use that thing or have I convinced you that I'm not an alien from outer space?"

Hana allowed the aluminum baseball bat to fall to the ground with a hollow thud. "I suppose you think it's funny," she accused, tears beginning to cloud her vision. "Two are stone-cold dead and I don't have a clue as to how many more he stalked off with. See for yourself," she demanded, pointing inside the chicken coop.

Jayce peered inside, rubbing his chin pensively at the sight of the dead chickens. He took a quick head count then and ducked back out, staring at her as though he couldn't bear to tell her.

"There are three dead now and one is missing, so I guess that makes four."

"It's my fault. I forgot to close the door as I should have. I'll leave the premises first thing in the morning," she looked down at her shoes.

Jayce couldn't help but be somewhat moved by her sense of failure, and while she was busy staring at the ground, he found himself compelled to stare at her.

He was taking advantage of her guilt and he knew it, but she deserved it, or maybe it was he that deserved it, just a tiny glimpse into the soft and attractive woman that dwelled beneath all the cold conviction. It was a small return for all the work he'd been doing for her. In fact, if he wasn't a gentleman, he might have made an obscene request via repayment. Of course he wouldn't be serious about it. He'd only be teasing, but throwing Hana Islander off her mental balance seemed to be the most interesting form of entertainment he'd had in a long time.

She was stunning as usual, and even more so when she wasn't trying to insult him. Under normal circumstances he'd play the hero and take her in his arms and tell her that it wasn't her fault, but he'd regret it later, that he was certain of. He'd be much better off to stick to his original plan, to hold her to her agreement, to be objective. Oh, who was he kidding anyway? The fact was, she'd been driving him absolutely insane. He hadn't had a moment's peace, awake or sleeping, since she'd arrived in Lone Prairie and it was starting to have detrimental effects on his emotional well-being. There was nothing objective about it.

And hadn't he dreamt about her in almost this exact same predicament—distraught, needing comfort, needing him?

In a moment of insanity he contemplated the notion of just kissing her and getting it over with. She'd probably slap him, insult him to the point of exhaustion and then tell him that she wouldn't have anything to do with him even if he were the last man on earth. Maybe then he could get her out of his system. But then again, what if she didn't reject him? What if she allowed it and reeled him in like a helpless fish, choosing a more opportune moment to fillet and sauté him like yesterday's stir fry?

"I'll dispose of the chickens. You get dressed." Jayce shook himself back to reality, opting for objectivity. "I could use a little help getting my cattle in."

"How soon shall I leave?" She asked, staring at a place just over his shoulder.

"You don't have to leave," he spoke too quickly. "The will stated that if there is a loss through no fault of your own, you should be given a second chance."

"But it was my fault," Hana interjected, while tears trickled down and into the scrape on her cheek, causing it to burn.

"What happened to your cheek?" Jayce quickly changed the subject.

"I fell in the bathtub when I heard the noise outside."

Jayce took a step closer until he was near enough to tilt her chin upward and turn her cheek into the shallow glow of the yard light. "That looks like quite a bruise." *He shouldn't have cared, but he was a Christian first.* "It's definitely starting to swell." *And Hana's competitive neighbor, second.* "We'd better take a closer look at it inside." *And finally, he was a man, completely exhausted from punishing himself for being one.*

Dressing quickly, Hana prayed that Jayce might leave in her absence, but when she returned clad in a faded pair of jeans and a t-shirt, he was waiting for her in the living room with a frozen package of sirloin steak and an incorrigible grin.

"See? There are a lot of useful purposes for cold, frozen meat."

She laughed unexpectedly and allowed him to press the brown papered package against her cheek. It stung at first but she endured it, realizing that it felt good to have somebody fret over her if nothing else.

The shrill ring of his cell phone broke the quiet that hung awkwardly between them and Jayce took her hand and held it up to the steak, encouraging her to continue with the remedy until he was off the phone.

"Yeah, I'm aware of it," he said to the caller as he sauntered over to the window.

She admired the way he walked, the way his back arched, not even a hint of a stoop. He was proud and confident without trying, and had a backbone strong enough to carry the weight of a generation and then some. For the first time, she could plainly see that his physical capabilities didn't come close to the strength of character beneath it all, and the soul within him that housed an unbreakable spirit.

"Well, I appreciate it. You bet. Thanks a bunch."

"Is everything all right?"

"Right as rain," Jayce returned his cell phone to the holder clipped to his leather belt. "Mr. and Mrs. Weinstead were making their way home from town and saw my cows out in the ditch. They lured them back into the fence and strung a makeshift wire across the break."

"Wow," Hana replied, genuinely shocked. "That was extremely nice of them."

"Yeah," Jayce nodded thoughtfully, "but it's not unusual. That's what neighbors do. They help each other." He glared at her with a purpose, as though he could drive the concept into her brain if he stared long enough. "Well, since the cows are in, I won't be needing your help. So, if you're all right, I'll be on my way. I'll dispose of the chickens on my way out," he headed stealthily for the door.

"Jayce?" she called out, stopping him before he could leave. "I really am sorry. I would never do anything intentionally to hurt those chickens."

Jayce turned back to her with a wide grin. "And here I thought just maybe you'd plotted revenge."

Hana remembered her first visit to Abner's farm and the rooster that had practically chased her to her car. It was a bit funny if she really thought about it—but just a bit.

"I suppose no matter what I do, I'll always be a bit out of place here. The chickens are as wise to it as the old farmers in the coffee shop," she quickly sobered, her expression turning to self-pity.

"What about the old farmers in the coffee shop?" Jayce took a step toward her, his eyes narrowing with curiosity.

"They just laugh at me is all, but it's okay. They have every right to," she shrugged as though it hadn't hurt to remember their sneers.

Jayce climbed back up the porch steps two at a time until he was standing directly in front of her. Her gaze dropped and he lifted her chin gently until her eyes met his and glimpsed the kindness that she'd convinced herself hadn't existed there. Together, their breaths mingled in the muggy summer evening, weighing as heavy as the heart that she'd exposed to him in a weak moment.

"Don't let them get to you, Hana," he said, his words somehow clearing the air and making it easier for her to breathe. "You hold your head up high and you show them."

She couldn't reply. What could she say to something so completely uncharacteristic of a man she'd nearly painted as evil? Then again, maybe he was just setting her up for another fall. Quickly, she squared her shoulders, but when Jayce turned around to walk away she felt immediate regret, like he had taken her heart and wrapped it up gently, guarding it from the cold.

"Jayce?"

"Yeah?"

He turned back toward her again, looking as though he expected, well, something at the very least. She wanted to tell him to stay, that she did need a little help once in a while, that she needed someone to talk to, someone to—love.

"The grasshoppers are here," she stared straight ahead, losing the battle once again with the stubborn impulse that had always made her cautious.

"I know," he replied with a hint of understanding and disappointment.

"We haven't had any rain for weeks. Do you suppose that the crops will, well...," she stopped herself and straightened, trying to snap out of the abyss that was sucking her into its sad and desolate pit of loneliness. "What is it I should be doing now?"

"Pray for rain, Hana Islander. Pray for rain."

Hana turned out all the lights and crawled into bed, choosing to ignore the silence. Instead, she filled her brain with all the things that validated her existence in Lone Prairie. She hadn't come here to make a life and an abundance of close friends. She'd come here to prove a point and ultimately to win a bet. Her real life awaited her back in the city of Saskatoon and friends awaited her, too. Well, maybe not real friends but acquaintances, people who cared about her. At the very least, she had Joanne.

Oh, who was she kidding? Her life had never been anything but lonely. Her mother had raised her to be independent, to be thrifty about whom she trusted. Priscilla had always warned her that true love didn't exist and it was a waste of time to think that it did. Eventually, she'd come to believe it. After a series of bad relationships, it had been easier just to stop dating than to be continually disappointed and she had the audacity to think that Jayce was strange for not committing to a relationship?

Hana flipped back the covers on the bed and stepped back out onto the weathered hard wood floor. Groggily, she crossed the room to the window, peering out into the hot summer night. Instinctively, she located Jayce's yard light. It seemed nearly close enough to touch.

She'd felt a connection tonight and she couldn't deny it. It was a ridiculous thought, almost as ridiculous as climbing into an antique brass bed in an old shack situated in the middle of nowhere. A few months ago if someone would have predicted she'd be here, she'd have laughed herself silly.

Taking a step backward, Hana glanced into the mirror of the antique dresser. It made her look short, fat and extremely distorted. *Distorted*, now that really wasn't a stretch. It was exactly how she felt, but refusing to allow negative thoughts to lull her to sleep again, she focused on the tangible reality of the things around her.

Everything in the house was old and dilapidated. It was hard to believe that anyone could live here and be happy. She couldn't, she decided, as she crawled back into bed.

If she was to make it through the next few months, she needed to make some changes. Maybe it wouldn't hurt to do a little shopping and buy a few things to brighten up the place. She wouldn't even use Abner's meager budget, since the changes were really not necessary. She had some money squirreled away. Besides, she wouldn't need much. She could improvise, stretch the budget. It could even be fun.

Hana looked around the room again, trying to imagine that her mother had once lived there. Her mother had never been one to cope with living on a small budget. Priscilla's spending habits had been as frivolous and dramatic as her personality, but Hana had prided herself on the fact that she could do a lot of things differently from her mother.

At times it even seemed as though her life was a direct result of deliberately attempting to head down another path; funny then that she should end up at exactly the same place Priscilla had started. But what had been so bad about Lone Prairie that Priscilla Islander had spent her entire life running away from it?

Disgruntled, Hana reached for her night stand and turned the small portable fan up another notch, simultaneously setting it to rotate. The thought that she might never know the answer to that question caused her to toss and turn. Restlessly, she attempted sleep and to swallow the sickening feeling that if only she knew the answer to that question she would finally understand her mother, her father and maybe even herself.

For a moment she contemplated Jayce's encouragement. It had been so sincere, almost as though he really had faith in her. *Faith,* that was another thing altogether. Jayce had told her to pray. Hana closed her eyes and gathered all her thoughts, heaping them into a huge pile of wants. "I want to prove to everyone that I truly am Abner's daughter. I want the people of Lone Prairie to have a good harvest. I want Jayce Harlow to...." What did she really want from Jayce Harlow?

Hana heaved a sigh. She didn't know a lot about faith but she was sure that God wasn't like a genie who granted wishes. Maybe faith started with something as simple as trusting *someone.* At least that was tangible. Was there anyone she could trust? Anyone she could place her faith in? The answer fell into the cracks of the night, shifting from complete darkness to dim shadows once again.

It was nearly sunrise when the soft buzz of the fan finally hummed her to sleep, along with the lullaby of the croaking frogs and crickets singing *eight more months, just eight more months.*

ChApTeR 6

At dawn on Sunday morning, Hana awoke with the sudden notion that it was the perfect day to take a trip into Saskatoon. It had been almost a month since she'd come to Lone Prairie and besides her new idea to do some interior decorating, it seemed only logical that she check out her apartment, empty out her mailbox, and spend some time with Joanne.

Joanne Spencer had been her best friend since high school. With mutual interests, they'd both attended college, Hana heading off into the world of commerce and Joanne in a completely different direction. Finding a budding interest in physical fitness, she'd taken a management position at a fitness center. Their friendship had remained steady and true to its original foundation, providing a certain comfort that hovered somewhere between close and distant. Until now, Hana hadn't longed for anything more.

As Lone Prairie faded far behind her, Hana tuned the radio to her favorite FM station. "Back to civilization," she mumbled aloud, although the thought didn't exhilarate her as much as it should have. For the first time in her life she realized that the day wasn't really hers. She had a responsibility to Abner's animals and even though she'd fed them well that morning, it wouldn't be fair to Betsy or any of the animals for that matter, if she were to be late. It was unfortunate that farmers had so little flexibility. There seemed to be no end to the facts she was learning about their life. She'd been happier in her little world of misconceptions.

When the city finally came into view, Hana took the quickest route to the nearest shopping center, deciding that she needed to be both efficient with time and money. As the traffic slowed and the single lane highway broke into several lanes, Hana found herself tensing and she turned off the music to compensate for her sudden attack of nerves. Driving in the city had never bothered her before, but it seemed busier today, extra crowded and congested.

At the next red light, Hana flexed her fingers which had become nearly stiff from clenching so tightly to the steering wheel. She glanced at the woman in the vehicle beside her and then quickly turned away as the woman peered at her with a hint of irritability. Strangely, Hana felt completely out of her element, like a foreigner. Had she been gone that long?

When she finally turned into the crowded Wal-Mart parking lot, she became even more annoyed, making several loops until she was finally able to squeeze into a tiny spot at the farthest end. It was Sunday after all. Who needed to be out and about today with the same need as she had? City people could browse on any day of the week.

Hana shook her head, dismayed at her change of attitude. Sunday back in Lone Prairie was quite different. She'd watched the steady stream of vehicles head to church around eight-thirty in the morning. She wondered as she watched them return a short while later if they had been given a gift that she had been exempt from, if the only way to receive God's grace was to be born into it like royalty.

It seemed easier at first to believe that was the case, but something, *something*, had told her otherwise. It had seemed at times that when she was really listening, soft invitations came in the breeze, in the kind gestures of Elizabeth and even in the root-bound ways of Jayce Harlow.

Walking cautiously up and down the jammed aisles, Hana let her list be her guide, careful not to be lured into the sections that held tempting items she really didn't need. She wasn't doing this to be fancy, she was just trying to make the old farm house more comfortable, but guilt shot its poisoning arrow, sucking all the fun out of the moment. If she was relying solely on Abner's bank account, she couldn't afford to be fancy or comfortable.

There were many women in Lone Prairie who hadn't enjoyed the luxury of a non-necessity shopping trip in a very long time. How could they? Their money was invested in the farm and hard times and making it through another tough year.

Closing her eyes, Hana attempted to slam the door on the realities of Lone Prairie. She'd be careful and practical in her choices, just grateful for the security of knowing that she, unlike half the people in Lone Prairie, did have money in her bank account that wouldn't be eaten up by another impending year of crop failure.

New curtains for the kitchen, the bathroom and the bedroom were of utmost importance and Hana searched through the piles of lace and frills to find something practical. Unable to find anything to suit her needs, she decided to buy material instead, figuring that the cost to make them herself would be considerably cheaper, assuming that the old sewing machine she'd spotted in the corner of Abner's garage actually worked.

Hana surfed the paint aisle next, deciding to brighten the kitchen with a buttercup yellow and eggshell white. Next, she found a few throw pillows for the sofa and an attractive but useful throw to cover its rough and snagged surface.

Temptation led her to the last aisle where she couldn't resist the urge to rummage through a few things in the craft section. By the time she'd purchased the items in her cart, two hours had passed. Something had to be rescheduled and the choice was obvious. She could phone Mrs. Baker, her landlady, in the morning and have her send anything important to Lone Prairie through the mail. Joanne, on the other hand, was non-negotiable. She'd have a fit if she cancelled.

Hana maneuvered her car out of the parking lot and into mainstream traffic, wishing she'd picked a more convenient spot to meet. Starbucks in downtown Saskatoon was nearly fifteen minutes out of her way, but it had always been their favorite hang out. Diligently, she focused on the destination, trying desperately to change hats. Strangely, nothing seemed to fit and when she caught herself tuning into the country music station for some peace of mind, she knew something was seriously wrong.

"Oh my, Hana? Is that you?"

Their cars reached the parking lot simultaneously, confirming their common denominator of being prompt. They'd shared other values too, such as shiny new cars and fashionable clothes, but today the only thing shining was Joanne, car and clothing alike.

"I'd never have guessed that was your car. It is still red, isn't it? I can't quite tell beneath all that dust." Joanne swiped her finger along the front fender, a smug expression escaping before she could control it.

"Of course it's red," Hana slid her sunglasses down her nose and peered over the top of them, the old familiar gesture that had always made her feel confident and in control. "It's just a little dust is all. It'll wash off," she pretended to be sassy, but failed miserably.

Joanne's eyes narrowed as she gave her friend the once over. "Plaid? Jeans? If I didn't know it was you Hana Islander, I'd put a search warrant out on you."

"Oh come on. I'm still me, just a little too busy to primp properly," Hana attempted to lighten the atmosphere, borrowing Elizabeth's words. "Besides, who needs to be dressed up to shop at Wal-Mart?" she cringed. It had slipped out in a moment of weakness and she waited patiently for her friend to flip out.

"Wal-Mart? Are you serious, Hana? Since when are you an avid Wal-Mart shopper? On second thought, maybe I should get the police to put out an APB on the real Hana Islander."

"Oh, don't be so dramatic. I really don't have any need to be fancy where I've come from," Hana explained as the two found a comfortable corner booth in the specialty coffee shop. But when had it become dishonorable to shop at Wal-Mart? Okay, maybe she hadn't made a habit of it, but it wasn't a crime. Had she really been that judgmental?

"I'll have a Caramel Cappuccino," she allowed Joanne to take care of the ordering and waited patiently, trying to remember what the delectable mix tasted like. She hadn't really missed it or many of the other amenities that came from the city. Okay, maybe that wasn't completely true. She did miss take-out-pizza. Someday, someone would have to invent a chain of pizza shops that delivered to people living in the country.

It seemed strange to think that she and Joanne had been regulars here. Now the only thing that was *regular* was the coffee she drank, and the truth of the matter was—it really didn't matter. A cup of plain old coffee in the early morning light, sitting on Abner's porch in the middle of the prairie had a delectability of its very own.

"Earth to Hana! Hello? Are you there?"

Hana regained focus to see the palm of Joanne's hand waving like a windshield wiper in front of her face.

"Yes, I'm here. I'm just a little tired from the three-hour drive I guess."

"Oh, now, stop your whining. I'm sure the drive here is the very least of your worries. How's it going out there in Hickville? I want to hear all the dirt?"

"*Dirt*...that just about sums it up. Dirt, dirt and more dirt." Hana slid her arms back and allowed Joanne to place the steaming cup in front of her.

"Oh come on. There's got to be more to it than that. Have you found some handsome rancher or are you too busy battling with that Harlow fellow?"

"Honey, there aren't any ranchers there. It's not something romantic like you might find in the foothills of Alberta or the

Rocky Mountains. This is Lone Prairie, Saskatchewan. It's flat and full of grain farmers, and while some of them may express an interest in horses, they have very little time for that sort of thing. They raise cows, pigs, chickens, and children, not necessarily in that order. There's nothing romantic about it," she spoke with conviction, attempting to convince herself that she truly believed her generic description, but then why was it that she wanted to tell Joanne about Harry and Elizabeth and some of the good people she met there. Then there was Jayce Harlow, who even though grumpy and primitive, had an amazing facet to his character that she longed to explore.

"Hello! I'm over here. Can you hear me?" Joanne was once again attempting to bring her back from the twilight zone of Lone Prairie. "What is on that mind of yours? I haven't seen you act this way since you went out on that date with Charlie Adams. Oh! Wait a minute. You've met somebody out there, haven't you? Come on, Hana. You can tell me."

"Well, I, uh…," Hana's thoughts were conveniently interrupted by the tall man walking purposefully toward them, and she couldn't have been more relieved. Was it that obvious that Jayce Harlow was affecting her entire view of the universe?

"Reggie! What brings you here?" Joanne turned to face the man with obvious delight.

"Hana, this is Reggie Dawson. Reggie, this is my best friend Hana Islander." Joanne slid over in her seat and allowed the man to cozy up beside her. With her eyes fixated on him for the duration of their visit, Hana could only assume that he was her new flame.

Glancing at her watch, Hana found her opportunity to leave. She was honestly behind schedule and if she didn't leave now she'd have to contend with a disgruntled Betsy.

Bidding a farewell filled with pleasantries, Hana left the city. Her car was full of the things she bought, but her heart felt empty. She and Joanne had never had the kind of relationship that allowed her to be completely open. In the end, it had just always been easier for her to allow Joanne to believe that she had it all together. Besides, what could she say? Her life had spiraled completely out of control, or in control, or that, for once, she'd found some calm in the middle of chaos? Whatever the case, she couldn't deny the fact that with every mile she grew closer to Lone Prairie, she felt as though she were truly getting closer to home.

The sun was setting when she returned. The yard light peered brightly through the trees and she was grateful that she'd remembered to switch on the porch light. It brightened the front step, welcoming her almost as warmly as the cat who rushed to her feet, causing her to nearly trip right over top of it on her way up the stairs.

"Did you miss me, Sugar?" Hana bent to pet the cat, the fresh country air filling her lungs to the brim and reviving her after her long and tiresome drive. She smiled despite the fact that she had a lot of work awaiting her.

With Sugar temporarily assuaged, she turned her attention to Betsy. On the verge of showing discontentment, Betsy swallowed her pride and exerted some patience with her master. Even King, the old gelding, neighed upon her arrival, and Hana stood for a moment and watched him eat the overgrown grass. He was regal and poised and she'd been intimidated by him from the start.

Normally when she reached out to pet him, he'd pull away, holding his head up high and condescendingly. Today, he let her touch him, and she felt privileged in knowing that he just might have missed her, too.

She wondered what stories he had to tell about his owner, her father. Ironically, King knew more about Ab than she did. In fact, the entire barnyard seemed to house secrets, important details it seemed she would never know.

The chickens, on the other hand, were less mysterious. They made no qualms about their feelings and clucked with disapproval as she entered the coop. They had not yet recovered from the fox incident and it was obvious that she would have to regain their trust. She laughed at the thought. Earning their respect seemed foolish. Yet, it was with a gentle hand that she gathered the eggs from their nests, watered and fed them generously and then closed the door tightly. She wondered what Joanne would have thought about her new-found compassion for all of God's creatures.

With the chores finally done and all the animals content, Hana walked slowly to the house, relishing in the cool, nurturing air. It actually smelled like rain. Could it be a sign that it just might? Even the possibility was exhilarating as she watched the dark clouds roll in from the west. Everything felt almost perfect, but wait, she'd forgotten something.

"Shamrock!" Hana called her old dog, suspicious of where and why he was hiding. When he didn't come she threw in a feeble attempt at a whistle, her mind going back to the day when Jayce Harlow had shown her how to whistle through a blade of grass. Plucking a blade from the grass that needed mowing yet again, she made a sorry attempt, deciding in the end that hollering out his name repeatedly would be more effective.

When he still did not respond, her mind quickly tabulated all the times that he had been behaving strangely. The night of the fox incident he'd been nowhere in sight. He'd failed to do his duty as a watchdog, and despite her own negligence in failing to close the door, she'd been disappointed in him.

This was even stranger still. He must be starving, so why wouldn't he come?

The eerie howl of a coyote off in the distance made goose bumps prickle every inch of her skin and she quickened her pace, deciding that she'd search for Shamrock in the morning, but Sugar rushed to her side before she could get inside, winding her way in between her feet so that she could not possibly avoid tripping over top of her once again.

"What is it Sugar? Is it Shamrock? Do you know something? Where is he?"

Hana reached down to pick up the cat and cradle her in her arms. Together, they went inside, but the cat immediately squirmed out of her arms and scratched anxiously at the door.

"Now what? You want out?" Hana pulled open the screen

door and watched as the cat scurried out, but just as the screen door swung closed the cat turned back, pawing relentlessly at the screen door once again.

"First you want out. Now you want in," she scolded, opening the door again to let her inside, but this time Sugar wouldn't budge.

Hana watched her suspiciously as she scurried down the porch steps, and then turned to wait for her. It was obvious that the cat wanted her to follow. Exasperated, Hana followed the cat feeling somewhat ridiculous, but when Sugar led her to Shamrock cowering beneath the porch steps, she had no reason to doubt the intelligence of the feline species.

Too concerned to be cautious with the old dog that lay helplessly at her feet, Hana reached out to pet him. She'd often heard stories told about rabid dogs or dogs that turned on their owners, but this was different. Shamrock needed her.

"What's the matter old boy?" she crooned as she attempted to ease him out from underneath the cold, steel framed steps.

Seeing that her coaxing wasn't doing any good, she ran to the house to fill a dish of water and to tempt him with his favorite, a strip of bacon.

It didn't work. She'd need a flashlight to investigate more thoroughly and she found one in the kitchen cupboard above the refrigerator. Relieved that the seemingly old thing still worked, Hana rushed back to Shamrock.

The sight that met her eyes was one she'd never forget as she allowed the glow to frisk his furry body. His nose was full of prickly white spikes which she could only deduct were the quills of a porcupine, but it was the huge gash on his leg that caused her to panic and to run to the house to phone the local vet as quickly as her brain would process. When she couldn't reach him she did the unthinkable—the inevitable—Ab had willed it so and for Shamrock's sake, she really had no choice.

Guilt pounded away at her soul again and she felt unworthy of the lives that Abner had entrusted to her.

"I'm so sorry, Shamrock," she whispered, but while Shamrock nuzzled his head gently on her lap, oblivious to blame, Hana wondered if her neighbor would be quite as forgiving.

ChApTeR 7

"Shamrock's getting careless in his old age. Older dogs have usually had their experiences with porcupines and know enough to stay away, but he's been out of sorts since Abner died. I'm not sure if this wound is from a barbed wire fence or a scrap he had with a coyote," Jayce examined the dog gently.

"Do coyotes usually come this close to the buildings?"

"Occasionally. They're usually not a threat, but if you do hear them, all you need to do is switch your house lights on. It'll scare them off immediately. Ab's yard light usually does the trick, but they're hungry. The drought affects them, too, so they take more chances, come closer to farm yards than they normally would. Old Shamrock was probably just trying to do his job. He doesn't have the energy he once had. I'd imagine it won't be much longer before he...," his voice trailed off.

"Just like Abner," Hana didn't need him to finish.

Jayce fixed his eyes on hers and for an instant their souls were locked together in an understanding, a common longing for a man whose significance was becoming like a magnet, drawing them together if they flipped their thoughts in just the right way. It lasted for only a few seconds, until Shamrock squirmed.

Jayce continued to work gently and efficiently at pulling the porcupine quills out of Shamrock's pointed nose with a pair of pliers. Then he cleaned the wound thoroughly with antiseptic.

"He'll have to spend the night inside," Jayce scooped Shamrock up into his arms. "And if you don't mind, I'd like to hang around for a little while just to see if the wound cauterizes. If not, we'll have to track down Mr. Demker. While I am good at a lot of things, stitching up wounds is not one of them."

Hana complied without question and was relieved that once inside, Shamrock seemed to perk up considerably. He took a few slurps of water from the dish she placed near his nose and even ate the bacon she'd tempted him with earlier. Then he curled up onto the old blanket she'd laid down for him and within minutes, fell asleep.

"Can I get you something to drink? I picked up some cola today but I didn't have time to refrigerate it. I do have some ice in the freezer though."

"Sure. Do you mind if I use your washroom to wash up?"

She nodded toward the hallway, taking in his appearance as he walked away.

He was dressed in black jeans and a black long sleeved western shirt, trimmed with a small red rose just below the left lapel. Black cowboy boots and hat completed the classic look and she wondered what she'd interrupted him from when she called.

The man in black, no wait, that was Johnny Cash, she attempted a private joke, but there was nothing funny about the fact that he looked handsome enough to be heading out on a date, his boots polished, his clothes crisp and unwrinkled and his smell always fresh and exhilarating.

By the time Jayce returned she had the cola poured into a tall glass and fizzing with three large ice cubes. For herself she poured a cold glass of water from the tap. She'd longed for it all day. Nothing else seemed to be able to quench her thirst, even though when she'd first come to Lone Prairie she hadn't been able to stand the taste of well water.

She sat adjacent to Jayce, he on the sofa and she on the armchair that she assumed from its level of wear had been Ab's favorite. An air of awkwardness and suspicion passed between them and she wondered if they would ever overcome it. Quickly she reminded herself that her friendship would never be worth as much to him as the land he stood to inherit if she faulted on one tiny detail. But she had faulted—on more than one tiny detail, hadn't she?

The notion that perhaps Jayce wasn't the big jerk she'd originally assumed him to be made her entire body tense. If he wasn't a jerk, then what was he? Frantically, she reverted to her competitive alter ego and eyed him up suspiciously instead.

He looked so at home in Abner's living room and she wondered what his intentions had been towards the old and ailing man. Secretly she longed to accost him with the questions that needled her brain into an almost constant migraine, but now was not the time. The man had just helped her out in a crisis. She wasn't going to attack him. There would be other and more appropriate times for that.

"So, how are things in the big city?" Jayce broke the long and agonizing silence.

Hana nearly choked on a sip of water. How had he known? Irritably, she made a mental note to check her car for an implanted tracking devise.

"Mr. and Mrs. Kelly saw you leave early this morning almost before the sun was up. I heard it in town after church," he grinned, amused by the fact that she still couldn't seem to understand how quickly news traveled in a small town.

"I shouldn't think my taking off to the city for the day would be breaking news," she scoffed.

"Well, it is if people were thinking that maybe you wouldn't be returning."

His eyes held hers in a questioning gaze. They looked bluer today against the earthy tone of his skin which was darker now than on the first day she'd come to Lone Prairie, but his hair took the opposite effect to the sun. It had lightened to become, not white and bleached like some of the artificial looks she'd seen in the city, but rather, golden with frosted tips. The effect was a total contradiction, a blonde beach bum in the middle of Saskatchewan. The image almost made her laugh.

"What's so funny?" Jayce's composure suddenly slunk with his broad shoulders, revealing a hint of vulnerability.

Of course! Why hadn't she thought of that before? If she wanted to turn the tables, she needed to appear secure, to laugh in the face of presumptions, even though what she really wanted to do was take out an ad in the local newspaper threatening everybody to keep their wrinkled little sun burnt noses out of her business!

"I'm just amused by the fact that people think I won't make it here. I've done well so far, haven't I?"

"Sure, with a little help," he corrected her.

Jayce straightened his shoulders, making himself look large and intimidating. He might as well have reached around and given himself a hearty pat on the back.

"Hey, I'll admit that I haven't managed completely on my own, but the terms of the will state that I should call on you if I need anything, and believe me if I had a choice I certainly wouldn't..."

"Hush," he interrupted, placing his cola softly back onto the coffee table. "Do you hear that?"

"No, what?" Hana became immediately guarded, taking a mental run through her chores and praying that she had not neglected anything. No, she hadn't. She was sure.

"It's raining!" He hopped up off the sofa like an excited child, and in just a few large steps he was at the window.

As he pulled back the tacky orange curtain, the first flash of lightening reflected off his face and the crash of thunder that immediately ensued made her curl up tightly into a ball.

"Come look!" he insisted, pulling her up off the chair and out onto the porch. Together they stood, quietly watching, and when the next flash of lightening edged across the black sky, he instinctively put his arm around her.

The loud crash of thunder that followed was barely audible as her senses numbed and her body froze to the spot. A twister could have been headed their way and she wouldn't have noticed. Jayce Harlow was holding her, protecting her, caring about her.

Sensing her body tense, he pulled her closer. "Let's get inside. It's getting a bit too intense for sightseers."

With his hand in the small of her back, Jayce guided her gently back inside, the kindness of his gesture nearly causing her to trip right over top of Shamrock who was still asleep, relaxed and comforted by the presence of his people. It was obvious that he would be all right, thanks to Jayce, but she clearly wouldn't— thanks to Jayce.

She was relieved that he'd interpreted her tension to be a sign of fear of the thunder and he was partially right. She hated thunderstorms, but the greater truth was that she hated the storm that brewed inside of her whenever Jayce was anywhere near.

She watched quietly as Jayce hurried to the kitchen gathering candles and placing them strategically around the room. It unnerved her. Like a child, she held her breath, counting the seconds until the next obtrusive crash of thunder, *one one-thousand, two one-thousand.* She pressed a pillow to her chest as the small house shook in response and the lights flickered, exposed and vulnerable to the wrath of a prairie storm.

In the city she'd experienced only one power failure and could still remember every detail of it. She was just a child, curled up on her mother's lap while her mother shook with fear, barely able to comfort herself let alone a child. It had instilled a phobia within her that she might not have had if she'd experienced it differently. Some children, the next day at school, had talked about how they'd made shadows on the wall with the glow of flashlights or told ghost stories.

Her own story had been a unique tale of fear scarier than any monster or ghost. It was the fear of a child not comforted or consoled by a mother. And maybe Priscilla had done her very best, but it had been a turning point in their relationship where the child had become the parent. The same dysfunction would manifest itself in different ways throughout her childhood.

"I hope you're not afraid of the dark," Jayce teased as he lit each candle with an old cigarette lighter he'd found in the kitchen.

When she didn't answer he turned toward her, his smile slowly turning into a look of disbelief. "How do you manage to stay alone?"

"Is it so absurd to think that an adult might be a little afraid of the dark?"

"I'll stay with you until the lights go back on," he teased, his tone a unique blend of macho protector and heroic gentleman.

"They haven't even gone off yet," she argued, her words trailing off into darkness. She watched in fear as the darkness molded and settled into the room, finding every corner and crevice. "You could have just used the flashlight," she said in her meager attempt to sound calm and unaffected.

"Yeah, but it's not as romantic," he said from somewhere off in the distance and Hana couldn't tell if he was being serious or sarcastic.

Jayce picked up a candle and made his way toward her, bringing with him a soft glow that illuminated his face and made him look warm and pleasant. He placed the candle in the center of the coffee table and returned to his spot on the sofa. "There now, isn't that nice?"

"Lovely," she grunted back and crossed her arms with obvious discontentment.

"Do you know what this will do for the crops?" Jayce chose to ignore her bad humor.

"I think they're damaged beyond help, aren't they?"

"Not exactly. The stalks may be stunted and shorter than usual but a good rain will help the heads to fill at least."

"I hope you're right," Hana replied dismally.

"You don't have much faith do you?"

The question caught her off guard and she wriggled herself deeper into the contours of the old chair, hoping to distance herself from his personal probing.

"Things aren't always as simple as a bunch of figures on a piece of paper. There are a lot of variables in farming. Having a little faith is one of the greatest variables of all."

"But you can't make decisions based on hopes and dreams. There needs to be some basis in reality," she argued.

"Have you ever gone out on a limb, Hana Islander?"

"Never, until I moved to this God-forsaken place and there isn't a day that goes by that I don't ask myself just what on earth I'm doing here." Hana frantically searched for a buffer to protect herself against the man who was getting uncomfortably close.

She hadn't really believed that Lone Prairie was void of the presence of God, and she waited for the inevitable wrath of a faithful man who would defend his home, his God, and his livelihood. From Jayce Harlow she'd expect nothing less. It was, in fact, what she loved most about him.

"First of all, this place isn't *God-forsaken*," he started out strong and passionate. "He is all around us and we are blessed despite the hard times, but if you think it's so terrible, then what are you doing here?" His voice softened as he leaned in toward her, invading her personal space.

For the first time since her arrival, she was grateful for the old clunky coffee table. It was nothing more than a thick block of wood, nicked and scuffed by hardships like the soul of the man who sat across from her. She wondered how in those impossibly slow and grinding hours of the morning she could even dare to dream that Jayce Harlow could be anything more than a man too different and too far removed from her own way of thinking.

"You know very well why I'm here," she snapped, her voice defensive and high-strung. "Land is a very valuable asset. There are countless things I could do with the money from Abner's land. I could invest in stocks and bonds or maybe…"

Jayce threw his head back and laughed.

"Stop that!" She was angry now.

"Oh, I'm sorry," he faked sincerity. "I didn't mean to offend you, it's just that while you may have *almost* convinced yourself that's why you're here, I know otherwise."

"Yeah, you're right. I forgot to include the part about wanting to make your life miserable!"

"You know, at first I thought that was the only reason you'd come, but now I know otherwise," his tone once again turned to serious. "You're here because you have a little faith too, Hana."

"That's just a bunch of bologna," she rose abruptly from her chair, completely infuriated. "There's no point in putting faith in fantasies or in things that just don't exist."

She walked to the window and peered out into the chaotic night, less afraid of the electrical storm than the electricity that was sparking between her and the man she wanted to despise. She was taking out her anger on him, anger that she should have been venting on the very two people who had left her high and dry.

"Is that why you read these magazines? Because they're grounded in fact and reality?"

She turned from the window to see Jayce thumbing through her most current issue of *Lady Love*.

"Give me that," she strode toward him and attempted to grab it, but he was quicker and turned away from her sharply, finding the page that she'd marked with a tiny fold at its top right corner.

"Let me see here, the five most romantic things to do with a man. Number one, take a trip to Paris, the city of love; number two, sip champagne and eat decadent chocolates in a hot tub filled with aromatic bubbles; number three…"

"Give me that!" Hana reached for the magazine, extending her upper body further than her muscles were willing to stretch. Her foot instinctively slid forward, catching on the spindly leg of the coffee table. Inertia took hold after that and sent her twisting through the air. She landed in a heap across Jayce's long and sturdy legs, like a child about to be spanked.

Jayce laughed himself silly as she righted herself and attempted to squirm onto the floor, but he caught her and held her still, his voice changing tenor to deep and husky in a matter of seconds. "Settle down or you're liable to knock yourself out on that thing."

"I think I've twisted my ankle," she reached down to rub the spot that had collided with the leg of the table.

"Here let me have a look," he sighed, as though taking care of her had become his lot in life.

"Not until you give me my magazine." She reached for it and snatched it away successfully, but only because his attention had now turned to her ankle instead.

"Looks like it's starting to swell," Jayce announced with obvious concern. Without another word, he went to get some ice, deciding on a package of frozen peas instead.

"I suppose you're going to tell me I should be growing my own peas," Hana winced slightly as he knelt at her feet, resting the wounded ankle in his lap and wrapping the bag of frozen peas gently around it. "For your information I planted some, but it looks like the grasshoppers may get their pick before I do."

"You know, this place really isn't as bad as it seems," Jayce looked up into her stubbornly set features. "It really is beautiful here, and you can find *real* romance right outside your back door if you've got a mind that's open to it."

"Yeah, right," Hana shook her head haughtily, "like there's anything romantic in this barren wasteland...oh, unless you're referring to the way women tend to dote on their husbands and are content to go to the farmer's market on Saturdays with the occasional perk of going out for the odd meal at the local greasy grill. That's about as romantic as it gets around here."

"So that's the way you see it," Jayce paused thoughtfully, as if to ponder the fact that she could be so out of touch with reality. Laying the bag of frozen peas on the coffee table he joined her on the sofa, intent on demanding her full attention on a subject that most people would have rendered completely pointless and unarguable. "How about this then, the five most romantic things to experience in Lone Prairie are, well, hey! You've already experienced one of them."

"Oh really? And just what might that have been? Milking Betsy?" Hana's ankle throbbed incessantly and her will power to escape Jayce Harlow had completely abandoned her.

"No, but there is hay in a barn and that could lead to...well, let's leave that for now. Let's just start with the basics. Number one, an intimate ride in the cab of a tractor, small, confined and…"

"Oh good grief! You call that romantic?"

"Well, it could be." Every time Mrs. Nelson's been seen riding around with her husband there's been a little one, nine months later," Jayce grinned, making Hana blush. They've got five children already so I'd presume that…"

"Oh just stop it! You people should mind your own business and give your neighbors a little privacy," Hana's level of annoyance was rising in direct proportion to the heat that now burned her cheeks and was making her palms sweaty.

"Well, that would be number two. What could possibly offer more privacy and romance than a power failure? The last time we had an extreme power failure was about six years ago, and you'll note that at the local school they have to split the grade one class into three separate groups in order to best accommodate their educational needs. It's the highest enrollment of any class in the history of Lone Prairie."

"That's ridiculous! Have you people nothing better to do than sit around and calculate?"

"Well, now, isn't that just the pot calling the kettle black?"

"The what calling the what?"

"Oh never mind," Jayce sighed near defeat.

"Well, carry on. I just can't wait to hear number three, probably has something to do with cooking while you're on the subject of pots. Oh wait, let me guess, the way to a man's heart is through his stomach. Even I've heard that one."

"Yeah, that could work," Jayce paused, pursed his lips and warded off the amusement that underlined the fiasco. Skillfully, he returned to serious mode once again. "But no, that's not it. You're not ready for number three. You haven't even experienced number two yet."

He leaned forward then, hesitating only for a second before kissing her like he had a right to. His lips were soft and compromising, offering her the option to pull away, but her body betrayed her, forgetting how to react to the signals of her brain. She was lost and found.

The lights came back on and they pulled away from each other simultaneously, reacting as though they'd been caught in the act of robbing a bank.

"Listen, the rain has stopped." Jayce quickly rose and strode to the window, his speculations confirmed. "Well, I better get home."

He was regretting it, all of it. It was the only natural thing to assume in response to his hastiness in changing the subject. Well, she regretted it too, she told herself a lie.

"Uh...thanks for coming over and...," she stuttered, searching for words that wouldn't allude to the moment that had just passed between them.

"And showing you one of the most romantic things to do in Lone Prairie?" The smile returned to his lips and was accompanied by a flirtatious wink. Clearly, he was not regretful. No, his response was worse. He was unaffected.

Hana winced and drew a deep breath. "I meant thanks for coming over and helping me out with Shamrock."

"Yes, Shamrock. It looks like he'll be just fine. Just keep him inside until he's healed up, and as for you, keep putting ice, I mean peas on that thing," he motioned to her ankle.

Hana closed the door softly and hobbled back inside, emotionally bankrupt and physically exhausted. A ton of ice or peas wouldn't ease her wounded heart if she let that man get any closer, but the lonely house surrounded her and she wished she could call him back. What would be the harm in experiencing a little romance in Lone Prairie? What would it cost to admit that if her heart had once been a block of ice, it was now a warm puddle, dripping slowly and filling up the hollow in her soul?

She knew the answer to both questions without having to think about it. It would cost everything she had within her, everything she'd ever known. Trusting someone, anyone, and especially Jayce Harlow was without a doubt, the highest price to pay.

ChApTeR 8

"Stupid, stupid, stupid." Jayce let the hot water spray into the hollow of his neck in attempts to decimate the hard lump that had formed there earlier. It was still persisting to choke him long after he had left Hana Islander's presence, and unlike the cold stings of rain that had drenched through his clothing and chilled him to the bone, this wouldn't wash away.

The evening had started out with a harmless invitation from some friends. A game of pool, a few drinks at the local bar—heck, it could have even been therapeutic. How many times had he told himself never to answer the phone when he'd been about to walk out the door? He knew better, but it was almost as though his subconscious had a radar set for anything *Hana Islander* related, but instead of flagging her down as potentially threatening, the wires seemed to get crossed and he wound up running toward the danger instead of away from it.

The only good thing to come out of the evening had been the rain, although even that had conspired to thwart his plans, stopping only temporarily to break the spell and trick him into leaving. It had started up again shortly after he left, leaving him with the notion that perhaps it had been his comrade instead, protecting him from the possibilities of near disaster. At any rate, whatever nature's intentions, it had been too late. He'd kissed the enemy, confirming what he'd believed from the first moment he saw her standing on Abner's front porch like a little lost soul, that Hana Islander was nothing but trouble

At the time he'd been convinced that he was protecting Ab. As far as he knew, Ab had no one, except a wife who had left him a long time ago, but at the time his brain hadn't been coherent enough to calculate.

Instead, the sight of Hana Islander standing there in her white trim cotton pants and red silk blouse made his stomach something akin to nauseous. From her pointed white leather pumps to her white silk scarf she was a city girl, modern, sophisticated, and untouchable. The very essence of her embodied all the things he hated in a woman and all the things he loved at the same time, and even though he knew in his heart that Hana Islander was not responsible for his high school sweetheart leaving him to find adventure in the city, she reminded him of Allison.

Still, the memory of an ex-girlfriend didn't give him any right to lash out at her so irrationally on their first meeting. It was unlike him to attack a person without hearing their story. He'd embarrassed her and Ab too, and then topped it all off by preying on Ab's loyalties to trust the ones he could and be wary of anyone else.

Yet, even as the hot water poured down, filling his lungs with steam, Jayce convinced himself that she really hadn't proven a thing and he owed it to Abner to continue to be cautious. Heck, people had been suspicious of his own motives in spending so much time with Abner and he'd lived in Lone Prairie his entire life. They should have known him better than that. Hana Islander was a stranger. There was no telling what her intentions were.

Jayce's stomach suddenly tied back into knots. He wanted to trust her. He shook his head with disgust. This time he was the one who should have known better. Letting a woman get close was not in his best interests. It was a fact that was tried, tested and proven true, not just by Allison Swanson but by a few other women besides. They'd wanted so much more than he could give them, and it had cost him a lot of pride to finally accept that he might never find a woman who just wanted him, plain and simple. So, how was it then that in one weak moment he was willing to risk a broken heart for the wrong kind of girl again?

Jayce turned up the heat, desperately trying to distract himself from his thoughts and the truth that chilled him. He would go through it all again. Given the right circumstances he'd throw his common sense right out the window just for a chance to be with a woman who had *mistake* written all over her.

Reluctantly, Jayce stepped out of the shower and into the damp, cool air. He'd left the bathroom window open, could smell the sweetness of rain and wet grass, but not even nature could clear his senses. The scent of strawberries and *Hana* lingered, and he wondered if burying himself in cow manure would do the trick. Probably not. She was like one of those scented dolls his little sister had as a child. What was it called? Strawberry Shortcake? Well, whatever it was, Jessica had taunted him with it relentlessly until he'd finally given in and smelled her hair. Well, he wasn't going to give in this time, no matter how cute, poised and tempting she was.

"Stop it," he shook his head, water spraying around him like a prairie dust devil.

He could still hear the soothing sound of rain and it cheered him somewhat. With the thick green terry towel he swiped the foggy mirror and frowned at his reflection. He could see it there already, that sappy glow of longing or idiocy. Well, whatever it was, it would just have to disappear.

Jayce focused on the small transistor radio he'd kept in his bathroom and carefully fine tuned it as he heard the familiar song introducing the upcoming weather forecast. Rain hadn't even been in the forecast, and even though it probably wouldn't amount to much, it was better than nothing.

"Just goes to show…weather men don't know everything."

He waited for the long term forecast then, hearing what he'd fully expected, *temperatures expected to be hotter than usual for this time of year—no rain in sight.*

A song from the Johner Brothers broke through the airwaves next, and Jayce cranked it up, hoping to dispel the thoughts that had reversed the effects of the soothing shower. Now his shoulders ached again with the stress of the day, and he closed his eyes, willing himself to enjoy the song and the sound of the rain while it lasted.

"Some days I was living and some days I thought I'd die, if I didn't have a country girl to keep the country boy alive," he sang along to the familiar song until he realized that it, too, seemed to be conspiring against him. Vexed, he turned off the radio.

The operative words had been *country girl*, not *city girl*. He couldn't take a girl out of the city and expect that she'd be willing to change her entire life to be with him, and this woman wasn't like any others he'd ever taken a fancy to. Hana Islander had the unique power of controlling his future in the tip of her ball point pen, and he had only a few short days to figure out how he was going to make up the payments he'd missed to the bank.

It seemed ridiculous now, putting his entire farm at risk for the sake of eighty acres, but it was more than that, much more. He couldn't really explain it, didn't have to explain. He just had to pay for it. The thought weighed heavy on his mind.

Well, he'd think of something. He always had in the past. In fact, his best ideas had come from being placed under pressure. Besides, she had a few things of her own to worry about, like how she was going to get through the harvest and through a long cold winter in Lone Prairie, even though deep down he knew he'd be there to help her, thanks to Abner and his crazy will.

Jayce slipped into bed and switched on his bedside lamp, fumbling for the *Western Producer* beneath a heap of magazines. It was a farming newspaper, not as interesting as *Lady Love*, but it was educational. Jayce pursed his lips tightly and closed his eyes, willing the vision of Hana Islander to go away. When he opened them again the words in bold black letters on the front page of the newspaper did little to comfort him.

"Saskatchewan grasshoppers predicted to cause irreversible crop damage," he read aloud, willing his eyes to proceed, but as the headline blurred new words came into focus. *Hana Islander predicted to cause irreversible heart damage.* He flung the newspaper across the room.

"Rosey, could you please find Jake Forister's file? He and his wife will be here any minute and I haven't even gone over their financial statement." Hana pushed her black rimmed glasses up onto the bridge of her nose, concentrating on the schedule in front of her.

Today was the deadline and even though her morning was filled with work involving several other clients, only one kept dominating her thoughts. She'd have to make a visit to Jayce's farm and demand financial action. She was relieved in one sense that the day had finally come. She'd committed herself to it on two levels, personally and professionally, and she couldn't back out on it now. Besides, she had her own set of professionals to answer to, board members who were concerned with the security of the bank.

While it was true that she'd found ways to grant some farmers special favors, she hadn't been able to waive the deadline facing Jayce Harlow. She'd granted Harry and Elizabeth a two-week extension to make their payment, claiming that there had been an error on the original documents. Harry had questioned her on the phone, almost sensing the dishonesty of her claim, but she'd finally convinced him in the end. She owed him after all, and if offering to pay him was out of the question, then pushing off his deadline was the least she could do.

"Miss Islander, here's the file you requested," Rosey responded formally.

"Thank you, Rosey," Hana extended the same stiff tone, not even bothering to look up from her work, but when it became clear that Rosey had planted herself firmly to the spot, Hana looked up, removed her glasses and placed them lightly on her desk, a gesture that she knew made her look conceited and self-important. "Is there something else?" She questioned without a smile.

"Well, it's just that I thought you ought to know that Jake's wife, Jessica Forister, used to be Jessica Harlow."

"Oh," Hana's mouth went dry. The fact that Rosey was offering her personal information that could be of some use to her was one thing, but the information itself was almost too overwhelming to process. Jayce Harlow had been married and his ex-wife was now remarried and living in the same town? Well, what could be worse?

"Thank you, Rosey, I appreciate your concern but I'm here to make decisions based on numbers, not on the personal affairs of my clients. Now if you'll excuse me, I really need to get to work."

Hana retrieved her glasses, adjusting them accurately on the tip of her nose, while Rosey spun around on her flashy red heels and stomped back to her desk, virtually slamming the door behind her. Hana choked down a sip of coffee and silently cursed herself for having been so rude, but the town and everyone in it was starting to wear on her.

It would take her years to understand all the webs that connected people here and even though she might have been interested in the juicy details, it had no place in her line of work. In fact, the more she knew about the people of Lone Prairie the harder her job would be, and it was becoming difficult enough as it was. Besides, if she allowed herself to become absorbed in the personal affairs of others, she'd be no better than the general populace of the town whom she abhorred for having nothing better to do than to spread gossip.

"Your two o'clock is here," Rosey poked her head in the door a few minutes later, making the announcement sternly.

"Thank you. Please send them in."

Hana rose slowly from her black leather chair, her ankle still a bit tender from her latest rendezvous with Jayce Harlow, but with firm conviction she pushed him out of her thoughts and focused on the couple reluctantly entering her office. Extending her hand in a gesture of formal handshake, she introduced herself and then invited the couple to sit.

Etched in tension and nerves, the couple took a seat on the opposite side of her desk. They held hands as though silently comforting each other against the wrath of Miss Islander, the big bad wolf. Suddenly, she didn't feel well.

"So what can I do for you folks today?" Her response was professional but without the usual cutting edge she usually strived to achieve. Today she softened her tone, wanting to ease the couple that sat before her and at her complete mercy.

Of course, it hadn't escaped her attention that Jessica Forister was a very attractive woman. She was countrified from her baby blue tasseled western shirt to her denim blue jeans. She seemed sweet and pleasant and it wasn't difficult to see why Jayce Harlow had married her, but why he'd divorced her remained a mystery.

"Miss Islander, we've come to ask for a loan. If you've reviewed our file you'll note that I've been keeping up with my land payments. My cattle have been generating some surplus income for the farm but the drought's taken its toll. Jessica here is a very talented hair dresser. She took a course in the city before we got married and, well, I hoped she'd never have to work but...."

Jessica squeezed Jake's hand, reassuring him with a smile as tears clouded her eyes. "I want to work, Jake. I miss my old job and you know it. Besides if all goes well, I won't be working out, I'll be working in."

Jake struggled to swallow his pride but the woman at his side gave him strength. "You see, we'd like to open up a shop in our home. We've got the perfect room in our basement. We just need a bit of an operating loan to get the necessary supplies and to spruce it up a bit. I can plumb in the sink. That won't cost a thing. I'm very good at that kind of stuff," he beamed, his pride returning, but we'll need a salon chair, the sink, some paint and start up supplies."

"How much do you anticipate you'll need from start to finish?"

Hana leaned forward and removed her glasses and then regretted the silly habit. Immediately, she offered them some mints from the jar on the corner of her desk to soften the gesture.

"Well, we think $10,000 should do it. We'd like to take the loan out over five years. That way, if business is slow from the beginning, we'll still be able to generate the payment, but once Jessica's able to build up a clientele, which I know she will," he stopped to smile at his wife, "the business will generate a profit. I know it will."

Hana looked at the files that held Jake's life story, the loan he'd taken out at the age of eighteen to buy his first half-ton, the loan he'd taken at the age of twenty-three to buy an engagement ring, and the loan he'd taken at age twenty-six to expand his cattle herd. The first two loans were now paid in full but the third remained, taken out at a time when interest rates were high. He'd faulted on only one payment. It was when he'd injured his back at his second job, was ineligible for disability benefits and had to borrow the payment from his uncle, who'd demanded repayment only three months later with interest. In the end, he'd had to sell off part of his cattle herd to get caught up on his payments, and work the repayment to his uncle back into the loan.

Hana sighed and closed the folder, setting it aside and out of mind. "Can I see the expenses and start-up costs?"

Jake handed her a sheet of paper neatly written out in a black fine point marking pen. "I apologize for the chicken scratch," he chuckled nervously. "A computer just doesn't fit into the budget."

"That's fine," Hana attempted to reassure him. "I see you've done your research. "When do you need the money?"

They stared at her, mouths gaping, barely daring to breathe.

"You're eligible for the loan," she reiterated, waiting anxiously for their reaction.

They hugged each other first and then came around the desk to pull her into their circle of happiness. She'd never been hugged before by potential clients, not even after having granted a

$100,000 loan. It was unprofessional but positively elating. Suddenly, she felt free.

"Thank you, thank you, thank you," Jessica grabbed her hand and shook it excitedly. "We won't let you down."

"I'm sure you won't. Have a seat and I'll prepare the forms," Hana smiled broadly, truly believing they would succeed.

As Hana busied herself with the details of the paperwork, Jake and Jessica prattled on happily, freely discussing with her their life histories. It seemed to Hana as though the two had never known any other loves. She envied them.

"I'll have these papers processed immediately. The money will be in your account by the end of the day. The sooner you get that shop set up the better," Hana smiled, offering her hand in one last gesture of closing the deal.

"Thanks again, Miss Islander," they beamed as they left her office, their happiness and enthusiasm lingering and making an impression on her heart forever.

For the remainder of the day, Hana watched in anguish as the minutes on the clock ticked slowly by. Forty-five minutes left until closing time and Jayce Harlow was a no-show. Secretly, she hoped that he would take some responsibility in the matter and drop in at the bank, or call at the very least. He'd made no attempts to make things right and the words of her boss pressed heavily on her conscience—*a deadline is a deadline*.

Packing up the necessary documents, Hana left the office, stopping at the local diner to purchase a ham and cheese sandwich and an iced tea to go. She'd skipped lunch again and even though the thought of seeing Jayce turned her hunger pains into nausea, she knew she should eat.

Hana eyed up the attractively wrapped sandwiches as she drove out of town, but couldn't bring herself to try one. The iced tea was all she could tackle for now, and silently she cursed the man who had tied her stomach into knots for the umpteenth time. *She* shouldn't have to feel guilty. Making a personal visit was above and beyond the call of duty. Most loan managers would have taken his well-worn file and handed it over to the greater hierarchy, washed their hands of it. For whatever reason, she'd chosen to give him the benefit of the doubt. Again, her stomach twisted at the sight of the familiar green tractor humming in the field.

It was the strangest thing she'd ever seen and she watched with dismay as Jayce Harlow plowed his crop under. He had already managed to make an entire loop around the field, revealing a strange geometric pattern of black framing the various shades of green wheat. He had to have some reason for doing something so preposterous and she couldn't wait to hear it.

Parking in the nearest approach, Hana killed the engine and waited, listening to the roar of the tractor grow in intensity. If she closed her eyes she could have imagined that it would swallow her up, just as Jayce Harlow would when she interrupted his busy schedule to petition him for money.

The tractor stopped abruptly only yards away from her, the hum gearing down from a loud full fledged roar to a dull sputtering idle, reminded her that its power was only temporarily harnessed. She respected it, along with the man who hopped down from the cab with ease. Her knees grew weak and wobbly.

"I would have been there within the hour if you would have waited," he chastised her almost immediately, a frown creasing his brows in a way she'd never seen before.

"Well, I just thought I'd head home early today, take a look at my crops on the way home," she lied sheepishly, wanting to turn around and run. She wished that she'd just been stopping by for a visit on her way home from work, to bring him a cold refreshment maybe. She wished that she'd come as a friend.

Jayce looked at her cross-wise, squinting against the intensity of the sun. His features softened. "I've got the cheque here. Jake and Jessica were going to pick me up in the next half hour and give me a ride to town. I've got a flat on my pick-up. It changed the pace of my entire day, and my cell phone's dead, too, or I would have called. I apologize."

He looked tired. It was the first time she'd seen him look slightly less than capable of tearing the world apart. She watched as he rubbed at the bristles on his chin. His light blonde features made them barely visible and she longed to touch, to feel for herself the contrast of smooth and rough. The dimples in his cheeks were gone now in the absence of a smile and the need to make them return became so great that she was suddenly struck with an idea.

"We'll get to that in a minute," she said, gesturing for him to put the cheque away. "I'll bet you haven't eaten lunch."

He shrugged. It was all she needed.

"I'll be right back," Hana tried to contain her excitement. Within minutes, she returned carrying a blanket, the untouched sandwiches, and the iced tea.

She led him to the other side of the tractor, away from the sun, and spread the navy and green plaid blanket on the patch of black. She sat down then, smoothing out the wrinkles and patting a spot with the palm of her hand, inviting him to sit and join her. He complied without question and rewarded her with a smile, revealing the dimples that made him look mischievous and handsome.

He watched her silently as she removed the wrap from the sandwiches and then used it as a makeshift plate. Carefully, she placed the sandwiches in front of him, but kept the iced tea.

"I'm sorry I've already taken a few sips out of it. I hope you have some water in the tractor. I can get it for you if you…"

Jayce smiled, winked, and then slowly and deliberately slid the glass bottle out of her hand. "I don't mind if you don't." His eyes never left hers as he unscrewed the lid and took a huge swallow.

Hana's mouth went dry.

"So, to what do I owe the pleasure of this *random act of kindness*?" He smiled and handed back the bottle of iced tea.

Hana could only manage a dismissive shrug.

"Well, whatever it is, I'm grateful for it."

"I'm not an ogre, Jayce," she suddenly felt the need to plead her case.

"No. At least Jake and Jessica seem to think that you're not," he stopped chewing then and placed the rest of the sandwich back down on the plastic wrap. "They stopped to tell me the good news on their way home. I'm extremely grateful to you for giving them a break. They needed one."

"It's good to see that you don't resent her. I'm not accustomed to seeing two people come out of a relationship and still be willing to communicate."

His eyes widened in surprise and immediately she regretted having tread onto the paths of his personal life. It wasn't any of her business but the miserable little town was starting to creep into her in ways she just couldn't control. Like a sponge that had soaked up more than its full capacity, something had to give.

"Just what kind of a relationship are you talking about?" he paused thoughtfully. "Oh! You don't think that Jessica and I were...holy cow, you do." He could read the guilty expression on her face. "Jessica Harlow, now Jessica Forister, is my sister, not my ex."

Rosey—it was all her fault, Hana was quick to blame. For whatever reason, Rosey had wanted Hana to know that Jessica's last name used to be Harlow. Of course, if she hadn't been thinking about Jayce in marriageable terms she wouldn't have naturally assumed that Jessica was his ex-wife.

"I'm sorry, Jayce. I was given some information that I guess I just misinterpreted. I apologize."

"It's all right. You couldn't have known," Jayce decided to leave it be. "My sister is the only family I have. She means the world to me and I'm grateful that you're giving her an opportunity. She and Jake have been trying to have a baby but so far haven't had any luck. Running her own business will keep her mind occupied as well as help out with their farm debts."

"Oh, I see," Hana replied sadly, again finding herself caught up in the heartstrings of Lone Prairie. It hurt her to think that Jessica and Jake had other problems besides financial ones. It wasn't fair. Financial problems were more than enough for anyone to have to deal with.

"Well, I better let you get back to work," she replied, noting that the sandwich was gone and she really didn't have any other reason to stay.

They rose from the blanket simultaneously, both gathering and cleaning and trying to cover up the awkwardness. When the wrappers had been properly disposed of and the blanket neatly folded, Jayce unsnapped the button of his chest pocket and removed the cheque.

Hana imagined the many hours of hard work Jayce had toiled in order to make that money, hours in which he'd probably been every bit as tired, hot, and dirty. Her friends had often scorned at the everyday worker in work boots and jeans, covered in dirt and grease. To them it had been unfashionable. They were wrong. *She* had been wrong about a lot of things. At this very moment, Hana couldn't imagine that any man on earth could look better in a business suit than Jayce Harlow could in a pair of jeans, a farmer's shirt and a layer of dirt.

"Here's the money." He held it in his outstretched hand.

"Thank you," she replied numbly, not feeling worthy to accept something that was worth so much more than the dollar value it indicated. Its value to the bank of Loan Prairie was certainly not worth much more than a speck in a dust pan either. There were so many overdue accounts of greater value and risk than Jake's measly loan.

With his hands folded across his chest he watched her, and the dreaded awkward silence passed between them again. Swiping the green John Deere cap from his head, he wiped his brow with the back of his hand and then scrunched the hat in his hands as though he were fighting a terrible demon. He had *hat hair*. His wavy locks were flattened around the middle where his hat had been and flared out in an unruly fashion around his ears, but it looked boyish and cute and she could barely resist the urge to fluff it up with her fingers.

"I meant to ask you what you're doing here," she found the distraction she needed as her heels sunk into the freshly cultivated dirt. "If this is a new method of farming, I sure am not aware of it," she teased trying to lighten the tension.

"It's a grasshopper barrier. They're moving in. It's not

foolproof but it has been known to deter them. They're fooled into thinking they've hit barren land so they reroute. It might not work but it's worth a try. Grasshopper chemical is extremely dangerous to work with. My land borders Mr. and Mrs. Harold's yard. They have three small children and the conditions would have to be perfect for me to spray. I'd rather just take my chances."

"I see, so you sacrifice a small portion of your crop in hopes that the rest will be saved?"

"Something like that," Jayce paused and tilted his head thoughtfully.

Hana sensed a change of subject coming on.

"It's going to be an early harvest. Do you think you'll be able to manage?"

"Definitely," she replied without thinking. She sounded starchy once again even though his question had not been condescending. It was just her natural reaction to a man questioning her ability to handle things on her own. Yet, for the first time in her life her natural reaction seemed completely unnatural. "The rain sure has helped to fill the heads. Do you predict an average yield?"

"If the grasshoppers don't devastate us, yes," he nodded, looking into the crop that stood proud against the elements.

"Well, I'll see you around." Hana hesitated only briefly before spinning around and starting to her car. She could feel his eyes watching her, but she didn't sense the same hostility as she had felt when she'd first met Jayce, nor did she reciprocate hostility. Things had changed. She had changed for more reasons than she could count.

How could she dislike a man who cared more about the neighbor's children than whether or not his crop was devastated by grasshoppers? How could she find fault with a man who'd just come up with $6,000 and came by it honestly, and there was no doubt about it that he had. She knew his account numbers off by heart and this one came straight from his savings account, which now would hold a balance of zero.

Jayce watched her walk away in her typical graceful manner, despite the fact that her heels were sinking into the dirt. When would she learn to dress properly for the country? It was the most basic lesson and he still hadn't managed to teach it successfully. It didn't seem to bother her though. She was adjusting well and he wondered what it would take to get her to really open up to the prairie, to surrender herself to it fully and maybe to him, too. But the fact that she'd believed Jessica to be his ex-wife proved that she'd assumed the worst about him once again, and had she not just done a huge favor for his sister, he might have told her that when he married it would be forever.

"Hana," he called after her and waited until she turned around, the anxious look on her face nearly rendering him breathless. Instantly, he felt driven by the same irrational force he'd felt every time he was with her. Why had he called her? Because it was the perfect opportunity to scold her about her shoes? No, he knew better than that. He'd called her because he didn't want her to leave.

Calmly, Jayce sought out the objective frame of mind he'd worked so hard to achieve in her presence. It wasn't too late to make an issue about her shoes, but he was too tired to be rational, too exhausted for objectivity and who needed a conscience anyway? His mother hadn't.

"Yes?" She probed, while catching a strand of hair that the wind had just snatched. Irritably, she tucked it firmly behind her ear.

"This is number three you know."

"What?"

"The third most romantic thing to do in Lone Prairie." He walked toward her, his eyes fixed on her lips which had opened slightly in shock. "A picnic in the field, beneath the clear, blue sky, amidst the gentle breeze, being kissed—by—the—sun...."

ChApTeR 9

His lips met hers softly, but they scorched her through and through. When he pulled away he was smiling, always in full control of the secret agenda that propelled him and left her brain completely disorganized.

Seeming completely unaffected again, he hopped back onto his tractor and drove off without another word, while her heart ached all the way home. Irritably, she flopped herself down on the old sofa like a rag doll. The man completely drained her, not unlike the hot and stuffy farmhouse that threatened to suffocate her if the temperature rose even one more degree.

What was he after anyway? Initially, she'd believed that he was merely trying to soften her resolve to get out of paying the money. But this time he'd handed her a cheque and then kissed her. Well, whatever the motive, Jayce Harlow had certainly succeeded in finding her weak spot. *He* was her weak spot.

Hana cringed at the thought that she'd refused to believe from the moment she'd set eyes on the man. He wasn't even her type. Yet, somehow he'd penetrated her resolve and challenged everything she believed about herself. She was strong, she was independent and she could make her mark on the world, but why had it become so important that she do it alone?

After a meager dinner of toast and peanut butter, the long evening loomed ahead, holding little comfort or distraction. Hana eyed up the Wal-Mart packages that had been collecting dust in the far corner of the living room. She'd tossed them there days ago, failing to find the time to do the makeover.

Now, she took a moment to scour the old house once again. It had potential. Even the word *quaint* popped into her mind for a millisecond before she snuffed it out and replaced it with a more practical descriptive.

"Home decorating...how hard can it be?" Hana mumbled aloud and then like any other time she'd set her mind to something, she attacked it head on, tearing the place apart. It didn't have to be a personal thing, even though she was adding a personal touch, she justified her efforts. She could be doing it merely to increase the value of the place, to make it more appealing to the average prospective buyer.

With that goal in mind, Hana worked recklessly, painting the kitchen walls and windowsills, and when she was through with that, she touched up the living room. In only a few hours she had accomplished more than she could have imagined possible.

After a meager lunch consisting of a banana, strawberry yogurt and black coffee, Hana decided to tackle the curtains next. She retrieved the old sewing machine from the garage, a place where Ab had collected and piled many things. He was a pack-rat, and it cheered her to think that even though he had not managed to attach himself to many people, he still had a sentimental side. Of course, it could be argued as a psychological dysfunction, but if she had believed that for a moment, the sewing machine changed her mind completely.

It was small and compact and very much like the one she remembered having used in her home economics class in high school. She lugged it into the house, set it on the table and then found a rag, wiping it meticulously until the case sparkled. With a strange feeling of reverence, she removed the case, her eyes appreciating the machine for all its facets of value.

It was in immaculate shape, almost as if it had never been used, and to some it probably screamed *Antique Road Show* possibilities, but it was the shiny gold name plate that really caught her attention. She bent lower and squinted to read: *To my darling Cilla, Love ABC.*

A sentimental fool just like her father, she reached for a tissue and soaked it completely in less than five seconds. Grabbing the entire box, she sat down at the kitchen table, for once just allowing herself to feel.

It had been a beautiful gesture on her father's behalf, perhaps not a romantic one, but certainly motivated by love, and her mother had completely misunderstood his intentions. It was plain in the fact that the machine had barely been used and that Priscilla had obviously not taken it with her. Instead, she had probably been completely insulted by it. In fact, hadn't she always said, *Hana, never let a man break your spirit. Your mission in life is far greater than keeping house for a man and tending to his needs.*

Hana pondered the words that, at the time, had seemed quite legitimate. Now she realized the dangers of accepting a belief system that had been presented to her completely out of context. Priscilla Islander was born and raised in a very different generation of women, and sadly found herself to be a woman-out-of-time. Or was it simply just a misunderstanding, an unfortunate case of failing to see the forest in spite of the trees?

Hana recalled the story she'd read in Ab's Bible about Jesus washing the feet of his disciples. The story advocated service to each other and in doing so, finding fullness of life. It seemed like a bit of a contradiction to the thinking of the present age, but its message was timeless and for the first time she could see it all differently.

Ab had only wanted to make Priscilla's life easier with the state of the art model, a classic now, and his way of thinking had become classic, too. He had recognized her special talent, and had wished to foster it in the best way he knew how. He hadn't meant for her to use it to patch his blue jeans.

Maybe Jayce Harlow was right. You could find romance all around you if you were open to the possibilities. How many men engraved a name plate on a sewing machine? Ab Crawford had. Suddenly, she couldn't think of anything sweeter, but with it came the bitterness of cold harsh reality. Priscilla and Abner were gone. It was too late to make things right, to fix the rift they had created. Yet, the sewing machine hinted of the possibility of patching the holes that had allowed years and years of cold, stinging winds to penetrate.

That night the hum of the sewing machine filled the old house until the early hours of the morning. She stopped only once to do her chores but the lure of the machine pulled her back into its magical snare, a snag in an endless seam of misunderstandings, attempting to bind three very different people together.

At times the thought occurred to her that perhaps God had made a terrible mistake. Priscilla and Ab were never meant to be together and she should never have existed. Her heart hurt at the thought. But what if He meant for it all to happen just as it did? What if He had a greater plan? It was a hopeful possibility worth the nine-month pilgrimage.

Using the old curtain rods, Hana slid the gaudy orange curtains off and cut them up for rags. New yellow and white checkered curtains replaced them, looking clean and fresh and modernly fashionable. Matching pillows were propped neatly into the corners of the sofa, the pillowcases sewn quickly and easily with enough material left over to sew a coffee table runner and two placemats for the end tables.

With an air of pride, Hana stood back to marvel at her work. She was talented, just like her mother. She remembered as a child, hearing her mother's sewing machine whir until the early hours of the morning. It had become a soothing lullaby, one that gave unspoken reassurance that her mother was happiest when she was sewing, and that they would be able to buy groceries for another week. Eventually, Priscilla had been hired on by a reputable designer in the city and had earned a very comfortable living, until her illness forced her to quit.

Hana recalled the day Priscilla had been diagnosed with cancer. She'd sold her sewing machine almost immediately, and Hana had always been a bit hurt by it. Why hadn't she given it to her? At the time she assumed that it had just been too hurtful for her mother to look at it. She'd become too sick to do anything almost immediately, and really had very little time to make natural, well thought-out decisions.

At the time her mother had teased her, had said that she'd never really shown much interest in sewing and truthfully she hadn't, but it would have meant something. It would have been a kind gesture, not unlike Ab's intentions, which was probably precisely why Priscilla hadn't given it to her. But it didn't really matter. What she had received was even greater and beyond her mother's abilities to withhold—the inherited talent that flowed throughout her veins, like an undeserved gift.

For the first time in her life she could feel what her mother must have felt after completing a difficult project. It was an incredible feeling of elation to have created something tangible out of a mere vision, but unlike her mother, so much more had happened in the process. Something new had been created inside of her in the untapped part of her psyche. Somewhere within all the emotional chaos, she finally understood the meaning of feeling blessed.

Now she understood what people meant about counting their blessings. It was very much like seeing the glass half full instead of half empty. It was realizing that while she couldn't fix the wrongs between her mother and father, she could refuse to perpetuate the hurt between them. In the absence of her mother and father, she could feel them both coursing through her veins, and mixed together, they balanced out just about right.

ChApTeR 10

"Good morning, Rosey," Hana placed a bouquet of pink petunias on Rosey's desk as she blustered by her in customary fashion. It was the last few flowers from her garden that had remained untouched by the grasshoppers and Hana decided that they had survived for a greater purpose, for a chance to start fresh in Lone Prairie, for the possibility of friendship, and in particular for Rosey.

Rosey was anything but what her name might have indicated, but the look on her face was definitely softening and Hana vowed to surprise her more often. It was much easier to try to get along with people. Didn't her mother always say that it took more effort to frown than it did to smile?

"You've got a couple coming in at nine thirty this morning, Mr. and Mrs. Sanders. They're newlyweds," Rosey added for good measure.

Hana thanked her, sincerely grateful for the added bit of information. She couldn't fight it after all. The people here were different than the kind she was used to, in a good way, and maybe it wasn't nosiness. Maybe it was kindness in caring enough about each other to want to know their business.

The morning flew by quickly and by the end of it she'd granted the newlyweds a mortgage on a new home, and an eighteen year-old without a trust fund, a loan to go to college. For the first time in her career she actually felt as if she was helping people, although ironically the one that had been helped the most was the strong and independent Hana Islander, every bit as sappy as Rosey who stole secret sniffs of pink petunias when no one was looking.

To make the success of the day complete, Hana booked the entire afternoon off to visit Jessica Forister at her new hair salon. She needed a hair cut anyway, and it had been a long time since she'd taken any extra time to fuss with her appearance.

Hana drove slowly through the autumn gusts that swirled the leaves and the scent of the ripening fields. The elders in the coffee shop said you could actually smell harvest in the air. She'd thought they were crazy as usual, but today she could smell it too.

Grasshoppers scattered as she crawled down the dusty trail, but she'd become accustomed to them, even though it was difficult to come to terms with the fact that there were some things that could not be controlled or mastered by human intelligence. Insufficient rainfall had also stunted the crops and she wondered what would be next—damaging winds, frost, hail?

It was unfair, and she couldn't help but wonder how the people of Lone Prairie would be able to afford the costs of seeding in the spring. What would carry them through until the next harvest if they didn't have any quality grain to sell from this one? How would the cattle manage if there was a shortage of feed?

She'd return to the city when all of this was over, to her old job, her old life, but she'd never look at a farmer in the same way again.

"Come in, Miss Islander. It's so good to see you again. I'm just finishing up with a customer and then I'll be right with you, but feel free to read a magazine or just have a look around," Jessica welcomed her with a warm smile revealing two dimples identical to that of her brother. She should have noticed the resemblance before, the wavy blonde hair, the denim blue eyes and long golden lashes.

Hana followed Jessica into the basement. The fresh smell of apple and apricots filled the air, appealing to her femininity. She'd been used to a weekly pampering at the beauty salon when she lived in the city and she'd have felt extremely guilty to even mention to anyone that she was in desperate need of a massage.

Mrs. Potter smiled brightly as she paid Jessica for the perm, fluffing her tight gray curls with her bright red painted nails. She looked too dramatic for Lone Prairie and reminded Hana of her mother and how she might have looked if she had stayed in the dusty prairie town.

"Well, you're next," Jessica beamed as she led Hana to the sink in the corner of the room. "How about the full treatment? Wash, cut, and style? It is Friday, after all. Most single women usually have something exciting to do on a Friday night."

"Yeah, right," Hana grumbled. "You're talking about the general populace of single women. I'm more likely to spend the evening reading a good book or…"

"Oh come on. You probably have a boyfriend back in the city that you're pining away for," Jessica teased as she worked a healthy lather of fruity shampoo into Hana's hair.

"I wish," Hana replied too quickly, not thinking about the consequences of allowing Jessica into her personal affairs.

"Do you mean to tell me that you have no male prospects in your life?"

"None." Hana began to relax as the hot water tickled and massaged her scalp. Her eyes closed automatically and for an instant she imagined that she was free, free to confide in someone who wouldn't judge her, someone who was truly interested in her well-being. She'd never had that, not even with Joanne. Hana pursed her lips at the thought, feeling as though she'd just betrayed her best friend.

"Well, I know a few eligible bachelors who've certainly noticed you."

Hana's eyes flew open. "I find that hard to believe," she nearly stuttered. The thought hadn't even crossed her mind.

"Oh. You're one of those women who...oh, never mind."

"No, please continue," Hana sat up while Jessica towel dried her hair with a pink bath towel. She followed her to the hair dressing chair that stood in front of a mirror outlined in a string of globe-shaped lights.

"I only meant that you appear so confident. You look like you're aware of your beauty."

Hana couldn't help but feel a bit insulted. Jessica had euphemistically portrayed her as being conceited, but she deserved it. She hadn't really given anyone a reason to like her.

"I knew that day in the bank that there was more to you than what met the eye," Jessica winked.

Hana shifted slightly as Jessica combed out the tangles until her hair and her spirit hung limply. "I work in a very competitive business. You have to look good and appear confident. Neither one of those things comes naturally to me," Hana smiled nervously.

Jessica laughed then, moving behind her and staring at Hana's reflection in the mirror. "Well, you can think what you want and I'll think what I want. We'll just agree to disagree. Now, what can I do for you today?"

Hana perused the pictures that Jessica had hung on the wall of super models who had dared the impossible. Short edges, angled bangs, no bangs, wacky colors. No thanks.

"Just the regular will do. About an inch off the back, some layers to freshen it up, and my bangs trimmed just slightly."

"Sure. I can see something face-framing maybe, soft wisps layered in through here," Jessica used her fingers to illustrate her intentions.

"You're the expert," Hana consented and Jessica started cutting then, creating the vision that only she could see in her mind.

"So, are you dating anyone back in that big city of yours or not?" Jessica pressed.

"No. I've come to terms with the fact that being alone isn't the worst affliction in life."

"You sound just like my brother. He's sworn off members of the opposite sex, too, and all the prodding in the world just won't budge him. It's such a waste. He's such a massive heap of male potential, don't you think?"

"Uh...yeah, sure," Hana stuttered, wondering how the topic had leaped into a Bermuda Triangle of sorts, with Jessica, Jayce and Hana as the three points encompassing inevitable disaster.

"He's always looked out for me. I'd just like to see him happy you know?"

"Yes, I can understand that," Hana responded, wondering how she could possibly understand. She was an only child. It was difficult to imagine the responsibility and the compassion you would feel toward a brother or sister. She'd wanted to know that feeling for as long as she could remember.

"Now if he was smart, he'd just leave it all up to me. I'd have him married off by now, but no! He insists on handling it himself, or rather, not handling it at all. I think the biggest problem is that he's attracted to the wrong kind of women. I know they say that opposites attract but there's an exception to that rule when it comes to farmers. I guess you can't help who you fall in love with, but it seems rather strange to me that the type of women that make him see stars have no appreciation for the country, no place here in Lone Prairie." Jessica stopped herself, but compensated for her lack of discretion by increasing the speed of her snips.

Hana tensed, hoping that Jessica wouldn't clip her ear or make a mistake and cut her hair too short. She seemed to be gone, probably slipped into the center of the black hole when she finally realized that Hana was one of *those* women. She was probably praying that Jayce wouldn't fall for her and make another mistake. Hana wished that she could console her with the first hand knowledge that that would never happen.

"I'm sure you'd rather talk about something else," Jessica finally found her tongue again and desperately attempted to engage Hana in a conversation that wasn't one-sided. "Why don't you ask me some questions? I bet you're just dying to know about some of the people here in Lone Prairie. I'm a native to the area. I know almost everything there is to know," Jessica encouraged.

"Why did Jayce buy the old school site near the creek?" Hana clapped her hand to her lips, unable to conceal the fact that she'd shot off her mouth in the worst way. Jessica's invitation had been exactly what she'd wanted to hear from someone, anyone, since the moment she arrived in Lone Prairie.

"Don't be embarrassed. It's a legitimate question," Jessica reassured her. "It's a mess isn't it? It's hard to imagine that anyone would want to own it." Jessica stopped cutting and stared off into the distance. "Mom used to go there when she was feeling blue and needed some inspiration. She called it her *little haven*. She'd ride her horse there now and then, sit among the trees and just think, *clear the cobwebs* she used to say," Jessica smiled, but Hana could see the sadness in her eyes. She wondered at the rest of the story that continued to play out behind her beautiful and innocent eyes, filling them to the brim with a pool of grief that seemed to come from the deepest place within her.

Her own desire to learn more about Jayce just didn't seem as important as Jessica and the despair that suddenly thickened the air, making it difficult for her to breathe.

"Are you all right? That really wasn't any of my business and I apologize."

"Don't apologize. I like to talk about my mother, as difficult as it may be at times. To tell you the truth, I used to feel good and sorry for myself until you came to town."

"Me? What difference should my presence here make in your life?"

"Well, you gave Jake and me the loan. That's changed my life, keeps my mind occupied in a good way, but there's more to it than that," Jessica continued to fuss with Hana's hair. "I used to feel sorry for myself for having lost my mother and my father, for being virtually alone in the world, and then I saw you, struggling completely on your own. At least I have Jayce, no matter how much of a pain he can be at times. He's the best memory I have of my childhood," Jessica paused, getting lost in her own thoughts again. "Anyway, I admire your courage."

"Was Abner a good person?" Hana continued to explore the long awaited opportunity. It was the closest she'd come to finding any answers and at the risk of over-stepping her boundaries, she had to try.

"Ab was a gem. He was kind to everyone, especially Jayce. I never could quite figure out how the two of them connected though, especially after, well," Jessica paused and shifted on her feet, the focus of her thoughts shifting, too. "They had a friendship not unlike father and son, or at least how a father and son ought to be. It took me a long time to see it that way, to forgive I mean, but the past is the past and even though we may not understand it, we have to live with it and the impact it has on our lives, but above all we have to forgive."

"Did Abner do something he shouldn't have? I mean, why would you need to forgive Abner?" Hana choked, the truth so close she could almost touch it.

"Nobody's perfect."

"But you harbored some resentment against Ab at one time. Why?"

"It's a long story," Jessica proceeded to squirt a generous heap of whipped mousse onto her palm and then work it through Hana's hair. " 'Let he who has not sinned cast the first stone,' said Jesus."

"Why does everybody resort to Bible quotations around here when things get serious?"

Jessica laughed. "Because faith is all we truly have in the end, Hana. Are you not a believer?"

"I don't know what I am," Hana allowed her irritation to show.

"Well, everyone is welcome to the flock."

"Easy for you to say. People around here are rooted in faith. How do you start in the middle of nowhere?"

"My mother always used to say that whenever you find yourself in the middle of a mess it really doesn't matter *where* you start to fix it, what's important is that you just start. Once you do, things will fall into place. Sometimes we waste too much time thinking when we should be doing, you know what I mean?"

"Yeah, I guess." Hana wished that it were really that easy. "But I still don't understand how people can tolerate years of drought and grasshoppers and hard times and still have faith."

"Faith is the one thing that remains when everything else abandons us," Jessica managed to turn Hana's thoughts around into a completely new point of view, even while a questionable sadness returned to her eyes. Jessica removed the pink plastic cape then, snatching it away like an artist that had just uncovered a masterpiece. "Well, what do you think?"

What she thought of the haircut had taken second place to what she thought about her visit with Jessica Forister. The haircut was fine, very good actually, but something wasn't quite right. She couldn't help but think that there was something Jessica hadn't wanted to tell her. Something about her childhood was atypical. She and Jayce obviously shared the pain of it together because she'd seen it in his eyes too, and what was it that had drawn Jayce and Abner together? Even Jessica seemed confused about that.

Frustrated with the reality that she would probably never know, Hana decided to focus on the concrete world around her, the things that she could plainly see and understand. Immediately, she was sidetracked by the number of farmers out in the fields who were already swathing down the crops that had ripened early.

It was harvest time and the responsibility of reaping what Abner had sowed, weighed heavily on her shoulders. Where would she start? The words of Jessica Forister came to her immediately. *Just start.*

ChApTeR 11

Her shallow breathing echoed loudly inside the old musty shop. Nervously, Hana stared at the huge metal machines, wondering what form of pride had convinced her that she could do this her own. No instruction manual in the world could teach her how to swath down a crop, combine, haul the grain to storage bins and then bale the straw for bedding for her cattle in winter. It was a process that was beyond the scope of her physical and mental strength and she knew it. Reading about it on the internet was one thing, seeing the actual equipment in front of her, ready to spring to life at any given moment, scared the conviction right out of her.

The only manageable contraption was Ab's old Ford farm truck. It was a rattle trap, but it sputtered to life on the first try and Hana was grateful. Equipped with a tool box, flashlight, fencing wire and other temporary repairs, it was a typical farm truck and would probably come in handy during the harvest season. As it was, her car had already been showing the detrimental signs of poor road conditions.

With the old truck rattling and shaking beneath her, Hana drove cautiously to Jayce's farm, searching for courage where pride had once been. At one point she stopped the truck and fought the urge to turn around and head back home. It was pure punishment to have to ask him for help again, but the magnitude of the burden upon her was so much greater than having to eat a few slices of humble pie.

If she failed to bring in Abner's crop she'd forfeit the terms of the will, yes, but there was something more. She'd be breaking the law of nature, the call to stewardship of the land. If God had entrusted a piece of His earth to Abner, then as his only surviving relative, it was her job to care for it. Truly, it was grand to think that there was more to life than what she'd known for most of hers. It felt as though she'd been invited to the greatest ball in the land and didn't have a clue what to wear. She killed the engine and peered around the yard, spotting Jayce near his swathing machine.

Gravel crunched beneath her feet. She wouldn't beg. She just needed to make a start.

"Haven't seen that old truck around for quite some time. For a second there I could have sworn that old Ab was back." Jayce greeted her with a smile as he wiped a greasy wrench on a rag that looked like it had once been a bed sheet. His swathing machine stood tall and ominous but he did not look intimidated. When had he ever looked anything less than comfortable and self-assured?

Hana glanced around the yard, formulating the words carefully in her mind. The whole thing was just so humiliating, just about as humiliating as—Hana stopped, her thoughts catching on the clothesline and shifting in the breeze like the assorted items that hung there.

"Dryer's broke down," Jayce followed her gaze to the backyard, where wooden clothespins held shirts, jeans and more personal items. "It will have to wait until harvest is over," he stared her down as though ready to pounce if she made even the slightest hint of a backhanded comment.

Hana forced a smile. Shoddy courage and ill-faith dangled from her psychological clothesline in plain view for Jayce Harlow to see. Everyone had to air out their dirty laundry at one time or another. It was just that for some strange reason, she'd thought herself above laundering, spiritual or otherwise. How many times had she convinced herself that she really didn't need him or Him? She steadied herself against the breeze that she fully expected would increase into a full-scale wind.

"So, do you plan on getting your crop off anytime soon?" Jayce interrupted her ridiculous thoughts.

"Uh, yes, that's why I'm here. I, uh, have a proposition for you," she stuttered. "I'm going to take a few weeks off at the bank starting tomorrow, so that I can get my harvesting done. I, well, the truth is I need your help Jayce. I'd like to offer my services to you in exchange. We can even start with your crops and leave mine for last. Anything you suggest, Jayce, just as long as you agree to help me." Hana squared her shoulders, trying not to sound desperate.

She'd rambled it all off so quickly that she barely caught the look of astonishment on his face, but true to his character he recovered quickly. She waited for the gust to tear her to shreds.

"I was wondering when you'd come around."

"Beggars can't be choosers," the wind settled to a calm breeze. Could it really be that easy?

"So, what is it exactly that you can do, Hana? Can you drive a standard? No farm vehicle is automatic, at least not around here."

Annoyance marred her perfectly planned presentation.

"You know very well I don't have the first clue about how to run any of that…that stuff," she motioned to the swathing machine with a dismissive wave. "It's why this whole agreement is nothing but a farce. You and Ab set me up for failure. I'm sure of it, but I won't be defeated. I'm going to prove to you and the rest of this sorry town that I belong here!" The wind increased, dangling items flapping mercilessly.

"Oh, so you have plans on staying if you succeed?" The sun threatened to parch and fade.

"I didn't say that. I just meant that...oh, you know very well what I meant. Now, do we have a deal or not?"

Jayce glanced downward at her sandals and followed the length of her thin and toned legs up to her chest.

Hana immediately cursed her choice of attire. How could she expect Jayce to take her seriously when she'd dressed as a city girl, in a khaki colored pair of shorts and a crisp white tank top?

"We've got lots to do before this equipment will even be ready to take onto the field, but you're going to need to change."

"Great! I'll run home and be back in a jiffy," Hana could barely contain her excitement and relief.

"Jeans, Hana, and work boots if you've got any," he called after her as she ran toward the old beat-up truck like a child who'd just received her first important job.

Elation replaced her disappointing behavior. She hadn't meant to chastise him, especially since she was the one who needed the favor. Still, the greater sacrifice had been hers. Like clothes that were over-dried and wrinkled and would now need to be seriously ironed, her pride had never been so wrung out. Emotionally, she prepared herself for the work ahead, confidence and pride ready to wear once again.

Jayce watched her drive away, perplexed with his lack of will power. Hadn't he just lectured himself on this very thing? Keeping his distance was the only way he could prevent her from getting under his skin, and into his heart. The very sight of her made his entire body shiver despite the prairie heat. It was an adverse reaction. Attraction and heat were the two things that usually made up the ideal passionate package, not distraction and the chills.

It was because he was fighting the natural pull between them, fighting it so hard that he'd confused his natural senses, but the woman was just down right intimidating, and now that they were going to be working side by side for days on end, he needed to come up with some sort of a coping mechanism.

He was pleased that she'd virtually had to beg him for help. It was what he'd wanted all along, wasn't it? To feel needed? Wanted? Just a tiny bit of pay back for all the hassle, but while he wasn't a mean-spirited person who preyed on other people's innate weaknesses, he didn't have a death wish either. Working beside a completely inexperienced city girl would be nothing but a high risk to his physical and emotional well-being any way he sliced it.

Jayce sought resolve in the memory of his father, a man who had allowed misfortune to take charge of and eventually ruin his life. He couldn't blame his father completely. Samuel Harlow had been dealt a difficult hand, but still, everyone had their own will, and it had to be stronger than the adversities that challenged it.

"I'm stronger than all of it," Jayce fought the urge to curse and steadied himself against the strongest adversity he'd ever had to face—a woman in a pair of designer boots and jeans and a deadly strong will of her own.

"Are you catching any of this?"

"Pardon me?" Hana stood upright, the calves of her legs cramped from crouching down by a u-joint on the swathing machine. "Uh, yeah. I understand. All joints need to be greased properly before use," Hana repeated his last words on swathing machine maintenance, knowing that they'd really gone in one ear and right out the other. Not on purpose of course, but merely by the fickle law of nature that clearly separated some men from some women. Clearly, she was among the ranks of the mechanically impaired. It wasn't a crime, albeit a bit of a safety hazard.

"Yes. Well, anyway, I thought that I'd swath ahead and have you follow me in the combine. It would probably be the simplest machine for you to operate."

"You want me to drive that thing?" Hana stared upward at the huge green beast that seemed to resemble a giant grasshopper.

"Well, it's the only thing I can think of, unless you want to haul grain, but that involves auguring it into the bins and I'm terrified of letting you operate an auger."

Hana paused, knowing that this time she wouldn't be able to prove her capabilities. It was as simple as that. Jayce knew best in this situation and she had to admit it. "All right, whatever you say."

Jayce gloated only momentarily before helping her up inside the cab of the combine. "My equipment is a little more modern than Ab's, so we'll use it for your harvest as well. That way, once I've got you trained on this machine there will be no need to change, unless we have a break down. Then we can always use Ab's as a back up."

"But won't that be breaking the terms of the will? I should be using Abner's equipment."

Jayce rubbed his left temple, the strain of the day taking a toll, and thinking about Ab's crazy will did little more than frustrate him to the brink of a headache. If he hadn't had so much at stake, he would have admitted that the will was totally impractical.

Truthfully, he hadn't expected that she'd follow it so religiously. In fact, there were so many times he wanted to tell her to forget about it, to take Abner's belongings and sell them for the money as he assumed she'd planned to do, but something kept holding him back. At first he'd tried to convince himself that he was just simply amused by her. Hey, he hadn't had a good laugh in a long time, and couldn't a guy have a little fun?

Jayce rubbed his aching shoulder now, the one that always told him he'd had enough for one day. It wasn't fun anymore. He was anxious and stressed and if he'd been paying more attention, he might have noticed when vindictive amusement had turned to something else entirely, something as crazy as thinking that Hana Islander belonged in Lone Prairie, that she belonged on Abner's farm, that she belonged to him.

"Jayce? You all right?"

"You know what? It's late. Let's leave this until morning. I'll give you a crash course on how to run this thing before we set out tomorrow and then it will be fresh in your mind. We'll start on Ab's wheat field say...around seven o'clock tomorrow morning, unless it's still damp and tough at that time. The evenings and mornings are starting to cool off now."

"But I thought we were doing your crops first. In fact, I insist."

"Oh no, ladies first, *I* insist," Jayce echoed, his argument somehow more persuasive.

Jayce helped her down from the bottom rung and she accepted his hand willingly.

"I'll see you early in the morning then?"

He stood only a few feet away, his eyes always scrutinizing and seeing more than she cared for him to see.

"You look a little stressed. You're not having second thoughts are you?" Jayce teased.

"It's just that I've never done anything like this. I just don't want to let you down."

"Don't worry. You won't. Everybody's a bit nervous their first time around. There's a boy from town that comes out and helps me harvest every year to earn extra money after school and on weekends. The first year he came here, he didn't know a thing about farming. Now, nobody drives that old grain truck better than he does."

Jayce followed Hana to Ab's truck, his hand touching hers as she reached for the door handle of the truck. "Make sure you get some rest tonight, Hana." He ignored her uneasiness. "You need a clear head to work around machinery."

"Of course," she replied numbly, staring at Jayce's hand upon hers. It was rough and almost completely black with grease and dirt.

There was a time when she would have been repulsed by such a touch, but now she wondered if she had ever really felt anything so caressing? His hands had toiled for many hours. They'd fixed machinery, mended fences, healed sick animals, cared for an elderly man, raised a little sister. His was the caress of the prairie, the pride of generations before him and the fortitude of all who carried on the legacy. She felt cold and empty as he pulled away.

That night, sleep wouldn't come. Jayce's words slipped in and out of her thoughts and she knew that she should obey. Proper rest was imperative to anyone working around machinery, but no matter how hard she tried, thoughts kept whirling around in her brain refusing to settle.

At one point, when she finally drifted off, she saw Abner's bedroom, the bed sheets strewn recklessly and the drawers pulled out of the dressers. She heard the overlapping voices of Ab and Priscilla arguing, although she'd never heard their voices in unison. They grew increasingly louder until they blended into one strange foreign sound that hurt her ears and her heart.

Out of breath, she sat up quickly, snatching her thoughts from the deranged place they'd taken her. She clutched the blanket to her chest, her heart pounding out of control as a cold sweat ran down her neck and into the hollow between her breasts. Was it a sign? Did Abner's room hold a secret she might have overlooked?

She'd kept his room intact and slept in the spare room instead, unable to deal with the thought of sleeping in Ab's old room. Upon her arrival she'd been curious, of course, and had rummaged through Abner's closets and dresser drawers just a bit, not really searching for anything in particular. She wasn't a detective or a psychological analyst after all.

What did it mean that he kept a stack of old western novels on the floor beside his bed? Did the white monogrammed handkerchief with the letter 'D' embroidered in blue and placed inside the drawer of his nightstand mean anything? Wrapped neatly inside of it was a pine cone. It all seemed completely irrelevant.

Hana stumbled drowsily to Ab's room. It was eerie and still, a perfect haven for shadows and overactive imaginations. She ignored the hair that stood up on the back of her neck and focused instead on the facts rather than the ethereal.

If she were to describe Abner by the state of his bedroom, she'd say that he was a very typical man. There were no frills, no curtains on the window, no lacy doilies on the dressers and nightstands, no lamps even. A stark light bulb without a shade hung from the center of the ceiling and a long string, an old shoelace, cascaded downward. She pulled it and the bulb immediately complied, lighting up the room and making her squint.

The lack of a woman's touch was evident everywhere and it saddened her that Ab had never known the unconditional love of a good woman, but there was nothing she could do about that now. He hadn't known the love of a good daughter either. If he and Jayce Harlow had given her half a chance, Ab might have at least died with the knowledge that—that what? That she loved him? Well, she couldn't go that far. She didn't even know him, but at least he could have died knowing that his relationship with Priscilla had not been in vain.

Bitterness replaced her logical analysis of the clues. She would never have made a good detective. You had to be objective for that. "Focus," she reminded herself. "Keep your emotions out of this."

Again, she strained her eyes, stripping every corner of the room of its secrets. There had to be more to this man than the *poor jilted husband* syndrome. She could feel it in her bones. There was something more than good neighborly conduct that drew an old man and a young man together. Ab would have given his entire belongings to Jayce without question had she not come into the picture. Anyone in their right mind would question that.

Hana opened the tiny closet behind the door. It was dark and musty, even a bit creepy, and as she rifled through the few items hanging side by side, she felt like a wretched sneak.

What would Abner have thought of her and all her crazy suspicions? Hana paused as she spotted an old suit hanging in the back of the closet. She pulled it out and tried to picture Abner inside of it, but the gray haired, tired man she had seen on the porch didn't look like he'd fit into it at all in either size or style. Immediately her imagination took hold, envisioning the young version of Abner, a tall, dark and handsome groom. He would have been proud and dignified as he stood at the altar with the vivacious *Cilla*. It was probably the first and the last time he'd ever worn the suit.

Carefully, Hana hung the suit back where she'd found it and

carried on the little charade in the deepest freest part of her psyche, imagining that the black and white striped shirt had probably been his town shirt, clean and crisp, snap buttons down the front and on the pockets. He had probably looked very respectable in it. Then there was the solid blue shirt, sharing its hanger with a cherry red tie. She assumed it must have been his Sunday best.

For a brief moment, Hana allowed herself to mourn the man she'd never known and the mother she'd never understood. The two of them had certainly left her to pick up the pieces. And maybe it wasn't right to think of the dead with such irreverence, but how could she let their souls rest in peace when her own felt as though it were breaking in two?

Hana slammed the closet door and proceeded to move around the room, stubbing her toe carelessly on the bedpost. Reeling to the floor with tears of pain, she cursed her father, her mother, herself and all the reasons that had brought her here to this pitiful moment in time. But then, as if the old wooden bedpost, and her klutziness had conspired, she saw it. Carefully, she slid the old musty shoe box out from beneath the bed.

Her hands shook, and her sixth sense hummed with a vibe she recognized. It was her inner voice speaking to her with seamless clarity, telling her that the box meant something.

She opened it slowly, the dust making her sneeze violently, but when her sinuses finally cleared, divorce papers stared up at her cold and heartless with Priscilla's signature sprawled boldly on the dotted line. Abner's line remained blank with an x marking the spot of finality.

"Great," she grumbled sarcastically. It was no surprise. Her mother had remained single and so had Abner. They'd made each other's lives miserable. For Abner, refusal to sign the papers was probably some form of pay back, the last bit of control he could exert over a woman who had left him high and dry without so much as a genuine forwarding address. The address on the forms belonged to a lawyer, out of province. It was obvious she'd meant to side-track him into never ever finding her.

Hana pulled the papers out of the box wanting to light the horrible things on fire along with any other evidence that merely reinforced the fact that Abner and Priscilla had tortured each other like cruel children. It was then that she noticed the lock of hair, bound together with a thin silky yellow ribbon.

It would have been shocking enough if it had been her mother's auburn locks, a sweet token of affection they'd had for each other in the beginning, but the lock was black, an infusion of color against the faded box, imposing and completely out of place. Her mother's hair had never been black. Priscilla often griped about the fact that some women chose to alter the color of their hair. She'd been a red head her entire life. Even the day she died, only a thin streaking of grey could be seen sporadically throughout her brilliant locks.

Frustrated, Hana closed the box and shoved it back beneath the bed, resigning to the fact that she might never understand Ab and Priscilla's quirky past. They had chosen their paths and she would choose hers, to live a life that reflected neither of them. It was a stark contrast to the feelings she'd had the night she'd found the sewing machine and she wondered why she'd become so uncertain all over again.

To that question she could think of only one answer. There was something left for her to discover. She just needed to use her time more wisely, to exhaust her resources. And what exactly were her resources? Well, the people of Lone Prairie for starters. What did the people here know about Abner and her mother?

Jessica knew something, and Harry and Elizabeth knew even more, but Jayce Harlow—somehow she had the stabbing suspicion that it was he who was withholding the most. She could feel the untold truth weighing as heavy as the hot humid air in Abner's farmhouse, that made her toss and turn until the hours on the clock ticked away another restless day in Lone Prairie.

ChApTeR 12

"Are you sure you're going to be okay on this thing?" Jayce shouted above the noisy combine engine.

"Sure," Hana nodded with false confidence, feeling that the minute he left her alone inside the abominable contraption she'd be physically ill.

"Just remember, when you turn the wheel, the back end is going to swing around. At first it'll feel a bit like you're fishtailing in the mud with a truck, but you'll get the hang of it after a while.

"Sure," Hana replied casually, while attempting to steady the quiver in her voice. His comparison had been nothing more than something else she hadn't even the tiniest bit of a clue about. Fishtailing? What in the wide world was that? Quickly she tried to think of a time she'd driven in mud. Her mind drew a blank. She had driven on ice though. That wasn't an uncommon occurrence in the city. Maybe it was something like that? Somehow she doubted it.

"I've adjusted the pick-up to the height I feel will be

appropriate to pick up the swaths after I opened up a round with the swather this morning."

Hana nodded. Numbly, she stared at the controls in front of her, mentally repeating the instructions he'd given her earlier.

"Would you feel better if we made a round together?" Jayce smiled down at her, crouching down so that his head wouldn't bump against the domed roof of the combine.

He knew. He always seemed to see right through her and it was down-right humiliating, but you didn't look a gift horse in the mouth. Even she knew that.

"I hate to put you through any trouble," she replied, talking herself out of begging him to do just that.

"It's no trouble. Hit the gear and start driving. I'll explain things as we go along."

Jayce's neighbor, Nathan Peters had taken a day off school to help out. He was leery of Hana and her capabilities and scoffed at her whenever she did something that didn't quite suit him, but he was sixteen, just a few months past drivers' license age. Already he knew all there was to know about the world.

She'd been intimidated by his cocky demeanor from the start, and it was highly unlike her to succumb to anyone's ego, but the truth of the matter was that at sixteen, Nathan knew more about farming than she knew at thirty. It took skill and a tremendous amount of it, more than she'd ever imagined, and she had the *easy* job as Nathan had so graciously informed her.

By the end of the day, every muscle in her body ached with stress, and the whir of the engine persisted to ring in her ears long after she'd stepped down from the combine. They'd need a little more time the following day to finish Abner's wheat crop before moving on to Jayce's if the weather cooperated, and it would be slower since Nathan would be unable to take another day off school. He would come after school instead, and Hana was relieved, even though his absence would considerably hinder the process.

In hindsight, she had to admit that Nathan had been a

tremendous help, and it was clear that the pecking order had already been established long before she came along. Consequently, on the ride back to Jayce's yard in the grain truck, Hana found herself stuck in the middle, the gear shift her enemy once again, while Jayce and Nathan talked around her about rads and horsepower, like it really mattered. Had her ears not been ringing, she might have felt confident enough to change the subject, but the slightest word seemed to come out as a shout and she vowed that first thing, end of harvest, she'd be getting her ears checked. With irritation, she watched Nathan drive away in his spiffed up '79 Chevrolet Silverado, his window rolled down and loud music hailing his exit as though he'd just saved the day.

"So, what kind of wages are we talking about for a boy that works well but carries a cloud of arrogance with him everywhere he goes?"

"Nathan?" Jayce seemed surprised. "Oh, don't worry about Nathan. I'll take care of his wages and his attitude," Jayce dismissed her concern easily and pulled the grain truck up to the fuel tanks.

Without even waiting for her, he hopped out of the truck and proceeded to refuel it. Hana decided to follow.

"Sure. Easy for you to say. He respects you," she shouted over the sputtering hum of the grain truck that had seemed, like her, to have had just about enough for one day. "But me, well, I might as well be the dirt stuck in the grooves of his work boots."

"He just needs a little time to get used to you," Jayce stuck the hose inside the tank and squeezed the lever. The diesel gurgled inside the empty tank. "You have to admit, it is a little unnerving to see a city girl behind the wheel of a combine."

"I did well today for a first timer, even you have to admit that," Hana demanded stubbornly, angling her chin upward. She was immediately punished by the kink in her neck that begged for a massage.

"Yeah, I'll admit it, you did do surprisingly well today," he pushed away from the truck and leaned into her, reaching out casually to wipe a smearing of dirt from her chin. "And don't you worry about Nathan. He'll mellow out. You know, you do tend to grow on a person, even though initially you come off being rather unlikable."

"Me? I'm unlikable? Have you ever stopped to think how you might come off looking?" Hana couldn't resist the urge to needle him back. She was too tired and vexed to care that Jayce's comment had been in the spirit of fun.

"No. Worrying about what other people think about me has never really been a concern of mine," Jayce replied arrogantly.

"Well, maybe it should be," Hana snubbed.

"I just always try to remind myself that I won't be judged if I don't go around judging, especially on the basis of appearances. For example, anyone who'd take a good look at you in those flashy boots would probably assume that you haven't done an honest day's work in your life. I know different. You've done at least *one* honest day's work and I can vouch for it."

"Now just hold on a doggone minute. I work very hard at the bank. Besides, it was you who told me to wear boots," Hana accused, angrier with the fact that he'd side-tracked her from a clairvoyant glance into his character with his goading.

"Well anyway," Jayce took a step backward and glanced around the yard, taking a deep and exhausted breath. "You might as well get on home to bed. I have a few things to do before I pack it in."

"Like what?" Curiosity made her sound desperate. She had wanted to go home, hadn't she? A long soak in a steaming hot bath couldn't possibly be outdone by any other alternative.

"Like moving the auger to a new grain bin and servicing this grain truck." Jayce paused to remove the nozzle and return it to its holder at the side of the tank. "Nathan said it was grinding a bit in third gear. I'd better check on that before it leads to a disaster tomorrow. What's that old phrase? A stitch in time saves nine?"

"Could you use a hand?"

"I wouldn't want to tire you out on your first day."

"I can handle it," she shrugged her shoulders with an attempt at indifference, but her neck protested against the sudden motion once again, conspiring with her conscience every time she tried to get up on her high horse.

"You alright?"

"Fine, it's just a kink I think."

Jayce reached out and rubbed at the spot, moving her hand gently out of the way.

"Sometimes a good hot shower is best for stiff muscles. It'll probably feel better in the morning but I've got some liniment for aching muscles if you need."

At the moment *need* took on a whole new meaning. She needed a lot of things but there was a fine line between want and need, wasn't there? Wanting Jayce in her life was nothing more than that, a want. A woman did not *need* a man, her mother's words seeped into her thoughts like tainted air filling her lungs. But, if that was so true then why did she feel so empty the moment Jayce pulled away? Why did she follow him like a hungry puppy starved for affection?

Together, they took the truck for a test drive and after a few adjustments Jayce was content with the sound of the shifting gears. After that they turned their attention to the grain bin in the back yard, rushing now to complete the day's work before dark.

"You can hear how full it is just by knocking." Jayce rapped sharply on the side of the metal bin. "Listen as I climb the ladder. I'll keep knocking and you tell me when you hear the sound change."

Hana stood beneath the ladder listening intently but the sound didn't change. Jayce clambered up the side of the roof top to the very peak. "No change in sound. That means it's full," Jayce shouted down to her, a wide grin on his face.

"Why don't we store Abner's grain in one of his bins?" Hana questioned suspiciously. Logically, she had some doubts about Jayce's intentions, although the desire to not offend him had somehow become just as important.

"Ab's bins are all wooden. They're old and they're falling apart. Metal storage bins are the way to go in this day and age," he shouted back while he peered inside the top of the bin. "I'm going to need you to crank the lever on the auger clockwise to raise this thing up. Can you do that for me?"

"Sure," Hana replied apprehensively, finding the lever on the side of the auger. It wasn't as easy as it looked. Nothing ever was with farming, but she exerted every bit of strength she could muster, refusing to be beaten. After all, she'd said she wanted to help.

"That's good," Jayce shouted down to her.

She watched as he shimmied quickly down the ladder. The sun was setting but not even the tiniest trace of a breeze blew across the prairie. It was still stifling hot and she could feel the sweat beading on her forehead.

Jayce removed his shirt and tucked it into his back pocket. It reminded her of the day she'd first come to Lone Prairie with nothing but vengeance on her mind. Things had changed.

"Wait. I'll help you. Where are we moving this thing?"

"To the next bin, right beside," Jayce lowered the end of the auger, wiping his forehead with the back of his arm.

She'd seen lots of men with toned muscles, but something about Jayce was different. There was a distinguishable quality in the kinds of muscle that the prairie could build as opposed to a gym, or maybe it was the strength of character that was different, she couldn't be sure. All she was certain about was that *this* man made her stomach do flip-flops.

The auger was heavier than she could ever have imagined. Jayce picked up the end of it effortlessly and she pushed by the tires until they'd swung it around successfully, repositioning it properly at the neighboring bin. They were both out of breath when they finally finished the task and Hana was extremely grateful when Jayce invited her inside for a glass of lemonade.

She followed him to the house in silence, being patient as he stopped to do his chores and to check out a few more details around the yard. Jayce took note of the fact that the fuel tanks were nearly empty and that he'd need to call the local fuel station for a refill first thing in the morning, and then unabashedly he grabbed his clothes off the clothesline before ushering her inside.

"Welcome to my humble abode," he teased as he held the screen door open for her, tossing the starchy over-dried items onto a wooden deacon's bench in the corner of the tiny entrance.

Hana slipped past him, resisting the strange urge to fold the clothes. What did the inside of Jayce Harlow's house look like? Wondering about the inside of other people's homes was a normal curiosity, after all. In the city she remembered taking Sunday walks and peering curiously inside the big white colonial house on the corner of 9th street and Main, conjuring up grand images of European furniture, intricately woven area rugs, and a shiny black grand piano.

She'd always thought that the way a person decorated their home was an insight into their personality. If that was the case, then she had Jayce Harlow profiled all wrong.

Jayce caught her scrutiny and smiled. "Not what you'd expect from a bachelor pad, huh?"

"I didn't think you had it in you."

"Well, don't go giving me too much credit. My sister had pretty much over-stayed her welcome before she married Jake. Even still she keeps fussing over this place, keeps telling me I'll never find a wife if I can't offer her a decent home."

It wasn't fancy, but it was tidy and fresh, and Hana followed Jayce throughout the house as he went on to explain how he'd put in the hard wood flooring himself, having salvaged most of it from an old school house a few miles down the road. He'd refinished the kitchen cabinetry on his own, too, and painted the walls a beautiful taupe, touching up the crown molding in a soft white. It was nothing more than a little elbow grease, he'd conceded, but still she was impressed.

After a brief tour of the main floor, Jayce pointed to a half bath just off the entrance where she could wash up, and she was grateful for a bit of privacy in a day that had challenged every aspect of her being. It didn't surprise her that she looked a sight.

It had been a long day, but it was nothing a little soap and water couldn't fix, and diligently, she scrubbed at the dirt, wishing that she could wash away the feeling of uneasiness that swept over her once again. There would be no animals to distract them, no noisy engines, just she and Jayce and, well, heavens knew what, male companionship maybe? She hadn't had that in a very long time.

Satisfied with her clean reflection, she followed the sound of ice cubes clinking harmoniously against glass. It was the most pleasant sound she'd heard all day.

They sat together in the kitchen nook, both tired and silent, sipping their lemonade politely rather than gulping it. When Hana's glass was empty, Jayce poured her another and then sauntered to the refrigerator.

"Are you hungry? Jessica dropped a pan of lasagna here yesterday and I haven't really had any time to try it out. What do you say we warm it up and call it dinner?"

"Sure," Hana replied, wondering why she just couldn't resist the invitation. As always, she thought of an answer that pleased her when the truth seemed too much to handle. She was just tired of being alone and who wouldn't be? She probably would have been content enough to dine with Betsy if she could talk.

Jayce navigated around the kitchen expertly, and she would have been impressed had the whole thing not seemed so sad. A man like Jayce should have someone to come home to, someone who would greet him at the door with a kiss and have a warm meal waiting for him. He shouldn't have to worry about his laundry and keeping the house clean.

Good Lord, Hana shook her head in disbelief at her own traitorous thoughts. Her mother, the eternal feminist would have fainted at such an idea, but did cooking meals and doing laundry for a man create an unequal partnership? From watching Harry and Elizabeth, she really didn't think so. It had nothing to do with equality. It was all about serving God by serving each other, helping each other whenever help was needed without keeping score.

"Is there anything I can help with?" She waited a safe distance behind him as he placed the lasagna inside the oven.

She startled him and he turned around to face her, nearly burning himself on the hot oven rack.

"I'm sorry. I didn't mean to scare you," she laughed.

"Why do women always do that?"

"What?" Hana replied defensively.

"Sneak up on a guy. It's as though you enjoy watching us come completely unglued." Jayce shook his head, a pleasant smile overshadowing his scolding.

Momentarily, Hana was struck with the thought of the *other women* Jayce had been referring to. The thought of there being other women who had passed in and out of his life depressed her, before the false assumptions set in. Yes, he'd probably loved and then left many women. He was just that type, and even though she really had no proof of that, she tricked herself into believing it.

"Do you know how to make garlic toast?" Jayce handed her a loaf of bread, his endearing dimples making her stomach do funny things again. At the present moment she was the woman in his kitchen, and even though she attempted to legitimize her platonic reasons for being there, she knew they were just excuses.

"Of course I do," she nodded, the idea of rising to a challenge putting her right back into her element once again.

The kitchen was small, but convenient and cozy, and when Jayce bumped into her once while he was reaching for the oven mitts, she felt every nerve ending in her body prickle and again the flip flops. It seemed completely futile to convince herself that her stomach was just reacting to basic hunger. There were two very different kinds of that, and at the moment, she craved companionship more than a pan of lasagna.

"Well, ten more minutes and it should be ready. Can I offer you another drink?" Jayce placed the empty jug of lemonade in the sink.

"Sure, why not."

Jayce rummaged through the refrigerator once again, while Hana leaned against the cupboard trying to deny her eyes the advantageous view. It was unfair how he fit into the kitchen as well as he did onto the prairie.

"I've got just the thing." Jayce turned from the refrigerator with a bottle of wine in his left hand, and a devilish grin on his face.

Hana couldn't remember the last time she'd had a glass of wine. There couldn't be any harm in it, or could there be?

"I think the heat's just about right," Jayce's choice of words stunned her, as though he'd snagged her thoughts right out of midair and read them accurately.

"Pardon me?"

"Your frying pan, it's heated to 350 degrees if you're ready."

"Yes, of course," she stuttered, embarrassed as usual that she'd been thinking about him in less than respectable terms. She had no right to.

"You know, you could call this the fourth romantic thing to do in Lone Prairie."

"What's that?" Hana replied curiously, although for once, she could actually see where his thoughts were leading.

"Well, Mr. and Mrs. Sanders always make Friday night, steak night. No matter what they're doing, they prepare the meal together and sit down with a glass of wine or beer and just take the time to enjoy the accomplishments of the week."

"Sounds romantic," Hana nodded, wondering if he were insinuating that they were sharing a bit of romance. She could envision it without a stretch of the imagination, she and Jayce, creating their own special rituals, but they had a long way to go before that would happen, and maybe it never would. She shut out the thought. Rome wasn't built in a day. She'd just have to settle for a small stepping stone, she decided, and then vowed to stop thinking and to just enjoy the moment at hand.

While Jayce set the table, Hana flipped garlic toast in the electric frying pan, taking extra care to toast each piece just right. They indulged in small talk then, much to her relief, and when the oven timer rang, Jayce retrieved the hot steaming pan of lasagna, carefully placing it on a ceramic hot plate in the middle of the kitchen table.

She sat opposite him in the cozy nook that jutted out slightly, offering a zoomed in view of Jayce's farm. It was beautiful, with the sun setting and the knowledge that they'd put in a hard and successful day's work. It was all so simple somehow, and Hana couldn't imagine why things had become so complicated for her mother and father.

"Do you mind if we say grace?" Jayce cleared his throat, seeming to sense that her thoughts had been elsewhere.

"No, not at all," Hana complied by bowing her head.

"Heavenly Father, bless us and the food we are about to eat through your goodness, Lord."

"Amen," Hana resounded softly, the word suddenly catching in her throat. She wasn't sure where the knowledge had come from to respond so properly. It was, of course, technically the correct thing to say, but the word had come from her heart rather than from her memory bank, and at the moment she really did feel *blessed.*

Jayce cast a suspicious sidelong glance as he dished out a generous helping of lasagna for each of them. "Praying makes some people uncomfortable. I hope I haven't..."

"Not at all," Hana interrupted. "I don't know much about it, but I have tried it. I think if I ever get it right, it would probably become a very comforting experience," she remarked thoughtfully.

Jayce laughed. "Well, there's one for the books. I didn't know there was a right or a wrong way to pray. I think that everyone talks to God in their own way. Besides, the talking is easy. It's the listening that's the hard part."

"I suppose you're right, but I can't help thinking that faith is something you have to grow up with. You can't just start in the middle of nowhere."

"Well, seems to me like it's just as good a place to start as any."

"I suppose." Hana pondered the thought. Hadn't Jessica told her the same thing? "I know He's here. I can feel His presence." Hana spoke the words she'd wanted to share with someone for so long.

155

"Yes, He is," Jayce agreed, his gaze holding hers with a look of comfort and understanding. "He's everywhere."

"I guess, but when I was living in the city I just couldn't grasp it all, you know? I know that there are a lot of faithful people living in the city, but I just felt a little lost there."

"Ah! So then you are getting to like Lone Prairie," Jayce ribbed, his smile one more of relief than of personal satisfaction.

"I wonder why my mother didn't feel His presence. I find it hard to understand why she would leave here."

"Well, she had her reasons I guess," Jayce suddenly became uncomfortable and crinkled his napkin into a tiny wad in his hand.

"I can't forgive her, you know."

"Well, you're going to have to eventually," Jayce's fork seemed to be suspended mid-air, the last morsel of lasagna balanced carefully on the end of it.

"Why?" she asked solemnly.

"Because if you don't, you'll never have peace, that's why."

Jayce quickly ate the last bite and then left the table with his empty plate, signaling that the conversation was over, but Hana had felt somehow that it had just begun. Jayce had left her hanging for one reason or another and she presumed that she'd said something that had made him uncomfortable. But now was not the time to start, she decided, not while she was a guest in someone's home and had just eaten one of the best meals she'd had in a very long time. While she was at it, she couldn't complain about the company either.

They worked together to clear the table, piling all the dishes into the dishwasher. With the kitchen thoroughly cleaned, Jayce offered her another glass of wine and she took it gratefully, joining him in the living room while he tuned into the ten o'clock farm news on channel eight.

The topics never strayed from the light and comfortable aura they'd established in the kitchen, but it was enough, and seated at opposite ends of the soft brown faux suede sofa, Hana felt safe. It was so nice to be with someone, to know that someone else was worrying about the creepy night time noises and the ghosts of the past that permeated her dreams.

When she'd finished her second glass of wine her eyelids grew heavy and as the newscaster started talking about grain prices, she drifted off to sleep.

"Grain prices are better this year than they were last year at this time, although that tends to happen when there's a grain shortage due to drought, hail and other natural disasters," Jayce tried to keep the conversation flowing, but when Hana did not reply he turned to her curiously. She was sound asleep, curled up on his mother's favorite throw pillow. He drew in a short breath, wondering what it was about a sleeping woman that was so beautiful.

Her hair had tumbled slightly out of the same blue butterfly clip she always wore. Reaching for it, he released it, allowing her hair to cascade softly around her cheeks. She squirmed a little and he feared he might wake her, but she was tired and continued to sleep carelessly, as he covered her with the quilt he kept on the old wooden rocking chair.

Jayce dimmed the lights and switched off the television set, remembering almost instantly then that Hana still had chores to do. He wouldn't wake her. Instead, he slipped on his boots, locked the door behind him and drove to Ab's.

It was a full orange harvest moon, his favorite kind, and he marveled at the warmth the perfect glow created, like the soft glow inside his house where he'd left Hana to sleep. She wasn't waiting for his return, but she was there nonetheless. It was a far cry from sitting alone night after night, a state of existence he'd never really grown accustomed to.

Together the moon and Ab's yard light allowed enough visibility for him to get old Betsy into the barn and milk her, to feed the pig out back, to give King some fresh water and to feed the chickens as well. Shamrock and Sugar were there to keep him company and Jayce had to admit that all the animals looked healthy and happy. Hana was doing a good job, despite his former opinion of her.

When he returned home, Jayce unlocked the door quietly and snuck inside, finding himself compelled to go to the living room almost immediately. She was still there, still sleeping, still beautiful. Her face was paler now as she drifted off into deeper sleep, and immediately he felt guilty for watching her. He was invading her privacy and he forced himself up the stairs and into his own room, taking a quick shower before climbing into bed.

He slept restlessly and a few hours passed stubbornly by, but he'd never been one to grapple with the night. His time could be better spent getting a jump start on the day, and it was nearly three o'clock in the morning when he slipped on a pair of jeans and crept quietly back down the stairs.

She was still sleeping soundly and he was glad of it. At least one of them would be ready for another hard, long day of work. Then again, maybe she'd take off running. It wouldn't be the first time a woman had run out on him after she realized just exactly what the life of a full-fledged farmer entailed.

Jayce slid into the rocking chair uneasily, knowing that he shouldn't stay. What would his mother think of him? She wouldn't approve of what he and Ab were doing to Hana, that was for sure. Well, there were things his mother had done that he hadn't approved of either, things that were worse than holding a woman to the terms of a will and testament no matter how silly it was. He wasn't holding her against *her* will. She could leave anytime she chose to do so.

Jayce rose abruptly and left the room, deciding to occupy his thoughts with something more productive. Quietly, he spread his accounting ledger out onto the kitchen table and sorted through the piles of bills he'd been neglecting for too long.

He hated book work, especially when no matter how hard he worked to juggle the numbers nothing seemed to balance. Farming expenses were atrocious, his loan payments were high, and farm income was extremely low due to the years of drought and fallen grain prices. He'd been working as hard as he could, had taken some risks, particularly in the cattle industry which had proven to benefit his financial situation, but the one risk that produced absolutely no benefits on paper was the land.

It was only eighty acres, but farming had taken an unpredictable down-turn. This was a time in Saskatchewan when fathers were encouraging their sons to leave the farm after high school and get an education instead. His father and grandfather wouldn't have approved. They would have been shocked at the changes—yes, but they wouldn't have excused him from it all. He had inherited a legacy, and one day, if he had a son, he, too, would know the life of a farmer and have the same responsibility of maintaining and passing on the Harlow heritage.

Jayce paused. Now that was a thought worth laughing at. He hadn't even managed to find someone to share his life with yet. The entire Harlow lineage was hanging by a tattered thread, dangling from his inadequacies. Not a one of the Harlows, living or dead, would have approved of that.

Penciling numbers for what seemed like hours, Jayce tried to tally his expenses and balance them with a practical prediction of income, but his crop wasn't even off the ground yet. He could lose a grade or two in the quality of his grain due to the possibilities of rain, frost, hail, or even an early snow fall. Wearily, he closed his ledger with a feeling of defeat, knowing only one thing with certainty. At the end of harvest, he would owe another quarterly payment to the bank.

Wearily, he closed his eyes. He was tired now but it was almost morning. Deciding to brew a pot of coffee, Jayce waited patiently, and then filled a travel mug before heading outside. He could do some work around the yard and then do Hana's morning chores. He'd check on her later, maybe make them both some breakfast before starting out again.

Satisfied with his plan, he closed the screen door quietly behind him and headed out into the prairie dawn, this time resisting the urge to peer at the woman sleeping soundly on his living room sofa.

ChApTeR 13

Panic set in almost immediately. She'd broken the deal, again. She'd fallen asleep and left her animals to starve. Poor Betsy probably hadn't slept a wink all night because of her negligence, and Jayce Harlow had allowed it.

She'd given him the perfect opportunity to take advantage of her, and he had. Hana rose quickly off the sofa and folded the blanket neatly. She secured the clip back into her tangled knots and walked to the kitchen in a haze, enticed by the luring aroma of freshly brewed coffee. She was sure Jayce would be there, looking refreshed and smug and victorious, but he wasn't. Instead, she found something quite unexpected.

She hadn't deliberately sought it out, although in her present state of mind she couldn't testify that she wouldn't have done just that. Nevertheless, an accounting ledger and a small stack of files sat on the table. She just couldn't resist.

Inside of the first file she found a copy of the very same loan contract she had at the bank. Nothing new there. She'd read every clause and stipulation, but the document beneath it had suspicion written all over it, like a trail of cookie crumbs leading somewhere beyond the cookie jar.

"Put it back!" The screen door slammed behind him, confirming Jayce's untimely entrance.

His eyes shot splinters of anger. Immediately, she felt like a thief in the night.

"I'm sorry, Jayce. I was just..."

"Sticking your nose where it doesn't belong!" Jayce shot back.

He came towards her, his eyes transforming from kind blue to solemn gray.

"What's the big secret Jayce?" Hana pressed. "You and I both know that you're hanging onto a piece of land that has very little value. In the end you're going to lose it if you're not careful!" She waved the file in the air like a dangerous weapon, anger getting the best of her.

Jayce stopped short. He was close enough to snatch the file out of her hands, but resisted the opportunity to do so.

"And just how would *you* define value?" He folded his arms tightly across his chest. "Oh, that's right, with dollars and cents."

His tone was a unique mix of sarcasm and disappointment. He didn't have to grab the file. Suddenly, it seemed to be burning a hole in the palm of her hand, singeing her soul, and crumbling her conscience into a heap. She sat motionless, buried somewhere beneath the rubble.

"A piece of land can have a type of value that has absolutely nothing to do with money! Can't you see that?"

She couldn't see it, although somewhere inside she wanted to. For a moment she wanted to feel what the people in Lone Prairie could feel, but there was no point in it. Why couldn't *he* see it from her point of view? Sentimentality wouldn't help him out of the bind he was in.

"That kind of value won't make your next land payment!" she accused, wishing she could have said it better. Immediately, she regretted the advice that could only be taken as an insult. With a shoddy attempt at indifference, she dropped the file and then regretted that, too.

Jayce swallowed hard, took the books and slammed them into the drawer of the old desk that sat in the corner of the dining room. His boots scuffed heavily across the floor as he went to the kitchen and poured himself a cup of coffee. He brought one for her, too, and she was ashamed by his polite gesture.

"I did your chores last night and this morning, but if you'd like to go home and take a shower that's up to you, or you can use mine, up the stairs, second door to your left. If not, I'd appreciate it if we could get started as soon as possible. There's a storm moving in. They're forecasting that it'll be here by the end of the day, so we better get a move on if we want to get your crop off."

He spun around on the heels of his work boots and left then, restraint apparent in every step. Somehow, his remarkable sense of self-control was even more lethal than if he'd given into anger. At the very least, it made her feel even more ashamed.

Why he hadn't run her off his farm remained unclear to her. He'd been nothing but polite, and she'd crossed the line as a banker and as a friend, if she could be as presumptuous as to call herself that. It wasn't her right to know why he valued the land. Many times in her career she'd been curious about clients and the financial decisions they'd made or the risks they'd taken, but as long as the money and collateral were in place, it wasn't any of her business. Jayce had made good on his payments. For now, he was completely caught up. She had no right.

Deciding to skip the shower, Hana found Jayce greasing the hoist on the grain truck. She hopped into the passenger seat and waited for him quietly, confident that her silence would be appreciated in lieu of congeniality. For once she was prepared to just shut right up.

They'd left the swathing machine and combine where they'd stopped the previous evening. Things would move more slowly with Nathan in school but they'd get the work done, if there weren't any mechanical break downs, and if the weather held out. There were so many *ifs*.

Jayce was silent on the way to the field. He rolled down his window as he drove and hung his elbow out in attempts to catch a bit of the morning breeze. Hana caught herself watching him as he looked out into the neighbor's field. He was probably thinking about her, the slow and agonizing pain, gnawing on his very last nerve.

She could see the fed-up look in his eyes. He looked tired and Hana wondered if he'd slept at all the previous night. How could he possibly have slept? He'd done her chores, not once but twice, and had obviously spent some time in the books, all while she'd been having the best sleep she'd had in months. She'd been careless and selfish and not even her stubborn ego could come to her rescue this time.

Yet, despite the rocky start, the morning passed by without any mishaps. They stopped only once, when Jayce returned after dumping a load of grain and brought back with him a bag lunch, a thermos of coffee and a fresh jug of water. Her hands and face were gritty, but somehow it made the food taste exceptionally good, despite the fact that the sandwiches were dripping in mustard and mayo and all the things she swore she'd never eat.

It would have tasted even better if Jayce had taken the time to sit and eat with her, but he'd taken off abruptly, returning to the swathing and leaving her alone with her thoughts. She deserved it though, and anything else he could dish out, but instead, he remained polite, a strength of character greater than anything she possessed.

The day flew by quickly, and all too soon, Nathan's old pick-up pulled into the approach. Jayce would probably be relieved that real help had arrived. Defiantly, she cranked up the air conditioner in the combine cab.

It was only a few agonizing hours later when *defiance* had worn out its welcome. If she'd managed to convince herself that she didn't need Jayce Harlow, the broken air conditioner had other ideas. It was inhumane to work under such conditions. Wearily, she reached for the blue jug beneath her seat and drank the last drop, the jug now empty, along with her resolve.

Grabbing the square speaker of the two-way radio system, she pushed the button. "Jayce, are you by?"

A mass of static pelted back first, making her ears ache. "I can't hear you!" she shouted back, annoyed.

"Well, I can hear you loud and clear so don't shout." she heard him through the squeals and muffles. "Turn the grey knob back a notch. It's the button to the left of the volume dial."

Hana swerved and missed a chunk of swath as she searched for the button. "I think I've got it," she responded, looking back over her shoulder at the missed swath and wanting to scream in frustration.

"Don't worry about it," Jayce always seemed to be able to read her thoughts. "What can I do for you?" He came back clearly now, and ever the gentleman.

"The air conditioner doesn't seem to be working," she tried not to sound whiney.

"Get used to it, honey," another voice shot back, and Hana immediately recognized it as Nathan's. She hadn't realized that he would be listening in on the conversation. While it was extremely practical for all parties involved in the harvest to be a part of the communication system, it was also unnerving, and Hana reminded herself that in the future she'd avoid the radio altogether.

"Nathan, pick me up and take me over to the combine. I'll have a look at it," she heard Jayce say.

Hana stopped the combine and waited, wishing that she hadn't caused such a fuss. Nevertheless, the break felt good. With slow movements, she flexed the muscles in her arms and legs, stretching them out cautiously until the cramps dissipated. She'd forgotten her glasses, and her eyes, like the rest of her body were starting to feel the strain. A migraine would be the next symptom of the day's disasters, and she felt it coming on with a vengeance as Nathan and Jayce arrived in the grain truck, equipped with smug grins and egos.

Hana's blood pressure rose in direct proportion to the mounting tension as Jayce entered the cab. Diligently, he fiddled with the dials, adjusting and fine tuning until he was perfectly satisfied.

"Yep. It's broken," he nodded, biting his upper lip hard to keep from laughing.

"Tell me something I don't know."

"Well, it can't be fixed, at least not out here. If you're going to be all right without it, we'll just carry on. One more hour and we'll be done. The clouds are already starting to build in the west."

Hana drew in a deep breath, finding it difficult to satisfy her lungs.

"Well, look on the bright side. At least you still have an AM radio. Neither one of us have air or radio."

"Are you serious? With the price that these darned machines cost, you'd think they'd be equipped with every modern convenience," Hana mused, finally seeing the humor in the situation. "What do you do without a radio? You must go crazy in there."

"I have a lot of time to think," he raised his eyebrows matter-of-factly, "and pray."

"Does He answer you?"

"If you listen, Hana Islander, you will hear," Jayce turned to leave.

"Jayce?" Hana called, not wanting to let him leave again without finally saying it. "I'm sorry," she paused. "I had no right to go snooping through those documents."

Jayce's expression softened, much to her relief. "It's all right. I guess you owed me one. That day you came to introduce yourself to Ab, I kinda' stuck my nose where it didn't belong, too."

"Kinda'?"

"Well, let's just call it even."

Hana watched Jayce walk away and her spirit felt like it could float to the moon. Quickly she reeled it in again, keeping her emotions in check, mindful of the fact that while he had forgiven her, he still had not entrusted her with the truth.

Shifting the combine into gear, Hana glanced at the dark clouds that churned violently now in moody layers of black and gray. Where had the rain been when they needed it? They certainly didn't need it now in harvest time.

Tuning the radio into the weather forecast, her observations were confirmed. She shook her head irritably, wondering what had been the biggest disturbance of the day, the fact that she was starting to sound like a typical farmer, or the fact that rain was inevitable.

It shouldn't have mattered to her. Ab's crop was nearly harvested, but for Jayce and the people of Lone Prairie, bad weather would cause a major delay.

"God, if you're listening, could you help me out here?"

She felt ridiculous. How did you just start up a conversation with God? She started out slowly, formulating the words carefully, but she couldn't pray for herself when all she could think about was Jayce—his crops, his future, his well-being.

Daring to enter the center of silence, she prayed, "Dear God, I ask you to help Jayce Harlow. Please grant him a good turn, even if it be at my expense, Amen."

She couldn't exactly explain what she'd meant by it all in logical terms. She'd simply just said what she truly felt, even though she was certain that God did not balance good deeds with bad ones like debits and credits in an accounting ledger, but if He did, she would take a little bad luck for Jayce's sake.

It was a foreign thought, but one that generated a feeling nearly equivalent to what she'd felt when she'd performed a good deed. If nothing else, it was an honest attempt at prayer—a long anticipated start to a journey that she hoped would lead to a place beyond her wildest dreams.

ChApTeR 14

The predicted weather disturbance came in the form of a two-day wind storm, mixed with sporadic showers. It delayed the harvest and succeeded in making a complete mess out of the swaths that had been ready for harvesting. Hana's grain was safely inside the bins and ready for sale. Jayce's crops were still out weathering the elements, and she felt guilty once again.

With no valid excuse to be absent from work, Hana dressed for work the following morning in her black pinstriped suit. She smiled at the memory of the skirt that had ripped directly up the back seam on the first visit she'd made to Jayce's farm. A lot of things had happened since then.

She'd mended the skirt. That part had been easy, but there was no way she could repair the rift that existed between she and Jayce.

There were other rifts that had been mended though. She and Rosey were now on very good terms with one another, and today Rosey was the first to greet her with a smile and a quick reminder that Harry and Elizabeth were overdue on their next loan payment.

Immediately, she regretted coming into work. At this point, they were probably extremely stressed by the harvest conditions. The last thing she wanted to do was add to their troubles.

Hana went through Harry and Elizabeth's files, searching for anything she might have missed, any loop hole that might allot them more time to make their next payment. She found nothing. Grabbing her purse and a coffee to go, she left the office, her mood as bleak as the weather.

They welcomed her anyway, just as they had on her first visit, and Hana accepted their offer of coffee, pie and kindness. When the time came for her to broach the subject of the payment, Harry ventured into the topic first and she was grateful.

"We can't make our payment, Miss Islander," Harry's soft brown eyes looked up from the old white china coffee mug. His fingers were white, too, from holding onto it so tightly, and Hana feared that the cup and his spirit might shatter simultaneously.

Hana's heart clenched tightly in her chest and she looked to Elizabeth for some sort of reassurance, but Elizabeth placed her fork softly down onto her plate and pushed it forward, clearly having lost her appetite even for lemon meringue pie.

"Our daughter is starting into her second year of college. Her tuition was due and we just couldn't afford both." Elizabeth continued to stare into her half-eaten pie, the fluffy meringue looking much too pleasant for the nature of a conversation that was as flat and tasteless as a piece of plastic.

"Have you ever considered looking into a government funded student loan for your daughter? There are some options you might be willing to explore if..."

"We've already tried that, Miss Islander. The government denied us a loan for Raelene. They asked for a detailed summary of our income. We spent a lot of time filling out the forms. Somehow they determined that our income should be high enough to manage on our own."

"That's ridiculous. I've seen the figures. I know it's impossible for you to fund your daughter's education, at least at this point." Hana attempted to balance her anger with proper decorum. In no way did she want to make Harry and Elizabeth feel that they had failed to provide adequately for their daughter and her future.

"The government sometimes fails to take into account the present changes in farming, the direct effects of drought and falling grain prices."

"Yes, the information they required was from the previous year. That hardly gives them a clear picture into our current financial situation." Elizabeth's face regained some color.

"Harry, with your permission I'd like to reapply for a loan for your daughter. I'll look after filling out the forms and attaching a special note if necessary so that they can get an accurate picture of your current financial situation."

"Now, Miss Islander, I wouldn't want to trouble you. I should have called about being late with our loan payment, but we were doing so well with the harvest until it rained, and then my combine broke down and needed some repairs, and..."

"It's all right," Hana came to Harry's rescue.

"But I just can't ask that of you, Miss Islander," Harry continued to argue gracefully.

"You didn't ask. I offered," Hana reached out to touch Harry's arm. "Please, let me do this."

Harry answered her with a smile and Elizabeth, much to Hana's relief, slid her plate back and began to eat again.

By the time Harry excused himself to return to his work, Hana and Elizabeth had slipped in and out of several different topics with the ease of two women who had known each other for a very long time. They hardly even noticed Harry leave with a look of relief on his face to be escaping the presence of women who shared a common view of the world unbeknown to himself.

Hana even accepted a second piece of pie, the look of pride on Elizabeth's face worth much more than the extra pound she stood to gain as a direct result of too much pie eating.

"So, I've been dying to ask you how things have been going with you and Jayce? I hear the two of you struck a deal in helping each other with the harvest and I think that's fantastic. The man works himself to death. Lord knows he can use the help."

"I think it's me who really needs the help," Hana gave a defeated sigh, but the fact that Elizabeth knew about it was actually a bit of a relief. She wanted so badly to talk to someone. Everyone needed a bit of a splashboard, even strong, independent women.

"Well? How are things going?"

"Elizabeth?" Hana paused and mustered up her courage. She needed to ask. "Can I trust you?"

"Well, of course you can trust me, dear!" Elizabeth reached out to touch her hand. "Your mother and I were good friends. I see a lot of her in you, all the good things anyway."

"So you did know my mother?" Hana became immediately side-tracked.

"Of course," Elizabeth seemed to disappear inside herself, remembering things she hadn't thought about in a very long time. "Priscilla was incorrigible. She brought out a side in me I didn't know I had, a wild and crazy side."

"My mother, wild and crazy? I find that hard to imagine."

"Oh, she was definitely a woman to reckon with."

"Is that why she left? She was just too different? Didn't fit in?"

"That's part of the reason I guess," Elizabeth shrugged.

"What's the other part?" She desperately needed to know. She hadn't assumed there was anything more to it than a woman who'd found herself in the wrong mold."

"You haven't answered my question about Jayce," Elizabeth seemed uneasy as she bustled to the kitchen, returning with the coffee pot. "How about a refill?"

"Sure," Hana replied, sensing that Elizabeth had closed the subject on her mother.

"Well?" Elizabeth prodded, sitting down again and helping herself to another piece of pie.

"Jayce has been extremely helpful. I couldn't have done it without him. When he harvests, I'm going to help him in return. There's nothing more to it than that."

"Well, that's funny. Jayce has been harvesting all day on the section just north of his place. Didn't you see him on your way to work?"

"No. I left early." Hana was stunned. They had a deal. She'd never have accepted his help if she couldn't return it. It was just like him to alter the deal to suit himself, but how could it possibly suit him? He needed help, and even though she probably wasn't the best hired hand he'd ever had, she did the job.

"Elizabeth, if you'll excuse me, I'd better head back to the office. I want to get a jump start on those student loan papers. Thanks so much for the delicious pie and coffee."

"Oh, wait dear. I'll send you a piece to go. Jayce will probably be hungry."

She handed Hana a piece of pie on a paper plate wrapped with plastic seal, a disposable fork placed conveniently inside. Hana accepted it speechlessly, wondering how Elizabeth could possibly have known. Were her thoughts and intentions that transparent?

Well, it didn't matter. All that really mattered was that Jayce had humiliated her once again. She'd give him a piece of her mind and then maybe a piece of pie.

What was it with these people anyway? She couldn't read minds for heaven's sake. If Elizabeth knew more about her mother, then why wouldn't she tell her? If Jayce was ready to harvest, why couldn't he call her?

Understanding Elizabeth's intentions weren't quite so simple, but Jayce, well it didn't take a genius to figure him out. He was Jayce Harlow after all, too proud and arrogant to accept help from a woman!

Hana drove recklessly, verging on too fast for road conditions. She should have known that it might be dry enough in some fields even though others remained wet. Nothing was consistent on the prairie. She found Jayce out in the north section just as Elizabeth said. He was tightening a belt on the combine and had already swathed several rounds. Hana assumed that he wanted to pick them up with the combine before the wind could cause any destruction.

She slammed the car door to announce her presence, but he ignored her as she stepped slowly across the field in her heels as though walking on broken glass. The stubble snagged her nylons and scratched her legs but she ignored it, the feeling of rejection causing more hurt than anything.

"You could have called," she fumed, hand on her hip. The other hand clutched the piece of pie and seemed to shake with a will of its own.

He turned around in a gesture of surprise as though he hadn't heard her arrival. With his wrench in hand, he leaned against the combine and eyed her up, whistling an approval that merely succeeded in making her see an even brighter shade of red.

"Never could resist a beautiful woman in a striking outfit. Not having a lot of luck with those danged heels out here though are you? Hopefully those will be salvageable," he laughed as he watched her dump the dirt out of her left shoe.

"Jayce, you should have called me," she ignored his jibing, her mission much more serious than a ruined pair of shoes. "I want to uphold our deal. You help me, I help you, remember?"

"I don't need your help Hana. I've been doing this on my own for years, and I imagine I'll be doing it on my own for many more."

A sullen look of annoyance creased his brows and he returned to his work, ignoring her presence again. It was the first time he'd ever looked anything else but pleased and confident with the choices he'd made in his life.

"Well, have you ever dared to *imagine* anything else?" Her question was a loaded one and it hung in the air between them intangibly, neither one quite able to grasp it completely.

"This is my life, Hana. Next year at this time you'll be long gone and whether or not you helped me with this harvest isn't really going to matter."

"Well, it'll matter to me."

When he turned away again and continued to ignore her, she tempted him with Elizabeth's pie.

"Elizabeth sent something for you."

"Don't tell me you were over there bothering those people again," his elbow swung up and down as he worked the wrench to tighten the troublesome bolt.

"I wasn't doing anything of the sort. In fact, I'll have you know that sometimes I do come up with ideas that help people with their financial problems."

"Really?" he grumbled, finally relenting to taking some interest in the pie.

He took it from her with a hint of suspicion and sat down on the bottom step of the combine. Again she had the silly thought that the moment could have been better if she'd come on a more positive note, if she'd baked the pie herself, if—Hana closed her eyes tightly, willing the unwelcome thoughts away.

"Headache?"

"What?"

"I asked if you have a headache. You look pained."

"No, I was just thinking that I'm not going to take the time to go home and change," she lied.

"What are you talking about?"

"I'm helping you Jayce, whether you want me or not. If we get this combine moving now, you can keep swathing. Will Nathan join us after school?"

"That's the plan."

"Good. Let's get started then."

Whether he wanted her or not—now wasn't that just the million dollar question? Oh, he wanted her all right, but not necessarily her help. He wanted her heart and soul, but most of all he wanted her in his life forever, and it was down right disturbing.

He knew the feeling. He'd felt it before, but it was different this time. It was better. It was worse. It was impossible.

He had wanted a relationship, to find someone that could renew his hope in the possibilities of *forever*, but a relationship with Hana Islander? He wanted that about as badly as he wanted a root canal. Besides, if she had a choice she'd be as far away from him and Lone Prairie as she could possibly get. She'd made that perfectly clear when she first arrived.

Then there was the whole other fiasco that he dared to call the past. Really, it was much more than just the past, it was what predestined their demise if they should ever even attempt a relationship. The bitter past had selfishly taken hold of his future, and he wouldn't make the same mistakes, but did that mean he couldn't enjoy it while it lasted? Well, he was enjoying it, even if he shouldn't have been.

He was enjoying the sight of her every time they crossed paths, her poise, her wit. He loved the innocent way she asked so many questions and then the very next day pretended to have all the answers on her own accord. She smelled like strawberries and vanilla, and her scent lingered, assaulting his senses all day. The fact that his fields were yielding some of the worst crops he'd ever seen, rarely crossed his mind when she was anywhere near.

There was no doubt in his mind either that she was Abner Crawford's daughter. She had farming in her blood. He'd never seen anyone catch onto things so quickly, not even Nathan, but it really hadn't come as a surprise. He'd known it all along, could feel it whenever he was around her, that a piece of Abner was somehow present, too.

For her sake more than his own he wished it wasn't true, that she wasn't really Ab's daughter. Maybe then things could be different between them, but she was, and once she found out the truth she'd feel the same shame. She was better off not knowing.

For the time being though, she yearned to know and understand her father, and for that he couldn't blame her. Ab's plan was working. She'd come to find her father, and found herself instead, but she wouldn't stay. She did have some of her mother in her, too, Jayce constantly reminded himself.

She wouldn't stay.

ChApTeR 15

"Well, this is it, the last load of straw."

Jayce removed his leather gloves and reached for his jean jacket which he'd hung on an old nail in the barn. His sun-bleached hair was slightly darker now, his farmer's tan fading. Fall permeated the air, altering the countryside to amber. Like a city traffic light, it was nature's reminder. Time was running out.

They'd worked together side by side quite successfully, had nearly worn a groove in proper decorum, but like the waning power of the autumn sun, Hana could feel her resolve weakening. She should have forfeited by now. It was a thought that started out small and then grew larger and more obvious every day. It made sense in more ways than one, and if she hadn't been so blind she'd have known all along that it was practically inevitable.

Jayce could have been rid of his financial stress and his annoying neighbor, and she could have been back in Saskatoon and settled into her old life. So what was the delay? A few months ago she couldn't have thought of anything more pleasing. Now, it was as if Abner had rerouted the course of her life and she was entirely lost. No way to go back; no way to go forward, just stuck in the mucky clay of the prairies. But clay was a funny thing. It was hard and unyielding at first, but it softened the more you worked with it. With warm hands, in time, it could be shaped into anything. Somewhere in the ruts of the past few months, she'd become the clay.

"I can't remember ever having finished the harvest and getting all the bales hauled in by this time. It's true what they say about many hands."

"Pardon me?"

"You know the old saying? Many hands make light work."

"Oh, that one," Hana feigned familiarity even though she'd never heard the expression before. It was just one more thing she'd learned to accept about the people in Lone Prairie. They had an expression for everything.

Jayce tucked his gloves into his back pocket and peered outside of the barn and into the early afternoon. "It's going to be an early winter. I can feel it."

"Would you like to join me for a cup of coffee or a hot chocolate?" Hana couldn't stand the thought of him leaving. It was the last thing they'd do together, she assumed, now that the harvest was over. She'd be gone before seeding time next spring, maybe even sooner.

"No thanks. I'll be by tomorrow morning to haul your pig to market like we discussed."

Hana cringed. She couldn't stand the thought.

"There's no need to have it here if you aren't going to put it to good use," Jayce had suddenly taken a step forward as if to comfort her, but then quickly stepped back again opting for the safety of the wide open farmyard.

She followed him out of the barn, desperate for him to stay, and for some sort of affirmation that—that what? She was still no better off than when she started. He still hadn't trusted her with the truth.

"Well, see ya' around," he kept walking, his paces quickening, her heart racing to catch up.

"Jayce, about the will, I..."

"Forget it, Hana." He stopped in his tracks and then turned around slowly, his expression tired and grim. "Just forget about that ridiculous thing. It was a stupid idea. I wish Ab had never..."

"So it really was Ab's idea?" Hana seized the opportunity.

"You mean after all this time you still think that I had something to do with it?"

His reaction hadn't been at all what she'd expected. It was as if she'd disappointed him in the very worst way, after all he'd done.

"Has it ever occurred to you that this whole thing has nothing to do with a will, nothing to do with a piece of land or money?"

"Well I..."

"You what, Hana? You continue to assume the very worst about me? Well, let me set things straight. I had nothing to do with that will and if you'd just open your eyes, maybe you'd see that there's a lot more going on here than...," Jayce stopped himself.

This was it. This was what she'd been waiting to hear, she could feel it in her bones, but Jayce bit his lip and spun quickly around on his heel, the past, the present, and the future hanging dangerously between them.

"Where are you going?"

"I'm going to help the neighbors. There's still some daylight left. Just because we're finished doesn't mean the harvest's over."

His words stung her, making her feel ashamed and selfish.

"You know, at first I thought that just maybe you and I, well that we could...," he shook his head, unable to even speak the words. "But we're just too different, and I've worked too hard to gain people's respect."

"What does that mean?" She shouted after him, and then watched helplessly as he walked away, his boots pounding hard on the ground.

She couldn't be Abner Crawford's daughter. If she was, she would have remembered the neighbors and volunteered to help them. She was guilty of thinking only about herself yet again, but

Jayce was guilty too. He was playing on her sensitivities and he knew it.

It was obvious that he'd meant to sidetrack her and he'd succeeded, leaving her with unanswered questions once again. Why would Jayce Harlow have to *earn* anyone's respect and what threat was she to all of that?

Brushing the straw from her clothes, Hana stomped to the house, mumbling a prayer to the God who knew and wouldn't tell. Yes, there was a God. She knew it now, because something had entered her heart that had never been there before. It was faith, faith in the man who had made her feel things she thought she would never feel, and faith in a father whose spirit led her from day to day in a place that clearly held no promise.

Snow came a few weeks later, covering the prairie like a thin sheet full of holes. She'd seen pictures of countrysides laden with snow, perfect and serene, but hadn't realized just how much snow it took to cover the landscape, the stubble in the wheat fields, the tall weeds left in the ditches.

Hana prayed that Lone Prairie would get its fair share of it. They needed all the moisture they could get, especially after another summer of virtual drought. It was evident in the pile of farmer's accounts that she studied and pondered day after day, never finding a solution beyond the obvious. They needed a good year, a year when the moisture level was more than sufficient, when grain prices were up, when the cattle market was stable at the very least. They needed some good luck, and if the snowfalls were any prediction of their future, she failed to see any positive changes.

There'd been no positive improvements with Jayce either. When his next loan payment came due, he arranged for payment with one of the tellers when Hana had gone out for lunch. She was disappointed to see his cheque on her desk when she returned, his name scrawled neatly on the dotted line. He'd sold a few head of cattle to make the payment, and it hurt her to think that he'd had to resort to that. It had taken him years to build up his herd. Abner's assets could have saved him from having to make such a rash decision.

Sadly, she entered the transaction into the computer as she would have done for any other client, taking note of the fact that his next loan payment would be due in early spring. She'd be gone by then.

With resignation, she returned his file back to the filing cabinet, annoyed with the temperamental drawer that didn't seem to want to close. Something was jammed inside, and she resisted the urge to slam it shut. Forcing the issue would probably just cause more problems. She'd had to learn that the hard way.

Looking around for Rosey, she sighed defeat. It was strange how the woman was always there when she hadn't wanted her, and never there when she needed her. Resisting the urge to curse, she reached inside, feeling with her hand a file that was severely stuck near the back.

It was like it had beckoned her from the beyond, choosing this exact moment in time. With a forceful twist, she wrenched free the crinkled culprit that read *Doris Harlow*.

"Who is Doris?" Hana questioned under her breath as she snuck the file into her office. With an eerie sense of something amiss, she opened the musty file and slid her glasses down her nose simultaneously. Every tiny little hair on the back of her neck prickled in anticipation.

She read it quickly, as though quenching a desperate thirst. It was a land title for the infamous eighty acres, but it was in Doris Harlow's name. Beneath it was a copy of her will and testament in which was highlighted that Doris Harlow bequeathed the said piece of land to Abner Crawford.

Abner? Now what on earth did Abner have to do with it? Hana made a dash for the filing cabinet again, this time grabbing Abner's file. In it she found the same land title. Attached to it was a document stating that the land had been sold to Jayce Harlow. Immediately, Hana's brain began to work overtime.

When Rosey returned from her lunch break Hana was waiting for her, her level of anxiety dangerously turning to anger.

"Rosey? Could you come into my office please? And close the door behind you!"

Rosey complied without question, curiosity arching her brows. She spotted the files immediately and a worrisome look edged with guilt immediately gave her away.

"Hana, I…"

"You what, Rosey? You thought it would be better to hide the truth from me? I'm not just some employer who came here from the big city to cover a leave of absence. I'm Abner Crawford's daughter. I have a right to know what this is all about."

Hana pointed to the scattering of papers angrily, knowing that she was venting on Rosey when she should have been venting on Jayce.

He had made her feel badly about all her doubts and suspicions, but worst of all he'd made her fall in love with him and then feel badly about that, too.

"Look, Hana, the people in Lone Prairie might know everything about everybody else's business, but we also know when to keep our mouths shut. If you want to know why Jayce bought the land from Abner then you'd best ask him yourself."

Rosey left her alone then to ponder the thought of approaching Jayce. This time, she'd go as Abner Crawford's daughter and not as the Loans Manager of the Loan Prairie Bank. She had a right to know why he'd kept it a secret from her. In the meantime, her mind continued to conjure up all sorts of devious and underhanded motives behind the deals that had taken place.

The land had to be worth something. Jayce knew its value and sucked it right out from underneath the poor and innocent Abner. It was why he'd paid full price for it. Perhaps there was oil on the land, but then who was Doris and why had she willed the land to Abner to begin with? The entire thing was far too complicated for her to figure out on her own.

"Rosey, I'm leaving for the day. I'll be back tomorrow." Hana grabbed her purse and headed out the office door.

"But Jessica is scheduled for an appointment in five minutes. You can't just run out."

"Yes, I can!"

"Miss Islander? Did I come at a bad time?" Jessica spoke from somewhere behind her and Hana's face went red with embarrassment.

"Cancel the rest of my appointments for the day," she whispered sternly to Rosey before swinging around with a jaded smile. It was Jayce's little sister after all, another criminal in a long series of hurtful omissions. Surely, she could find a way of using the appointment to her full advantage.

"No, you didn't come at a bad time," Hana painted on a bright smile before ushering Jessica into her office.

"I wanted to show you the financial statement from my first few months in business. We'll be able to make our payment and make a profit as well. Jake is so excited. We want to use some of the profit to increase our cattle herd. Every little bit helps."

"Yes. I see you two have things well in control."

"We couldn't have done it without you," Jessica beamed.

"Well, obviously you've developed a lucrative clientele. You should be proud of yourself."

"Yes, well, I might say the same of you. You've made it through the most difficult part of your term here. You must be so relieved."

Hana thought for a moment. Relieved? Was she relieved? While it was true that she wouldn't be responsible for the crops next year, she could hardly describe the feeling in the pit of her stomach as relief.

"It's been an experience."

"So you'll probably be leaving at the end of March? You're contract is up then, isn't it?"

"Yes, I guess it is," the thought threatened to deflate her anger. Was everyone calculating her departure? Hana closed her eyes. Now was not a time to feel sorry for herself. Avoiding questions and sticking to an agenda was key to finding answers. It was working already, as she could see Jessica starting to fidget in her chair.

"Miss Islander, Hana, I don't want you to take this the wrong way, but I'm his sister. He's always looked out for me, and for once, I want to return the favor."

"I don't understand," Hana shook her head trying to make sense out of Jessica's discomfort.

"Please, don't hurt my brother."

"What ever makes you think that I would?" Hana reeled back slightly in her chair, suddenly beginning to understand.

"I'm not blind, Hana. I can see the chemistry between the two of you, and you're a wonderful person, but there are things you just don't understand, things about Jayce, about the past."

"That's just it!" Hana fumed. "How can I ever understand if no one will tell me?"

"I can't."

"Why?"

"I promised."

"Promised who?"

"Jayce."

"For heaven's sake! What's the big secret?"

"Please Hana, just leave peacefully and unattached. You'll have won fair and square."

"I can't just leave without knowing, Jessica. You don't know what it's like to know that something is horribly wrong and that no matter how hard you try, no one will let you make it right."

"I've spent my entire life trying to make things right!" Jessica snapped and then immediately took a deep breath to calm herself. "You're a good person, Hana. I don't doubt that your intentions toward my brother are honorable, but you won't stay. Deep down you'll always long for the city and eventually you'll leave. So please, just do us all a favor and go back to where you came from. And don't look back."

Tears mingled with anger, a deadly combination, but Hana saved it for Jayce and allowed Jessica to walk out the door. They'd never let her into their circle. It was almost as if her father's reputation perhaps hadn't been honorable. Lord knows her mother's hadn't been. Well, she could resort back to plan A.

When she'd first arrived in Lone Prairie she hadn't been trying so hard to please everybody.

Hana grabbed the files and headed out the door, not even attempting to hide her disappointment. They all knew exactly where she was headed, and Rosey would probably warn Jayce before she got there, if he was anywhere near a telephone. That was none of her concern. All that really mattered was discovering the truth and then biding her time, and if Jayce Harlow thought he could try to run her off again, well this time he would be sadly mistaken!

"You've got to get your cattle home, Hana. There's nothing for them to eat out here anymore," Jayce seethed as he twisted a strand of barbed wire off the scrawny post. "This makeshift fence just won't hold them. They've been out on the road twice since harvest."

"Well, why didn't anyone tell me?" Hana crossed her arms firmly, the air seeping out of her carefully orchestrated plan once again. She'd assumed that since all the snow had melted due to the mild temperatures, there wasn't any rush. There were still patches of green grass, well, maybe not so much anymore. Her shoulders slumped. She'd been negligent again.

She'd found him after quite some search. The last place she expected him to be was across the road from Ab's farm, fixing Ab's fence, *her* fence. She'd rather have found him anywhere else.

"There are never any breaks with farming, Hana. There's always something to do or something to fix."

"I'll get my cattle home tomorrow, first thing in the morning." Hana spoke firmly, finding that old confidence that had at one time made her actually believe she could do anything. "As for the fence, leave it. I'll hire someone to fix it once I get my cattle home."

"Well, as far as I know, no one's started up a fence repairing business around here. Besides, what do you care? It won't matter after you leave. You can sell the place and then none of this will be any of your concern."

"And just what makes everyone around here so sure that I'll leave? What if I stay?"

He turned to her sharply, his eyes nearly freezing her to the spot.

"That's right, Jayce Harlow. What if I stay and take over my Dad's farm for good? And what if I finally get wise to all the secrets you people have been keeping? What then, Jayce?"

"What secrets?"

He spoke so calmly that she wanted to strangle him. Stomping back to her car she retrieved the papers, throwing them at him shamelessly. The wind scattered them violently in all directions and Jayce reached for the one that clung to his ankle. He read it slowly and deliberately and then pulled three more from the fence, chasing one sheet nearly thirty feet until he finally caught up with it. He didn't read anymore and didn't need to, she presumed. Instead, he walked to his truck and got inside, motioning for her to join him.

She got in reluctantly, slamming the door behind her. Together they sat, both out of breath and too angry to speak. Finally, Jayce started the engine and drove calmly and deliberately to the place that had captivated her from the moment she arrived in Lone Prairie.

His silence unnerved her as he drove through the tall grass and over the rough terrain leading into the heart of the valley. It was a place of tranquility beyond what the eye could see from the road, and she was stunned by the contrasting beauty of the tall evergreens that stretched to the sky, and the pine cones that were scattered beneath them on the ground.

Jayce got out of the truck and drew in a deep breath of cool, early November air. She waited for him to say something, but instead, he walked. She followed blindly until he stopped in front of a poplar tree growing amidst the evergreens. It stretched upward, barely higher than the rest. Jayce pointed to it with a desperation that chilled her.

"This is it? This is your explanation for why you've all been acting so crazy? ABC + D carved in a tree? What's so enlightening about that? This used to be an old school site, right? Children probably came down here to play. It's just the alphabet, Jayce!" Hana rambled on, her nerves so strung out she could hardly stop her body from shaking.

"For heaven's sake, Hana, figure it out! ABC was the way Abner Crawford spelled his name."

"Yeah. I found a sewing machine that he gave to my mother. He inscribed it with those very initials. So? It still doesn't make any sense."

"Well, just whom do you presume the D stood for?"

"I don't know." Hana fumbled, her brain whirling with ideas. Then it came to her as suddenly as the gust of wind that made its way into the calming shelter of the valley to hit her as harshly as a slap in the face.

"Doris Harlow. Was she your mother?"

He closed his eyes tightly and nodded, shame apparent in the muscles that tightened his jaw and the eyes that could not look at her. Hana took a step closer to the tree, reaching upward to feel the letters, to carve them into her own heart until they finally made sense out of the past the present and even the future.

"I found Mom's old love letters to Ab after she died. She loved him more than she loved my Dad. I don't know what kept her here, with Dad and us. Jessica found out, too, even though I tried to protect her from the truth."

Hana covered her mouth to smother a sob, her world rocked as hard as the day she discovered she still had a father. It changed everything once again, spinning things around and shaking her in the process. She felt nauseous. All the things she'd thought about her mother? About her father? Everything had been backwards. She wanted to scream.

"Your mother found out. I think she would have left Abner eventually, she just left sooner is all. My Dad found out too. He was never the same after that. I can look back on my childhood and see it all clearly now, how pathetic it all was. Dad took to drinking and just kind of let things go, the farm, his marriage. I've spent the last few years just trying to pay off his debts."

"So why do you keep the land?" Hana finally found the courage to speak. She willed herself to look at him, but the pain in his eyes made her look away and back at the heart that told the story of more pain than she would ever be able to grasp or erase.

"I don't know. I'm ashamed of it. Sometimes I think I just want to hide it away from everybody, but then I think that I'm keeping it for them, for Mom and Ab, because I think that when she was here with him, it was the only time she was really happy."

"You must have hated Abner. Why were you so nice to him?"

"I didn't know about it all at first, not until Mom died and willed Ab this land. She always loved this old school site. It was where she went to school, met my Dad and Abner, too. When I learned that she'd willed it to Ab, I accused Ab of a lot of things. I thought he'd swindled it off her somehow and that it was worth something, kind of like what you must have thought when you discovered I bought the land from Abner, but Ab didn't put up any resistance. He wanted to give it to me. I insisted I pay top dollar. When I came here, then, and saw this, I figured it all out. I was so mad at him, threatened to beat him to a pulp, but I couldn't do it. It was her fault, too, and then I found the letters."

"Did your Dad ever confront Abner? It must have been so hurtful to him that Doris would will a piece of land to Abner. It was almost like she wanted to confess, like she wanted all of you to know."

"Seems crazy doesn't it? It tears me up inside just wondering how she could be so cruel. She always believed that the truth sets you free though. It's the only explanation I have for her confession when she so easily could have taken the secret to her grave. And no, Dad never confronted Abner. He died shortly after Mom. You see? Our pasts aren't that different."

Hana turned to look at the heart again and then back to the man who had suffered so long for the sins of his mother. "I wish you had told me, Jayce."

"Would it have changed anything?"

"Yes."

"It wouldn't have, Hana. You were better off not knowing. I wanted to save you the agony of feeling like I do…of feeling like a mistake as a result of a relationship that should never have been."

"You're still angry with your mother, then?"

"She was unfaithful to my father, Hana. I can't forgive her for that."

"Well, you're going to have to," Hana echoed his very words. He'd told her just a short time ago that she'd have to forgive her mother for the secrets she'd kept, for leaving her father. Now she knew why. She'd blamed Priscilla all this time and it really hadn't been her fault. What wife wouldn't leave after finding out that her husband had been unfaithful?

Hana closed her eyes and let the knowledge she'd craved for so long settle into the pit of her soul and fill it up. Knowledge was a powerful thing. It replaced ignorance. The truth, no matter how hurtful, had set her free. When she opened her eyes again, Jayce was watching her, his jaw clenched tightly as though she'd just chosen sides, leaving him alone with the burden once again.

"She made a mistake one way or the other, but you can't make yourself pay for her mistakes," Hana struggled to find the right words. "You're not a mistake either, Jayce, and you can't deny yourself happiness forever."

"I'm not denying myself anything," he snapped.

Hana blushed, knowing that she'd been presumptuous. Maybe Jayce didn't have any feelings for her, but when she was with him it felt as though all of nature's chaos was calmed and properly ordered. If Jayce Harlow was willing to give her a chance, she'd prove to him that she was worth it.

"Jayce, what Ab and your mother did was wrong, but it doesn't mean that we, that you and I, have to pay for their sin."

"Well, maybe not, but two wrongs won't make a right."

"Yes, but maybe we're not two wrongs. Just maybe we're the only way to make it right, you and me."

"And just maybe we're two pieces of history just waiting to repeat itself. Maybe we're genetically inclined to be attracted to each other, and I can't deny the fact that I am attracted to you, but

I'm stronger than that. I won't let a bit of passion ruin the rest of our lives."

"So that's what you meant about earning people's respect. You think that the people here are constantly judging you, that you have to gain the respect our parents lost and that when you're with me it reminds them of Doris and Ab? Whatever happened to believing in God and forgiveness? Or are you all just a bunch of hypocrites sitting in your stuffy church pews every Sunday with nothing more Christian to do than judge each other?"

"Hey! Don't go bringing God into this. The good Lord has nothing to do with our sins. We all have our own free will."

"Yes, but what do you think Doris' will is in all this, and Ab's and God's for that matter? Do you think any of them would want you to live your life like this?"

Jayce turned away, but she persisted.

"And God forgives, doesn't He?"

"Yeah, if you're truly sorry," he grunted.

"Well, I'm sure that if Ab and Doris could do it over, they'd do things differently. Jayce," her voice softened as she scrambled for a way to connect with a man who had stilled his heart against the possibilities of redemption, "I'll admit when I came here I knew nothing about farming, but I'm learning. I knew nothing about faith but I'm learning about that, too. And you were right. He is all around us. I can feel His presence and Abner's, too, but you've been living here your whole life, surrounded by faith and truth and you can't seem to get beyond that one moment in time. Where is your faith, Jayce?"

They drove in silence back to the broken fence line where she'd left her car. Jayce had refused to speak any further and Hana couldn't find the strength to utter another word.

She drove off into the late afternoon feeling that she'd lived out a lifetime in that very moment. The lock of black hair bound with the yellow ribbon, the pine cone in Ab's nightstand, the monogrammed handkerchief, it all made sense now. Jayce's repulsion toward her made sense, too, and her head throbbed with the knowledge that there was nothing she could do to change his mind. He was deeply scarred by the people he'd trusted to be honorable. He was punishing himself for things he couldn't control. It was why he was such a control freak in every other aspect of his life.

She was being punished, too, for her father's sins, and wasn't that a strange turn of events when she'd believed all this time that her mother had been selfish in leaving him? She couldn't blame her now, at least not entirely.

Her father had committed adultery with Jayce's mother. The words echoed bitterly in her mind. If this was the valley of darkness, then where was the Lord? Where was He now? Was she not a lost sheep crying out for him in the wilderness?

Visions of the farmers in the coffee shop projected onto the windshield as she drove slowly into Abner's yard. How had Ab lived with the shame? He'd been left alone to carry it, long after Priscilla had left and Doris had passed on.

Hana choked back a sob and thought of Jayce, the man who'd picked up the torch of shame and diligently committed himself to carry it for the rest of his life.

She wouldn't join him in his futile quest.

ChApTeR 16

Hana dressed for midnight mass, wanting to experience all the blessings of the world that had once been her father's. Harry and Elizabeth had stopped to visit now and then, and even Rosey had become a close friend. From them she'd learned a few things about Abner, her mother, and Jayce's family, and all seemed just as relieved as she was that she'd finally learned the truth.

The discovery that Abner was a respected citizen in the community by most had helped to compensate the blow she'd received on that dreadful day, but it hadn't settled her nerves completely. There were still the whispers in the local coffee shop from the elders that had at one time worked right alongside her father. It was their cold stares that reminded her again of her father's follies, and she wondered what it was that drove a man to behave so dishonorably.

Yet, it was obvious in his relationship with Jayce that Ab had tried to do right by his past. Elizabeth had told her all about how Ab helped Jayce after his father passed away. Jayce was young, barely eighteen, with the responsibility of a farm, a large debt load and a sixteen year-old sister to take care of. It was Ab who'd taught him how to manage a farm. He'd taught him to appreciate the life of a farmer, too, and when Jayce was able to, he'd returned the favor and taken care of Ab, finding in Ab all those things his own father couldn't give him.

Yes, strangely enough, some good had come of it all. But still, there were moments when she was certain Ab must have regretted. Perhaps it was why he'd never signed the divorce papers. He'd hoped that someday he and Cilla would reconcile, or at the very least that he'd be granted her forgiveness.

Still she wondered how he was able to live with what he'd done. To that question she could think of only one answer. Ab had forgiven himself and had felt forgiven by God and the people he loved. But Jayce, on the other hand, harbored a resentment beyond her capabilities to mend. For him, she felt tremendous sympathy.

She saw him, sitting only a few pews ahead, and willed her brain to focus on the mass instead of his tall lean figure. He looked even leaner now, and his hair wasn't quite as wavy and vibrant as it had been in summer. Yet, he was still Jayce, handsome, self-assured and off limits.

With difficulty, Hana attempted to focus on the sermon. In brief moments of time she allowed it to lift her, to buoy her up in a place that had made her feel like she'd been sinking. Truthfully, she'd been up to her neck in it all, since she'd come. She wondered if that was, perhaps, why people came to church. The Gospel refueled them for another week in the unyielding world, giving them the armor they needed to fend off all evils. The thought seemed rather funny.

Most of the people in Lone Prairie looked like they had enough armor of their own to fend off an army, Jayce Harlow included. What did *they* need from God? Well, everyone needed something, or God wouldn't have given his only Son. He would not have sent him into the cold and needy world where one day He would suffer and die. Yes, everyone needed saving in one form or another.

The church bells chimed on cue as if confirming her thoughts. The mass had ended and they exited the church where snow was falling softly, transforming Lone Prairie with a tangible hope, despite the hardships. It all could have been so perfect, but there was no one to share it with, and even if everyone needed saving, Jayce Harlow still thought that he didn't, at least not from the likes of her.

"Merry Christmas, Jayce," she whispered into the snowflakes. Silently, they fell to the ground, carrying her secret with them. They sparkled like silver sequins in a long white flowing train of thought that always seemed to lead to the same ending. She had to leave.

When Hana returned home that night, she found a package on the front step from Jayce. She'd missed him by mere minutes, but was grateful for it. She really wasn't in the mood for a fight.

With shaking hands, she opened the tiny box wrapped carefully in golden paper. Inside it was a beautiful ornament made of wheat. Beneath it was a card. She read it to Shamrock and Sugar who'd come to join her on the porch:

I picked some wheat from your crop before we harvested...thought you might like a keepsake of the seed that Abner sowed and that you harvested. Jessica did the wheat weaving...wanted to apologize too. She's having Christmas dinner tomorrow. You're welcome to join us.

Jayce

Hana went inside and hung the ornament on her tree. It was beautiful, woven into the shape of a tear drop with a red velvet Santa glued inside. She smiled, despite the ache in the pit of her stomach. *Santa* had been about the only thing her mother had allowed her to believe in and even then when Priscilla had felt she'd believed longer than she should, she'd told her the truth. There really wasn't a Santa. He was just a character built around the memory of a generous man named Nicholas.

She'd been crushed and had felt betrayed. Even now the sight of a Santa had always stabbed her, but not today. As the white twinkling lights on her tree illuminated Abners's wheat twisted intricately around the smiling Santa, suddenly it all made sense.

Of course she'd felt empty to discover that there wasn't really a Santa. She'd had nothing to replace him with, but for children who believed in God, for children who'd been fortunate enough to be instilled with a sense of faith, for them there was still hope. For them there still existed a magical presence, someone who watched over, someone who guided and loved despite faults and follies, someone who forgave and could do the impossible.

Hana read the invitation again, her cheer deflating as quickly as it came. She wanted to go more than anything, to believe in the power of forgiveness, but—there was always a *but*. Like the woven wheat, it was an intricate situation where the delicate strands of nature had wrapped themselves around the transcendent world. Time had taken Doris and Abner and Priscilla. No one could go back and change things, or try to make sense out if it nearly thirty years later. It never would make sense, but somewhere, within the two worlds touching, was the answer so obvious it nearly screamed. Jayce Harlow couldn't be at peace with the past or with her until he was at peace with himself.

Jayce sat before the fire losing his focus within the hot orange mirage of flames. Every now and again a spark darted outward and fizzled onto the concrete tile, escaping the protection of the screen. He watched as the bright glow of the spark faded to blackness, knowing that even though it appeared to be nothing but a tiny cluster of ashes now, it would still burn to the touch. It was him in a nutshell. Even though on the outside he seemed to be fine, he still hurt so much inside. It shouldn't have been wrong for him to want to be with Hana. It was a perfectly natural attraction between a man and a woman, but he knew it couldn't work. Like the deceitful ashes, one or both of them would eventually get burned.

"Jayce, can I get you something? A hot buttered rum? Apple cider?" Jessica pressed.

"No, thanks. I should probably just be heading home." He

glanced at the large oak school house clock that hung above the fireplace. Simultaneously, it chimed ten times, announcing that it was at least four hours passed even hoping that Hana would come.

"It's my fault, Jayce." Jessica plunked herself down beside her brother, her shoulders sagging in unison with her frown.

"What's your fault?"

"It's my fault she didn't come. I was too hard on her. Maybe we've both got this thing all wrong, Jayce. Just maybe she's the missing piece of our past, you know? The piece that makes everything whole and right again."

"And just maybe she's not. Maybe she's a piece from another puzzle," Jayce nearly sneered. "I never was any good at puzzles anyway."

"Well, who are we to judge anyway, Jayce? Hasn't there been enough judging, enough accusations? I always say when things get messy you have to start somewhere, but sometimes you have to know when to stop, too. Do you know what I'm saying? Sometimes you have to know when to say enough is enough."

He knew what she was saying. He knew exactly what she was saying, but he just couldn't get there—to that place in his heart or his mind. He was still miles away and he wished he knew why.

Hana's light was still on when he drove by, and her Christmas tree lights shimmered through Ab's picture window. His own house looked stark and drab.

Grabbing the package that Jessica and Jake had given him, he sulked to the house, every step echoing in the quiet night. Once inside, he placed the package carefully on the bench in the foyer, taking care not to sit on it as he sat down to tug off his boots. It was a fancy black western shirt with silver trim, the kind of shirt he might wear on a date if he'd ever had one. The prospect seemed foreign.

Jayce flung his boots onto the shelf, hung up his parka and went to the kitchen to grab a cold cola from the refrigerator. On his way to the living room he paused by the answering machine, daring to hope that the flashing red indicator might mean that she had called.

There were three messages, all from Sally Redding and he erased them with some annoyance.

Sally Redding had been chasing him since tenth grade. She was bold and forward and giddier than any girl he'd ever met. Definitely not his type.

The first message had wished him a Merry Christmas. The second was just an affirmation call to see if he'd received the first message, and the third message was an invitation to Harry and Elizabeth's New Year's Eve party. Now had there been even one call from Hana Islander, he would have believed in the magic of Christmas. Turning back to the phone, he checked the call display. Maybe she had called but failed to leave a message. Nothing.

She was angry and had every right to be. He'd treated her terribly from the day in fall when they'd finished the harvest to the day she'd come hell-bent on getting some answers about her past, their past, the pasts that had been intertwined and tangled up so badly that he'd been nearly strangled by it all.

It had perplexed him that he could be so attracted to her, as if something within his genetic make-up had the dangerous tendency to defy any sense of good reason. Oh well, it didn't matter now. He'd finally succeeded in pushing her away.

Jayce threw crumpled newspaper into the fire and built a teepee of wood above it, lighting it with a barbecue lighter. Within minutes the flames burned brightly and he stretched out onto the colorful Aztec rug, only inches away from the flames

Again, like a thousand times before, the image of her came to him and he imagined her there with him, just enjoying the fire and each other's company with no drama for a change. Could they ever really have that? No drama? Just an ordinary relationship?

The fire spit out dangerous sparks as if to answer his question. Jayce took a bitter slug of cola and closed his eyes tightly, willing his thoughts to burn up and disintegrate. His father had often times found consolation in a bottle. Jayce wouldn't. He'd promised himself that a long time ago. It was the one thing about the past that he could set right. As for Hana, well he'd overcome that too and even though he couldn't right the past, he could certainly spin it off in a new direction even if it meant being alone for the rest of his life.

ChApTeR 17

Harry and Elizabeth's home was decorated impressively with sparkling streamers, homemade Happy New Year banners, and a huge table with every treat and drink imaginable. Hana poured herself a glass of punch and stole away into the corner of the living room when Elizabeth gave her a moment's peace. She felt out of place and avoided the glares of some who wondered what kind of nerve she must have to show up at a traditional community event, as though she didn't have a life outside of the office and didn't deserve one either. Well, even if she didn't deserve one, she decided that she needed one, or something at least to take her mind off Jayce.

The invitation had come the day after Christmas when she was feeling so blue she couldn't even imagine how she'd get through the next week. Things were slow at the bank and there was very little she could think of to keep her mind occupied. Instead, she found herself thinking about Jayce and the secrets of their past. Even a phone call from Joanne couldn't cheer her, especially when she announced that she and Reggie Dawson were engaged to be married.

They'd only known each other for a short time. The prospect of them getting married seemed ridiculous and totally *Joanne*, yet she'd congratulated her cheerily, trying hard to keep her opinions to herself. The old Hana would have thought it was marvelous. Reginald Dawson the Third was a very prominent citizen. He wouldn't have to work a day in his life because of his father and grandfather's accomplishments.

"Miss Islander?"

Hana heard her name and quickly snapped back to reality, relieved to see a pleasant face staring down at her.

"I'm Raelene, Harry and Elizabeth's daughter."

"Oh, it's a pleasure to meet you." Hana rose from the sofa to shake the hand of the pretty girl who stood before her, looking every bit like Elizabeth as was genetically possible.

"I wanted to thank you for all the trouble you went through in getting me a student loan. Mom and Dad just can't say enough about you. You really helped to take the pressure off things for us."

"That's my job," Hana smiled back, not wanting to take too much credit for something that Harry and Elizabeth were so deserving of. Instead, she encouraged Raelene to sit beside her and proceeded to ask her questions about the accounting and business classes she was taking in the city. Raelene was only too happy to discuss her blossoming life and Hana couldn't help but feel a bit envious, especially when a young man from across the room spotted Raelene, his face lighting up as though he'd just seen an angel.

Hana excused herself politely and slipped to the beverage table, keeping a safe distance away from the man in the black shirt, her angel with black tipped wings. It was what her mother used to call her when she was a child and had gotten into trouble. It was funny how things like that came to you when you had a place to put them. The expression fit Jayce Harlow perfectly, better than sugar coated poison.

He looked extremely handsome as usual, like he intended to impress someone, and Hana wondered if he'd brought a date. Then she saw Sally Redding grab hold of his arm and she knew he most certainly had an admirer if not a date, and while she didn't perceive Sally Redding as being a threat to any woman, she still felt a pinch of jealousy.

Deciding at that point to escape to the washroom, Hana sought relief with a splash of cold water. Her cheeks were flushed, her vision slightly blurred. *Brother, she really had it bad*, she shook her head in disgust, and what was even worse was the fact that even though she didn't know anything about Sally Redding, she was quick to believe all the tidbits of gossip she'd heard about her in the coffee shop. It was as if Lone Prairie had sucked her into its pathetic, narrow-minded thinking almost completely.

After another splash of cold water and lipstick carefully reapplied, Hana deemed herself fit for round two, but when the crowd began to count down in unison the seconds to the New Year, the room began to spin. Her stomach felt queasy too, and she bee-lined to the porch, rummaging through the pile of coats. When she failed to find her own, she aborted the mission and struggled into her boots, her cause becoming desperate as her stomach began to churn.

The cool air immediately cleared her head as she stepped out onto the cement landing. Carelessly, she dumped the contents of her glass into the snow, the blotch of red looking intrusive and disgusting, like a blotch of blood scattered across the pristine snow. "Humph," she groaned. "Just like me, an unsightly stain marring their perfect world."

Hana leaned against the porch rail and inhaled the bitter air. If she didn't get inside soon she'd probably freeze. Well, no one would miss her, she was certain of that, but why give them the satisfaction?

Taking a step toward the door, she paused and then quickly scrambled to grab hold of the rail, her legs wobbly and nearly giving out beneath her. It was a familiar feeling. She knew this feeling well, but what? Suddenly it struck her. She was having an allergic reaction to the punch! That was it, and her fuzzy brain attempted to process the amount of drinks she'd had. Elizabeth had reassured her that it contained no alcohol but Hana hadn't even bothered to ask if it contained pineapple.

She'd been severely allergic to it since she was a child, although then her body's reaction to it had been almost immediate. Now, it had taken several drinks before she began to feel the effects, but the reaction was just the same—dizziness, nausea, even her tongue felt heavy and numb.

Turning around slowly, Hana carefully balanced her way to her car, having trouble remembering with accuracy exactly where she'd parked it. She knew that she shouldn't drive but she really couldn't think of an option. It would be much too embarrassing to go back inside. Everybody would think that she was drunk and that was the very last thing she needed right now.

Hana searched frantically for her car, moving quickly despite the patches of ice that connected like tiny islands across the yard. She was half-way across the yard before she severely misjudged what appeared to be a thin layer of snow.

He reached out a hand, looking concerned and a bit angry. She hadn't even heard him approach.

"Need a hand?"

"No! I'm fine," she snapped. "Just wasn't watching where I was going is all." Hana struggled to her feet but couldn't seem to manage to get her legs to cooperate. Jayce reached for her again, steadying her with both arms, but she shrugged him off, losing her balance completely in the effort and falling hard against his chest.

He was warm and enticing, and the sight of him caused her thoughts to scramble, adding to the ill-effects of the punch. In a daze, she watched as his breath and her own mingled together, two visible white puffs in the chilling air, joining together despite the invisible antagonisms that separated them.

He held her tight until her feet stopped kicking and then carefully pulled her back onto the snow, laughing harder than she'd ever heard him laugh. It annoyed her.

"Oh and I suppose you think you're my knight in shining armor now. I'll have you know that I can do just fine on my own!" Struggling free from his embrace, she stomped to her car.

He ran after her and grabbed her elbow, spinning her around to face him. "Oh no missy. You're not driving home on your own! How much did you drink tonight anyway? I've been watching you and I think you've had more than enough."

"You've been watching me? Well, that makes you no different from the rest of them. You're all just waiting for me to screw up. You have no right."

"Well, maybe they don't, but I do. It's my job don't you remember? If you don't get home in one piece, who will do your chores in the morning?"

"Oh, yes, the animals," Hana sneered. "Far be it from me to assume that you might for once be worried about me." She had more to say, had formulated the words carefully in her mind, but they wouldn't come. Jayce stared down at her, his face turning fuzzy. He reached for her and she pushed him away, the blood leaving her fingertips and seeming to free-fall to her feet. Suddenly, the world went black.

ChApTeR 18

She fell heavily into his arms but he was prepared. He watched as her eyes flickered and then closed slowly, her mouth still prattling on and refusing to give into the signals of her brain. It would have amused him if he hadn't been so worried about her and a bit angry with her, too.

"Jayce?" Elizabeth came running toward him, bundled up in Harry's old parka. "Have you seen Hana? I've been looking for...," Elizabeth's words turned to silent horror. "What happened? I just knew something was wrong when she disappeared. We'd better get her inside."

"No!" Jayce was firm, catching Elizabeth off guard. "That would be like feeding her to the wolves. I don't want anyone to see her like this."

"You don't suppose she's had too much to drink do you?" Elizabeth reached out to touch her forehead. "Jayce, she's breaking out into a sweat and it's forty below zero out here."

Jayce felt her forehead and frowned.

"I only saw her drink punch. There's no alcohol in it, Jayce." Elizabeth paused, thinking hard. "Oh my heavens! It was the pineapple. I remember that she refused to eat my carrot-pineapple muffins one time. She said she had a severe allergy. Jayce, she's having an allergic reaction to the punch."

"Did she say anything about an antidote, Elizabeth?"

"Nothing, Jayce. I haven't a clue what to do."

"Well, the only thing to do is take her straight into the health center in Lone Prairie. Phone Dr. Johnstone and tell him I'm on my way."

"Right away, Jayce," Elizabeth turned to leave. "And please call me as soon as you know something."

"I will."

Jayce drove his pick-up as fast as he could for road conditions, slowing every now and again to ensure that Hana was still breathing. She had allowed him to believe that she was drunk and he wondered why. Then again, he hadn't exactly earned her trust. She probably thought it was none of his business, despite the fact that her health was in jeopardy.

It was becoming increasingly more difficult for him to hide his feelings, and a few times that evening he'd caught himself defending her, once when Mrs. Bailey said she was a *hoity-toity* and had no business in Lone Prairie, and once when one of Abner's old friends said that she was an exploiter. He'd also kept a close eye on Max Whitefield who eyed her up like a porcelain prize with no further intentions than a one night stand.

In fact, when Hana escaped outside, Max had followed in hot pursuit until Jayce cleverly detoured him at the door, offering to pour him another drink. It was the only thing he could think of to sidetrack the creep, and when the opportunity arose he'd left Max standing beside Sally Redding, finding that in one quick maneuver he had the opportunity to get rid of two problems. He'd peered back at them once before he left, finding humor in the fact that perhaps he'd actually done them a good turn. They were perfect for each other.

It was unfortunate, though, that the minute he was in Hana's presence all cupid abilities seemed to freeze in mid air. Now, peering at her in the passenger's seat of his pick-up, he couldn't find an ounce of humor or romance. She looked so vulnerable and pale.

Jayce reached out to stroke her cheek tenderly, knowing in that instant that he couldn't possibly live without her. Somehow, he had to make things right.

Less than an hour later, Jayce tucked Hana gently into bed, relieved that Dr. Johnstone was able to provide a quick and effective medication to counter the reaction of the punch. Hana had argued all the way home that she could take care of herself, but Jayce had barged his way through the door, refusing to leave until she was safely tucked into bed.

She hadn't argued much passed that point, and within minutes had fallen asleep. Jayce made himself a strong cup of instant coffee, hoping it might settle his nerves. Then he stretched out onto the sofa, listening intently to the sound of her breathing.

A strange feeling washed over him as he stared blankly at Abner's ceiling. Hadn't he done this very thing before? Yes, when Ab had been near his death, he'd fallen asleep many nights listening to the sound of his breathing, until one night he awoke to silence. It was a moment he would never forget.

Becoming uncomfortable with his thoughts, Jayce poured himself another cup of coffee. When he returned to the living room, Abner's old worn out Bible caught his attention.

Abner was a faithful man and through him Jayce had learned to rekindle his own faith, but there had always been something missing in his life, the very same something that now occupied Abner's home and Jayce's heart. But Hana Islander, farmer's daughter or not, just didn't fit the bill of farmer's wife. She would never last in Lone Prairie. Priscilla hadn't either, and she'd raised Hana to be biased to the world she ran away from.

Jayce recalled his own mother, and despite her faults managed a smile. *We don't always like the people we love*, she'd say, whenever he was angry with his father or his sister. Yet, he knew that those words had meant so much more.

Jayce paged through the thin and yellowed pages of the Bible, reading all the passages that he knew were Abner's favorite, but there was one, highlighted in yellow marker that he was sure Abner had not outlined, and he read it with great interest. It was a passage from the book of Ruth. *Wherever you go, I will go; wherever you live, I will live. Your people will be my people, and your God will be my God.* It was a loaded passage.

It had taken Hana Islander a lot of courage to come to Lone Prairie and to leave all the comforts and things she was accustomed to. She was honoring her father's will in the hope of finding him somewhere within the walls of his life, his mistakes, his dreams, his faith.

Jayce recalled the time she'd asked him if God really listened to his prayers. He'd said all the right things, but his actions, his example had been sadly lacking. Jayce scoffed. Who was he kidding? He'd been a terrible example of the faith so far and she'd been right about forgiveness. If God had forgiven Abner and Doris, then shouldn't he? Frustrated with his inability to let go of the past completely, Jayce checked on Hana one more time before leaving for home to do his chores.

The sun was coming up when he returned an hour later, and he parked in the shop safely away from prying eyes. The last thing either of them needed was to have anyone presume they'd spent the night together.

By the time Jayce finished Hana's chores, his head had cleared considerably. Ab's animals were all well fed and eyed him up as a stranger when at one time he had been their master. Even the reserved and magnificent King whinnied good morning and came to the fence to be petted, until he realized that the greeter was not whom he'd expected. Obstinately, he reared up on his hind legs and spun around, kicking up dirt as he ran to the other end of the pasture. It was clear that Ab's animals had learned to love Hana, too.

"Who wouldn't?" Jayce mumbled, and in one clairvoyant

moment found the courage he'd needed for quite some time.

Reverently, he thanked the God who had not deserted him, even when his faith had grown old and stale. With a happiness he hadn't felt in a very long time, Jayce carefully rehearsed what he'd wanted to say to Hana Islander since the moment she stepped foot onto Abner's front porch.

The rooster crowed and stabbed her brain in unison with the first rays of sunlight that penetrated her thin bedroom curtains. She sat up quickly, too quickly and immediately fell back down on the pillow, yanking the covers up tightly around her head.

"Are you awake? I thought I heard a groan."

When she heard his voice it came back to her, most of it anyway, but the sudden knowledge only made her want to bury herself even further beneath the covers. She should have asked about the punch. She wasn't a child anymore, although she'd clearly acted like one. She'd been careless and had fallen into Jayce's arms again, literally if she remembered correctly. Now, the consequence of her blatant negligence was to feel something synonymous to a severe hang-over, but the worst of it was the memory lapse. She could only imagine some of the stupid things she'd said or done.

"Oh, come on now. You can't be feeling that bad," Jayce laughed softly.

She heard his footsteps approach the bed and could smell the faint remnants of his cologne.

"Hana, you didn't do anything to embarrass yourself at the party." Jayce seemed to read her mind as always.

"Oh, thank God," she mumbled, her throat dry and parched.

"Yeah, you can say that again. It was nothing short of a blessing that Elizabeth remembered you were allergic to pineapple. You really should be more careful you know," Jayce scolded.

"I know," Hana squirmed, wishing that she hadn't been so irresponsible. "I'm sorry I caused so much trouble."

"Well, if we're really being honest, you've been nothing but trouble since you got here," Jayce couldn't resist a smile.

Hana nodded her head in agreement. "I know, Jayce, and I just wanted to tell you that you won't have to put up with me any longer because I'm..."

Jayce placed a finger softly on her lips.

"Hush. For once let's just quit trying to make sense out of the mess we're in."

Jayce's annoyance was different this time and he leaned into her, snatching away the pillow that she'd been using as a barrier between them. With his lips close to hers, Hana held her breath. She'd waited for this moment, wanted it so badly that she'd hardly been able to think about anything else. It was their last chance to make things right.

It was then that the phone rang.

"I've got to get it," he said as he left her sitting on the bed.

"Why?" She followed him to the kitchen. She really wasn't in the mood to talk to anyone and besides, she and Jayce had finally reached a breaking point. She couldn't imagine what it would take to get to that place again.

"I don't know. I just have this feeling."

She watched him pick up the phone and then observed his face turn from red heat to white wash in a matter of seconds. It was obvious that something was terribly wrong and after he hung up the phone he searched frantically for his coat.

"What's wrong, Jayce?"

"It's Jessica. She might lose the baby. Chores are done, Hana. I've got to go."

Baby? What baby? No one had told her Jessica was expecting and what went wrong?

Hana watched as Jayce backed his truck out of the shop. The shop? Had he been trying to hide his vehicle? He was embarrassed. He hadn't wanted anyone to see that he was there or to assume that he'd spent the night, and while a part of her argued that maybe he'd just been trying to protect her honor, belief in the worst took precedence. Tears trailed a jagged pattern down her cheek and her head began to throb.

The next few days were torture but there was a peace that had settled over her quite unexpectedly. It was the knowledge in knowing, that for better or worse, it was finally over.

After making a phone call to the hospital, Hana had been relieved to hear that Jessica and the baby were both fine, even though Jessica had been sentenced to bed rest for the next five months. Her hair cutting business would have to be put on hold and so would the payments, but Hana didn't care. That was the least of her worries and she scolded Jessica, telling her that the loan was the very last thing she should be worrying about. Jessica, however, insisted that Jake would be in to see her, and Hana had worked overtime, finalizing all the paper work.

She'd intervened and paid the loan off completely from her own personal savings, knowing full well that Jake would protest, but she really wasn't doing him a favor. The truth was that if she'd never come to Loan Prairie, Jayce would have inherited Abner's farm. He'd have sold it and paid his debts and Jessica's besides. It was how it should have been all along.

"Wait! You don't have an appointment, Jayce. She's scheduled to see Jake at one o'clock," Rosey's voice, stressed and urgent wafted through Hana's open door.

"Rosey, I made that appointment. I gave Jake's name because she's been refusing to take my phone calls."

"It's all right, Rosey. Let him in." Hana peered out from behind her desk and spoke calmly, despite her clamoring heart beat.

Jayce stormed in and slammed the door, his breathing ragged, his eyes tumultuous. "Why haven't you been taking my calls?" he demanded.

"I've been busy," Hana sat back down at her desk calmly and fumbled for the red button hidden beneath it. It was rash and incredibly distasteful but she didn't have a choice. She pressed it.

"Busy? You've been stewin' is more like it, about what,

though, I wouldn't have a clue. Care to share with me what's been naggin' you or do you expect me to guess?"

"Why are you here, Jayce?"

"You and I have unfinished business. I've been wanting to settle this for quite some time—just couldn't find a way to do it. I started it the other morning, but then the phone rang and I, well," he paused and drew a deep breath. "What I wanted to say was..."

"I forfeit!" Hana interrupted him desperately. She assumed that he was calling off the terms of the will and she couldn't allow it. It would spoil everything.

"What do you mean you forfeit?"

"I mean I quit. I'm through with Lone Prairie. I'm leaving."

"Well, now, that's just down right crazy. You won fair and square and you know it. You can't forfeit. You've almost made it to the end of the term," Jayce's voice was nearly pleading. "Okay, I'll even admit it. You're Abner Crawford's daughter. *I'm* calling off this crazy deal."

"It's too late. I've already contacted Ab's lawyer about my intentions. He's faxed the release papers and I've signed them and faxed them back. Abner's inheritance belongs to you as of ten o'clock this morning. I can't do it, Jayce. I really can't stay here a day longer," she lied, gaining strength from the change in his posture and the look in his eyes that shot unspoken accusations and affirmations.

Jayce straightened. A shadow crossed his face.

"Well, who couldn't see that coming?" He accused smugly. "You just go on and leave then, but you'd better be back by spring 'cause I'm not touching Ab's land, and if you don't seed it, you'll get a weed problem and this time I won't be here to help you."

"Oh, yeah? And just where are you going to be? Once a farmer always a farmer," she accused, pulling him into her tangled altercation and making a *farmer* sound like the worst possible thing a man could be. It killed her inside. She didn't really believe that. Being a farmer was the noblest thing Jayce could be and she loved him for it.

"Why are you doing this?" Jayce seemed to slip back into the rational state of mind that reminded him she couldn't be for real.

"It's what I should have done all along. I'm not a farmer. You can have Ab's land and all those useless animals," she added for good measure. "I'll be gone by the end of the day, but before I leave I want you to know that I've paid off Jessica's loan in full. If you and Jake feel strongly about it, you can pay me back when you sell Ab's place, interest free, of course."

Jayce stood completely still, his eyes cloudy and disbelieving as though she were a plague he'd avoided to contract by sheer luck. It was then that the sheriff arrived, responding to the silent alarm she'd pressed earlier.

"Miss Islander? Is there a problem?" The sheriff poked his head into the office as though *he* were the intruder. It was obvious that he was assuming the alarm had been pushed by accident, especially since the only customer in the bank at the time was Jayce Harlow, a well-known and respected citizen.

"Yes! This man is refusing to leave."

Jayce rose from his chair and stared at her in disbelief, hurt and betrayal tightening every muscle in his body.

"Look Charlie, I haven't been causing any trouble. Hana and I just had a few issues to sort out and things maybe got a little carried away. I'm sure when she comes to her senses she'll realize that she's wrong," Jayce turned back to her still fuming, but she was already gone.

ChApTeR 19

Hana sat at her desk and stared out onto the street watching the endless line of traffic and the constant flow of people walking purposefully passed her window. Where were they all going and what was the rush? It seemed odd to think that only a few months earlier she had been a full contributor to the rat race.

Things were different now and she couldn't help but feel grateful for the experiences she'd had in Lone Prairie. At times it seemed that a broken heart was a fair trade off for the rifts in her life that had been mended. She had come to know God, her father, and her mother and through it all had gained a greater understanding of herself. She was truly blessed, but still there was always the tiny hope. Didn't everyone, even people who knew they were blessed, have a tiny hope of something still to be accomplished?

Unable to resist the urge, she pulled open the top draw of her desk. It creaked open reluctantly and she realized with some amusement that she'd probably worn out the hinges. Inside, she peered at the blue hanky with the white polka dots, the one Jayce had given to her the day he'd taught her how to milk Betsy.

She was definitely Ab's daughter. Why else would she be acting like a sentimental fool? And just maybe being a Crawford wasn't so plain and common after all. Becoming a Crawford had expanded her view of the world and shown her that she'd been the narrow-minded one.

"Hana, your two o'clock is here," her secretary announced over the intercom, sending her thoughts reeling back to Saskatoon, where she sat in her tiny office feeling small and insignificant. She slammed the drawer and her memories shut.

"Don't bother getting up. Oh, and don't sound the alarm. I won't be staying."

Hana looked up from her desk to see—Jayce Harlow? Doubting herself, she reached for her glasses and slipped them on clumsily, the results being just the same. It was definitely Jayce Harlow in full focus. She fidgeted uncomfortably in her leather chair.

"Brought you a little something. Kinda' assumed you hadn't eaten yet."

She hadn't. He knew. He always seemed to know.

"It's your favorite, ham and cheese on rye, and some iced tea."

"Thanks," she choked, as he placed the wrapped sandwiches and drink in front of her, clearing a place on her over-crowded desk."

"Well, it's not as good as a picnic in the field, but it doesn't look like there's much room for that here anyway," Jayce took a moment to survey her office disapprovingly.

Hana remained quiet, still in a state of shock. She couldn't imagine why he'd come and for a moment she feared that something had happened to Harry, Elizabeth, or maybe Jessica. She prayed it wasn't so.

"I came here to tell you I'm selling the animals," he glared at her sternly and waited patiently for her reaction.

"My animals? I mean Ab's animals? You're selling Abner's animals?" Hana could barely manage to hide her disbelief.

"I can't take care of two sets of chores, Hana. It's almost seeding time and by the looks of it, it'll be an early spring. The snow's disappearing fast, what little of it we had. Some farmers are talking about cultivating next week. You've been gone for a while in case you haven't noticed."

Oh, she'd noticed alright. She'd been gone exactly two months, twenty-four days, eleven hours, and…

"Hana! Hello! Have you heard anything I've said?"

"Yes!" She shot back, annoyed. "I just don't understand why you can't take the animals to your place. They're yours after all. That way you wouldn't have to drive over to Ab's every morning and night."

"It's not that simple, Hana. First of all, I've got all the chickens I can handle. I'd have to build another coop to house Ab's. Secondly, I don't have time to be milking Betsy. I wish I did, but I don't. Shep's been moping around. He hasn't eaten much since you left and the cat…well she's just been down right ornery."

"What about King?"

"He hasn't been ridden since Abner died. If someone doesn't start working with him soon he'll be a real handful. Horses need to be reminded of the things they've learned or at the very least feel wanted."

The thought nearly made her sick. She had been negligent. She really hadn't given King much attention. He'd been too regal, too foreboding for her inept knowledge of horses, but she could have groomed him once in a while, or talked to him at the very least.

"Well anyway, I'm taking them all to market next week," Jayce continued to carry on a one-sided conversation. "I just thought you ought to know."

She wanted to say something, had formulated a few words in her mind and then lost them again, had even heard the cue from her brain to close her gaping mouth, but could physically respond to nothing but the mental conversation going on inside her head, making her feel guilty yet again.

"Well, I'll be seein' you around," he said, before turning and heading toward the door.

"Oh, but I meant to ask you," Jayce paused at the door and turned around to face her one last time, his expression unreadable. "What are you doing here?"

"What do you mean?" His question felt like a punch in the gut.

"I mean here, at this bank. What are you doing here?"

Well, certainly nothing as noble as creating a grasshopper barrier so as not to expose children to poisonous grasshopper spray.

"Well, I don't know," she responded dumbly.

"Thought so," he nodded, tipped his hat and walked out the door.

Jayce left the city immediately, having no further business there than his brief exchange with Hana. There was no denying that he'd touched a nerve, but still there was that tiny flinch of doubt. Perhaps she wasn't the woman he thought she was, or wanted her to be so badly that he hadn't slept properly since she'd left.

The past few months had taken their toll on him both mentally and physically, but time, aged and tempered was the only way to deal with Hana. If he'd have run after her immediately after she left as he wanted to, she'd have still been too stubborn to see things his way. Besides, if his plan worked, she'd be the one doing the running—straight back to Lone Prairie with a vengeance, and this time it would work in his favor.

Cranking up the radio, Jayce decided to just sit back and enjoy the last few sips of coffee and the final double chocolate dipped donut he'd picked up at Tim Horton's before leaving the city. Besides, it wouldn't be the end of the world if she didn't come back, he tried to convince himself. And since when did he let the actions of others dictate the outcome of his own life? The answer struck him as hard as a fist. *For as long as he could remember.*

Well, didn't everybody? It was the sad and glorious truth. As hard as he'd tried to be different from Abner and Doris, he wasn't. He was just the same—pining away for someone he couldn't have. But did that make him weak? Did that mean he'd failed?

Maybe he had things all wrong. Just maybe it meant that he, like everyone else, was human.

ChApTeR 20

The ramblings of the auctioneer unnerved her as she stepped into the market. The legalities of wrapping up thirty years had taken longer than she'd expected, and congested Friday afternoon traffic hadn't helped either. She was late.

She'd left the city as soon as possible after finalizing a few last minutes details of her elaborate plan. She'd dreamt about it, transformed it until it was absolutely perfect in her mind, and she couldn't wait to see the look on his face. Of course it would take a while for all of it to sink in. She could hardly believe she'd actually done it, but when she'd contacted Ab's lawyer and found out that Jayce had refused to take possession of the land, she decided that there really was no other choice.

Ab's lawyer was a very determined man. If he had failed to get Jayce to sign the documents, then there was little hope for anyone else. He'd called her only a few days earlier, at his wits end about how to wrap up Ab's estate when both recipients of the inheritance were forfeiting their rights to it. He'd explained with quite some anxiety that if neither of them claimed it before the said and final date, Ab's estate could fall into an entirely different legal process, a loop that might wipe out the possibility of either of them receiving it. It was then that she'd been so overwhelmed with a magnificent idea that she'd signed the papers the lawyer had faxed, quit her job, and immediately began to consolidate her belongings in the city.

She'd traded her fancy car for a practical, used, truck, sold most of her extravagant furniture, and gave her notice to her landlord. This time Lone Prairie's dust swirled up to greet her and the few meager belongings she'd kept that had actually meant something to her.

She appreciated it now, all of it, the dust, the wind, the sun, even the primitive roads that told the story of hard working people making their paths in unbroken soil with nothing but sweat, determination and faith to guide them. It was all so much more than she could have understood had she not spent so much time in their midst. She hoped that they'd allow her back, with the promise that this time she'd do her part to cherish it all as much as they did, and to use her gifts to give something back. She did have something to give, a lot to give in fact.

All she needed was Jayce. Without his love and acceptance she couldn't stay, but she was here now, and if she didn't get her head out of the clouds the next animal up for bids would go to someone else.

It was Betsy. She recognized her immediately.

As the young boy chased her into the ring she could see the fear and uncertainty in Betsy's eyes, and she cursed herself and Jayce a tiny bit, too, for putting her and Betsy in such a vulnerable position.

Hana watched carefully as the bidding began. Mr. Carpentor tipped the brim of his hat, Mr. Clairsholm waved his finger and Mrs. Stonewall nodded her head. The competition was stiff and the auctioneer continued to raise the price. Hana tweaked her ear lobe, catching the auctioneer's attention. It was the only sign she could think of in her meager attempt to be discreet. Within seconds, Mr. Clairsholm and Mrs. Stonewall dropped out of the bidding war, having decided that the price was too high, but Mr. Capentor remained competitive, his hat dropping lower and lower on his forehead with every indication that he was becoming seriously involved and committed to the process.

Hana began to panic. It was then that Harry appeared, an angel in gray striped overalls, squeezing his way beside her with an amused expression on his face.

"Are you trying to bid on that animal or do you have an awfully fractious itch on your ear?"

Relieved and annoyed at the same time, Hana inched over to allow more room . "I'm bidding, Harry! What do you think?"

"All right, don't have a fit. It's just that you've gotta sit back and relax. Make it look like you don't really care if you win the war or not. You see what I'm sayin'?"

"Yes, I see what you're saying," Hana whispered through clenched teeth, "but I do care. When I get a hold of Jayce Harlow, he's going to regret this. Where is he anyway? He must be skulking around here somewhere, watching me make a fool out of myself and enjoying every minute of it," she scowled as she tweaked her ear lobe again, indicating that she was still interested in the growing price of the animal at large.

"He ain't here," Harry replied bluntly, amusement seeping out of his face. "When you didn't show up for the sale of the chickens and old Shamrock and Sugar, he figured you weren't coming and left."

Hana pulled a little harder at her earlobe as the auctioneer waited for her response and when his attention turned back to Mr. Carpentor she turned to face Harry squarely. "Are you telling me that Shamrock, Sugar and my chickens are already sold?"

"They're gone, Hana. There weren't many small animals at the sale. It took only twenty minutes to get them all sold."

"Will you give me eight-fifty?" The auctioneer's ramblings indicated that it was Hana's turn to bid once again, but as she sat frozen to her seat, Harry waved his hand for her and magically Mr. Carpentor backed off, somehow feeling more comfortable with the prospect of losing the bid to a man.

"Sold to Harry Bolter for eight hundred and fifty dollars," Hana heard the auctioneer slam his gavel on the podium before focusing on a small herd of cow-calf pairs that were quickly ushered into the ring.

"Next time, you might want to consider using a different motion to bid. Your ear's as red as fire," Harry tried to joke, but Hana's eyes began to pool, and when the first tear fell, Harry couldn't take it any longer.

"Look Hana, if the truth be known, I bought your chickens and Shamrock and Sugar. Jayce told me to keep it to myself; said that if you did finally show up you should have to squirm a bit for bein' late, but personally I don't see the point. Seems like you two are torturing each other for one reason or another, none of which makes any sense to me."

"You bought Shamrock and Sugar and all my chickens?" The lump in Hana's throat quickly dissolved as she looked into Harry's kind and gentle eyes.

"Yes. Jayce had no intentions of letting your animals get away. He gave me strict orders to buy them all with the intentions of buying them back from me after the sale, but when you didn't show, he was awfully disappointed and left; said he was heading to the bank to rid himself of one more problem," Harry paused and squinted his eyes as though he could penetrate his thoughts right into hers by sheer osmosis.

With the sudden realization of what Jayce was about to do, Hana stood up quickly. "Harry, I've gotta go."

"I thought so," he smiled in immediate understanding of her intentions. "I'll bid on King for you," he nodded his head in affirmation, leaving her with no doubt at all that he would, indeed, bring King back home to her, too.

Like the first time she'd arrived in Lone Prairie, Jayce's John Deer tractor was parked in front of the fuel tanks and the cultivator was attached in preparation for spring seeding.

This time she took note of the pair of feet that stuck out from beneath the old contraption, like she'd gone back in time. For a moment her heart clung perilously to her rib cage, painfully threatening to free-fall to her feet, but the man that slid out from beneath the cultivator was not Jayce and she was immediately crushed.

"Nathan, I didn't expcct to see you here," Hana desperately tried to hide her disappointment.

"Can't say I expected to see you here either," he snapped, every bit as arrogant as when she'd left.

Not in the mood for small talk, Hana skipped the preliminaries. "Do you know where Jayce is?"

Nathan glared at her, sizing her up from head to toe. She was dressed in jeans, boots and a light denim jacket, not at all the woman he'd felt free to criticize, and for a moment she could have sworn she saw his features soften.

"He's at the old school site."

"Thanks," Hana replied and whirled around to head back toward her pick-up.

"Wait," he called out and the tone of urgency in his voice made her stop. "You can't get there in a vehicle. The spring run-off has practically washed out that trail."

"Run-off? But it's dry here. There hasn't been much snow."

"No, but that road has never been maintained. You'll have to go on horse back."

"Darn country roads," she cursed. "You'd think that after all these years the new generation could come up with a way to improve road conditions."

"Well, you can cuss about it all you want, but it won't get you there any faster. Jayce only has one horse but I think that's Harry coming down the road. We'll get a saddle for King from the barn."

Hana turned to see Harry pull into the yard, his stock trailer in tow and filled with the animals that she'd grown to love. When she turned back to thank Nathan for his shocking display of kindness, he had already disappeared inside of the barn. He had known, too, known that Jayce had set her up, known that Harry was bringing her animals there. The realization was too much for her to process.

On the one hand, Jayce had been nothing short of deceitful. He'd been sneaky and conniving, deliberately making her believe that if she didn't come to the sale, her animals would be sold to the highest bidder and dispersed throughout the countryside.

On the other hand, he'd been sweet in the way he'd figured out a way to get her to come to her senses, and in the way he'd confided his private problems to Harry and Nathan. She couldn't possibly hold it against him. Yet, she couldn't help but wonder what his real reasons were for going through all the trouble. Was it that he truly believed she should come back to inherit Abner's farm, or was there a part of him that wanted her to come back to inhabit his heart? It was too much to hope for, and Hana looked to the heavens knowing that hope wasn't enough.

When Nathan returned from the barn carrying a heavy saddle, Harry needed no explanation and released King from the trailer. Betsy waited her turn patiently and Hana couldn't resist reaching in through the open window to pet her on the nose and say hello.

"Have you ever ridden?" Harry seemed apprehensive as he came around to the side of the trailer leading King.

"No." Her heart quickened as she watched Nathan throw a saddle pad across King's back and then heave the heavy leather saddle over top of it. The horse flinched a little, side stepping to the left, and Nathan reassured him by stroking his thick brown neck. Fear pounded at her temples.

"King's well-trained but he hasn't been ridden in the past year. What do you say we let Nathan warm him up a bit first?" Harry suggested.

Hana watched as Nathan maneuvered the large animal around in circles, breaking him into a tired sweat. His face beamed with an inner joy and satisfaction and she watched with a touch of envy as he hopped down lithely to the ground and handed her the reins.

"He's all yours," he coaxed with a broad smile, free of attitude.

"Nathan, I'll be honest. I don't have the first clue how to ride."

Nathan stared back at her with an expression she couldn't read.

"Maybe I should just stay here and wait for him," Hana suggested, wishing that she really had that kind of patience, or that she could fly to him instead.

Harry cleared his throat from somewhere behind her and startled her. With a sheepish grin, his hands stuffed uncomfortably into his pockets, Harry said his piece.

"I don't claim to know much about the affairs between men and women. I'm not much good at it myself, but if you ask me, once a man sets his mind to something, it could take a long time to change it."

"What do you mean?" Hana struggled to understand Harry's awkward monologue. If the difference between men and women was a tall brick wall, she'd hit it head on.

"Well, he thought you weren't comin' and he's out there stewin' right now."

"Men stew? I thought just women did that." Hana attempted to stifle a laugh, despite the fact that poor Harry appeared as though he'd rather disappear into a gopher hole.

"I guess men and women really aren't all that different," Harry finally managed a smile and the ancient wall crumbled to the ground.

"Stick your left foot in the stirrup and swing your right over top," Nathan encouraged, deciding to refrain from participating in a conversation that had become embarrassing way back at Harry's claim to not know much about the affairs between men and women.

Hana did as she was told and within seconds found herself sitting in the saddle with a view of the world she'd never experienced. King was magnificent and intimidating. Her palms began to sweat. Sensing her nervousness, the horse side stepped again, but Nathan was quick to scold him, successfully getting King to stand tall and still once again.

"He's neck reined, Hana, which means that all you need to do to turn him left is to coax his neck with a light touch of the reins on the right side. To turn him right, you place the left rein on the left side of his neck.

It all sounded backwards and confusing to Hana, but she did what she was told and King responded in a way that made her feel powerful and in control. She rode him slowly around the yard, taking cues and tips from Nathan who strolled beside her, and when he felt certain she could handle things on her own, he helped her down off the horse.

"Well? Do you think she can manage?" he asked Harry, talking in a way that made her feel like an invisible child.

"I don't know. It's risky. King's a good horse but a year's a long time. He could spook at prairie chickens or anything else for that matter."

Nathan paused and looked at the ground thoughtfully. "How about we unload all the other animals and put King back in the trailer. Take them to junction forty-five where the dirt road branches off the grid. Then she'll only have a mile to ride on her own."

"Good thinking, son," Harry nodded and immediately the two set to work, unloading the other animals and getting King back into the trailer. Tired from the work out, King did not protest, and Hana was grateful for the plan that would cut three miles out of her riding time.

Hana thanked Nathan profusely and hopped into Harry's truck. They drove in silence the entire way, both feeling somewhat anxious about a situation that held no promises. When Harry finally stopped, he backed King out of the trailer, helped her into the saddle and then looked up at her thoughtfully.

"Thanks, Harry," Hana attempted to look confident, but failed miserably.

"You just be safe on that old guy, you hear?"

"I will," she smiled nervously and then immediately made herself strong, not wanting King to sense her fear.

"If you're unsure about where to go, let King lead the way. He knows it," Harry nodded. It was a comment that meant so much more than she could fathom. Yes, King knew it, Harry knew it, everyone in Lone Prairie knew that Abner Crawford and Doris Harlow used to come here so often their horses knew the way, but King couldn't have been the horse Abner used back then, and Hana wondered exactly how King could possibly know the way. Again the past and the present collided disagreeably and she wondered if she'd ever understand it all.

Hana rode slowly down the rough and rutted trail, careful not to make any sudden movements that would set the horse on edge. King picked up the trail of Jayce's horse almost immediately and followed it doggedly, giving her a moment to contemplate Jayce's intentions.

Why he'd come here, she couldn't be sure. She presumed it had been to face it one last time and maybe to find it in his heart to let it go, but she couldn't be sure, and as she came closer and closer to the spot that he had taken her to on that dreadful day in autumn, she grew uncontrollably nervous.

At one point King seemed to want to rush, perhaps spotting the place where Ab had tied him to a tree and let him graze in the tall lush grass. Hana quickly pulled back on the reins, inexperience causing her to be too abrupt. King reacted by rearing up and neighing his disapproval and Jayce raced toward her.

"Are you all right?" he grabbed the horse's reins and steadied him with words that seemed to scold and soothe at the same time.

"I'm okay," Hana hopped down from the saddle, glad to be back on solid ground. Immediately her leg and back muscles began to ache and retaliate, and she arched her back to work out the kink that had sprung from her tailbone and into her shoulder blade.

"A little stiff, huh?" Jayce smiled, but then his mood changed almost immediately and he led King away from her and over to his own horse, tying them side by side.

He turned to look at her then. She had not moved, couldn't seem to will her legs to transform back from their jellied state, and he glared at her in a way that made her feel naked inside.

"What are you doing here?"

"Nathan told me you were here." She took a step forward and hoped that he might meet her half way. Instead, he took a few steps back and leaned against the old poplar tree, chewing on a stem of grass with a shoddy attempt at indifference.

"I waited for you at the sale, thought you might actually show. I should have known better. It wasn't right of me to trick you into coming back. You wouldn't have, if I hadn't forced you to."

"That's just it, Jayce," Hana took another step forward, wrenching her hands together until her fingers turned blue. "I didn't *have* to come back. I wanted to. You just helped me to see it all clearly, is all."

"So, I take it you're the new owner of Abner Crawford's homestead?" Jayce spoke cautiously, making it clear that he was still unsure of her intentions.

"Yes. I accepted the inheritance, but under one condition."

"What's that?" Jayce pulled away from the tree now and dropped the grass stem which had evidently lost its flavor. He folded his arms across his chest in a way that reminded her of the strong, protected and guarded Jayce. Clearly, she had her work cut out for her.

"I've sold most of my belongings and put all my savings into a fund. I'm going to call it the ABC Farmer's Aid Foundation. I want to help people right here in Lone Prairie by donating or lending money to farming families who are in need of it."

"Sounds like a noble idea, Hana, but your assets can't be enough to do much good around here. Practically every second farmer needs help."

"Yes, I know. That's why I'm going to need your help. I own Ab's land but I want you to farm it for half the profits. The other half will go into the foundation to keep the money flowing. I can contribute by holding fund-raising events, researching government grants, and whatever it takes to keep the Foundation going. If it helps even a few people, it's better than nothing."

"Well, well, well" Jayce chanted. "I didn't think you had it in you."

"What?"

"Pure, unfounded and absolutely non-refundable generosity. The numbers will never add up on paper you know?"

"Yeah, I know," she laughed and stared down at her boots, choosing her next words carefully. "But I have a lot to give. I have a knowledge base about financial institutions and programs that have been set up to help farmers. I think that this is what I was really meant to do, Jayce. And if that isn't enough, I can whistle through a blade of grass," she teased, and stooped to pluck a perfect blade of grass, demonstrating her new-found ability.

"Impressive," he conceded, but Jayce was not to be sidetracked. "So, is this something you will be operating from the city or do I have a new neighbor?"

"Well, that depends on you."

Jayce paused for a long time before moving swiftly and pinning her gently between himself and the tree.

"I love you, Hana. You know that," he whispered, assuming something so preposterous she almost laughed.

"I do?"

"Well you should if you don't already," he scolded, kissing her finally and impressing a memory upon her heart deeper than the ones in the old poplar tree.

"But I'm not going to let you live a life that you're just not cut out for, and I won't let history repeat itself and allow our lives to end up in a knot of regrets. So, if this is not what you want, tell me now."

"Can't we just forget about history, Jayce? Can't we make our own history and bring our grandkids here. We can show them the tree and tell them about how much their grandparents love each other and how they overcame unusual obstacles to be together."

"You and me grandparents? Aren't we skipping a very important step somewhere in there?" Jayce allowed himself a second to enjoy that thought before pulling himself together one last time. One last time was all he had left before he would give in to her, and to the love and the truth that surrounded them.

"I'm like my father, Hana. When I love someone it's forever, in good times and bad."

"And I'm like mine, Jayce, stubborn 'til the end. You're just going to have to trust me when I say that I'll be yours forever."

He stood there quietly, wanting her so badly that he could hardly think straight. Did it matter? Did any of it really matter? The past wasn't his fault or hers, nor was it all disaster. Some good had come of it. The good Lord had seen to that. He'd met Hana because of it and any fool could see that they were meant to be together. Even Abner had known it. Besides, if he didn't find forgiveness in his own heart then he'd be nothing more than a hypocrite. Hana had shown him that his own faith could use a little polishing and she was a new sheep to the flock. He needed to set a good example. Oh, who was he kidding? He needed saving grace every bit as much as she did.

"So what do you say, Jayce? Is that heart of yours open for business, because if it is, I'm willing to make a lasting investment," she smiled slyly.

"You've just got it all figured out, haven't you?" His eyes laughed now, the doubt finally gone and replaced with a heap of trust. "I think old Ab had it all figured out, too," Jayce took her by the hand. "That crazy will wasn't so crazy after all."

"What do you mean?"

"Take a look on the other side of this tree."

Together they circled the thick body of the tree. The west side, illuminated by the late afternoon sun, glared back a reflection, a freshly carved heart with a new set of initials scrawled within it:

My HI + *Her* J COME WHAT MAY signed ABC.

"He did this?" Hana could barely comprehend the physical and mental strength required to perform such a task. There were other repercussions, too, like the realization that Abner Crawford never really had any doubts that she was his daughter. He knew. He'd just decided that there was more to it than just he and Cilla, and Doris, and the daughter he hadn't known. There was Jayce, and a woman who had stirred more emotion inside him than Abner Crawford had ever seen. He'd devised the whole will and testament as a ploy. It was all so completely obvious now.

"He rode out here once a week on King, until he got really sick. I followed him that last time, stayed hidden out of sight. I was worried about him."

Hana nodded, understanding now how King had known the way.

"He seemed to sit here forever that day," Jayce paused and shoved his hands in the pockets of his blue jeans as if burying the sadness that came with the memory. "He was so clear that day. It was almost as though he wasn't suffering from that awful disease. It was the last day, too. After that, things just went down hill."

"You took such good care of him. I'll always be grateful."

"I loved him. Mom did, too. I can't deny that. He took me under his wing after my father died, kept me on the right path. I wanted to hate him, but I couldn't no matter how hard I tried. He ended up being my best friend, seemed to always know what was best for me. I guess he knew that day on the porch that you were his…and mine."

"I guess he did," Hana allowed her fingers to trace the jagged markings in the tree.

"I'm going to miss this place," Jayce paused, formulating the words he regretted to say, "but I had to let it go, Hana. I had a payment due today; I let it go. There's just no point in keeping it."

"But there is Jayce, and it's still yours if you want it. I made the payment today, or rather, the ABC Foundation made the payment. It just seemed like the right thing to do."

Jayce expressed his gratitude with a soft kiss and held her close. "Well, what are two sentimental fools going to do with eighty acres of virtually unworkable land?"

"How about a community pasture, a place for farmers to bring their cattle if they're in need of it?"

"Sounds like a good plan," Jayce nodded his approval, "But there's still one more problem."

"What's that?" Hana frowned, wondering what could possibly be left for them to deal with.

"Well, I know what we're going to do with Abner's inheritance, I know what we're going to do with the land we're standing on, but just what the heck am I going to do with you?"

Hana's frown transformed into a smile and a sigh of relief. "Anything you want, Jayce Harlow," she folded herself into his arms. "Anything you want."

"Well then, I think I'm just going to have to marry you."

"I'll buy that," Hana teased, extending her hand in a gesture of a formal hand shake to seal the deal.

"Good, because it's about all you're going to be able to afford for a while, until things improve in the farming business. Are you sure you can handle that? I mean, the not knowing, the uncertainties, the risks?"

"My life has always been uncertain. I just convinced myself that I have it all figured out. Now I know that He's in control, and if I have faith, His will for me will always lead me in the right direction."

"Hallelujah!" Jayce responded to the accompaniment of ceremonial thunder.

They hadn't noticed the black clouds that encircled the valley like an impenetrable cloak, and when the first drop of rain fell, they looked to the sky. The same sky that had been void of rain for so long, now seemed to open up and release a spray of promises.

"I can't believe it. It's actually raining," Hana spoke the obvious.

"You know what they say about spring showers?"

"No, what do *they* say? Oh wait, let me guess…that standing in a spring shower is the fifth romantic thing to do in Lone Prairie?"

"No," Jayce laughed, "but you're close. Actually they say that spring showers…"

"Wait! Don't say it." Hana grew excited. "Is it…spring showers bring May flowers?"

"Well, yeah! That's exactly what they say," Jayce nodded his head in obvious approval, taking full credit for the pupil who had finally shown some progress. "You know, I think you're catching on, Hana Islander." Jayce held her tightly, as rain fell softly upon them like transparent confetti. "You're finally catching on."

"Like a house on fire, Jayce Harlow," Hana cast a smile to the heavens and the God whose promising whisper she could faintly hear in the falling rain. "Like a prairie house on fire."

ISBN 142511655-8

9 781425 116552